THE BLACK FIRE
CONCERTO

MIKE ALLEN

The Black Fire Concerto
Copyright © 2013 Haunted Stars

First edition: June 2013

ISBN-13: 978-0615838205

This is a work of fiction. All characters, places and events portrayed in this publication are either fictitious or used fictitiously.

Edited by C.S.E. Cooney
Cover artwork by Lauren K. Cannon

Haunted Stars
815 Oak Street
St. Charles, IL 61074

hauntedstars.com

PRAISE FOR
THE BLACK FIRE CONCERTO

"Mike Allen's *THE BLACK FIRE CONCERTO* is a dark, luscious feast of book. Allen is that rare and wondrous scribe that is both poet and storyteller and excels at both.

"Allen has created a fantastic world of fantasy and horror like a Bosch painting, like a Shostakovitch symphony—something out of a beautiful nightmare; full of horned demigods and trickster fox-men, dark forests, riverboat abattoirs, beasts of straw and monsters made of dust, civilized cannibals and murderous chefs, glowing rune-magic rifles and immortal ghouls.

"He's given us a duo of kickass heroines to lead us through his rich and dangerous world and I hope this is only the beginning of their adventures.

"Like a powerful musical performance, *THE BLACK FIRE CONCERTO* reaches into places in you and stirs feelings, summons visions and leaves you looking forward to the next performance."

—R.S. Belcher

For Claire
for whom this was written

For Anita
for whom I write everything

CONTENTS

And then she smiles a strange sad smile
And lets her harp lie long;
The death-waves oft may rise the while,
She greets them with no song.

— *William Sharp, "The Death-Child"*

PART ONE: THE RED EMPRESS

"*P*lay now, pretty plumpkin," said the Chef. His wide mouth twisted to favor Erzelle with a smirk. The oil on his bald head gleamed, reflecting the candlelight.

She settled in her chair on the stage, balanced the soundbox of her harp between her knees, braced its neck against her shoulder and caressed the strings. All twenty-two were in tune, and their song brought a sliver of comfort, for as long as she was allowed to play, she would live another day.

The dining hall awaited its patrons. Tables arranged four wide and six deep made an orderly procession back through the narrow, chapel-like space to the bronze dragon doors that served as main entrance. To Erzelle's right, past the corner of the stage, a pair of swinging saloon doors led to the kitchen, where the clank of dishes and utensils had fallen silent, though warm air still exhaled into the hall, bearing with it a stench of sour meat. Every mauve-draped table had its candle in place, a severed hand sealed in wax with a wick burning at the tip of each finger.

Satisfied, the Chef turned and nodded to the black-clad men by the bronze doors. He straightened, squared his shoulders, and given his inhuman height, his massive head, his black robe that swept to the floor, his red Roman collar, and the effusion of light through the room which rendered every drape, tablecloth and plate the color of bared gums, he resembled a demon carved from onyx and crowned with a moist clay skull.

The Chef's ushers opened the dining hall. The Family filed in, led by their roly-poly tuxedo-clad patriarch, who fixed his rheumy gaze on Erzelle as he wove between the tables toward the stage.

Erzelle wanted to fold inside her harp and disappear. Instead she plucked. Those assembling in the room would enjoy her desperate lullaby to herself, the same way ticks enjoyed warm blood.

The Family patriarch reached the Chef. Though he stood only half the black-robed man's height, they acknowledged each other with polite nods, a greeting of equals.

"So glad you haven't wasted her." The old man rubbed his ample belly in exaggerated anticipation of a meal. "She'll be your masterpiece. Just the thought gives me reason to keep on living."

If the Chef answered, Erzelle didn't hear his words. Her fingers alighted on string after string, exploring the limits of her three octaves, inventing melodies to bridge the scores she learned from her parents, the only parts of them she could keep.

Her notes competed with the babble of the old man's clan, many of whom she recognized. The Family visited the *Red Empress* often, and stayed in the boat's guest quarters. Here was the patriarch's gaunt, stooped wife in a shimmering snakeskin gown. Here, their gene-ensorcelled sons and daughters and sons-and-daughters in law, the men blue-eyed and black-haired, the women icy blonde, traits shared with their teenage children. One boy and one girl both looked to be Erzelle's age — she believed she was twelve, though she had no means to differentiate the days. The children showed no interest in her as their mother herded them to their seats.

Then came a commotion, surprised exclamations from the ushers. Erzelle looked up to see a woman whose like she'd never seen before standing at the entrance. Extraordinarily tall, with a heavy bosom and long arms thick through the biceps — physically to most women what the Chef would be to most men. And she was beautiful, with sloe eyes beneath arched brows and wavy blue-black hair that cascaded to the waist of her velvet opera coat. She towered a head taller than Rogiers, the chief usher, who was trying to take the leather case she carried. This was the cause of the row — the woman was refusing.

Erzelle faltered in her playing. The woman clutched a large mandolin case.

The Chef strode toward the door with a panther's grace.

But he didn't get far. The patriarch waved him off. "She's our guest. Let her in."

So instead the Chef aimed a glare at Rogiers, who shut up mid-sentence and bowed.

The woman joined the table nearest the patriarch's, set her case on the floor beside the chair an usher offered. She surveyed the dining hall with efficient tilts of her head, noticed Erzelle and gave her a brief, considering look. No expression moved her eyes or lips before she turned away.

She unbuttoned her opera coat to reveal a bright blue blouse, startling against the room's red palette.

Erzelle's heart sank at this dismissal from a fellow musician — and a chill spread through her bones. There was only one reason the boat's regular customers brought strangers.

She concentrated on her playing, even as the patriarch bellowed to the Chef in a voice meant for the room at large, "I've not yet had the pleasure of hearing Olyssa play her pipe. But clearly her skills are transcendent enough to open the heaviest purse, because when she came to us with her request to visit this boat, she even offered to pay for her place and was good for it." He brayed in laughter. "But, good sir, I told her that such a fine meal as you provide should be offered as a gift, or not at all."

Erzelle's eyes widened. The woman *asked* to come on board the *Red Empress*, with all its passages painted black and its rank cargo screaming in cages?

She nearly started from her chair when Olyssa laughed in return, her voice sharp and musical. "I've heard so much about the food served here, that its excellence cannot be denied. I am honored to be here."

The Chef inclined his head. "I am humbled. And I pray you find my labors worthy." Another curt nod, and his crew began wheeling out the meal. The kitchen doors swung open as the Chef's acolytes pushed out gurneys bearing covered dishes. The Chef remained in front of the stage, each subtle nod or finger twitch the wave of a conductor's wand, dictating every move of the service.

Erzelle tried to ignore the deceptively benign scents and sights of fresh bread loaves and cream-covered vegetables, but she noted the moment the long carving knife slid from the Chef's left sleeve into his hand. The writing etched along its edge began to pulse even before he raised the blade to shoulder height. When he did, his men lifted the cover over the largest dish.

She wanted to shut her eyes, but knew better. She fixed her gaze on the newcomer, hoping not to draw unwanted reaction.

Olyssa observed the proceedings stone-faced.

In keeping with tradition, the once-human creature intended for the main course had been prepared so that its head remained uncooked. Its throat and tongue removed, it grimaced as the Chef approached.

The patriarch chortled and elbowed his spouse. "Excellent choice, good sir. Remember when we brought him that one?"

His wife afforded him a smile both sly and exasperated. No one else among the patrons of the *Red Empress* would dare to speak while the Chef performed the grace.

"We thank you," the Chef said, "whose life, made everlasting, shall become ours." The etchings on the knife flared as he made the cuts required of the ritual. He partook of the first morsel before offering the next pieces to the patriarch and his wife on a small saucer. Together they spoke, "We thank you," and then ate, nodding their satisfaction.

The rest of the dishes were unveiled, revealing spare limbs from other ghouls deemed too feeble to suit as a main course.

Everyone at the patriarch's table watched Olyssa as the ushers brought her dinner. She showed none of the delight of the other diners, but neither did she seem repulsed. She raised her eyebrows ever so lightly as she sampled her first forkful, then continued to eat, nonchalant as if she dined on beans and bread.

Erzelle shuddered and withdrew into the rain of notes, a cascade that shut the dining hall out. She remained in that trance until she realized the Family was getting up from their meal. Olyssa, too, had risen, was approaching the stage. Approaching the Chef. Their heights made them oddly well-matched. Erzelle had never seen a woman so tall.

"I have to give you my compliments." The newcomer touched the Chef on the arm, casual as an old friend. Her other had gripped the mandolin case. "In my own experience, ghoul meat is the most difficult of all to make delicious."

The Chef's eyes narrowed even as his smile widened. "You are most welcome, madame."

Erzelle's heart lurched in her chest. Perhaps she misread this situation entire. Perhaps this Olyssa was in no danger at all. Perhaps the Family already considered her one of their own.

She peered down at Erzelle. "You play well," she said. "It is too bad your harp is so small." She turned to the Chef. "Surely the *Red Empress* can afford to buy her a better instrument?"

"Such instruments are rare, and it is rarer still to find one intact, as you surely know. We only expect this one to stay with us a little while longer, so my investors see no need for such an extravagant expense."

Olyssa looked Erzelle up and down. "Wise, then."

"Mistress," said Rogiers at Olyssa's elbow. "Your quarters?"

"Oh, yes, please," she said. "A meal that rich makes me just a little sleepy. I could stand to be refreshed."

Once the usher led her out, the patriarch waddled up the Chef, eyes gleaming. "A fine one, eh?" He actually patted the Chef on the belly, a bizarre paternal gesture. The Chef pursed his lips, staring into some far distance, looking as thoughtful as Erzelle had ever seen him.

"Indeed," he rumbled. "Powerful. Flooded with life."

And Erzelle knew that, fearsome as Olyssa seemed, she would not live through the night.

She continued to play, until the hall was empty. She knew better than to stop.

The *Red Empress* had once been a luxury paddleboat. Now it served as a floating fortress, permanently docked, admitting no one but crew, customers and those the customers brought. Erzelle was no longer certain how long she'd dwelt inside its pitch-black passageways. When she tried to remember the sky, it seemed like part of a story she'd once heard. So, sometimes, did her parents. She tried hard to keep them alive in her mind as more than memory wisps. When she curled on her pallet, she remembered her mother practicing the harp, and those notes would follow her into dream, or the drone of her father as he griped about the accounts he managed. The memories brought a lump to her throat. So often, she had tuned him out. She wished now that she'd treasured every word.

In her time inside the boat, months, maybe years, she'd found many places where a slender body could hide. So long as she was in her expected spot come mealtimes, the crew hardly cared where she was, though she didn't dare let them catch her spying.

The doors to all the guest cabins faced into a narrow atrium that might once have been illuminated by a skylight. Now electric chandeliers dangled from a ribbed metal ceiling. Stairs at either end led from the second floor balcony to the lower deck.

The atrium was empty when Erzelle slipped inside, though muffled voices, muted laughter, seeped through the walls. She scurried down the stairs, feather-light, and across the ground level to the opposite end, heart hammering at the thought that one of the doors to either side might swing open. She made it to the stairs at the opposite end, squeezed through a gap to one side, carefully dragged her harp in after her. She scooted as far back in shadow as she could and peered through the slats.

She'd seen this tragedy played out so many times her tears had dried up long ago. But Olyssa didn't come off as someone easily tricked or overpowered. Erzelle had to know what would happen.

Alerted by the creak of a hinge, she looked up. The Chef loomed at the entrance, chandelier light glinting from his scalp. Six crewmen filed in behind him. He set off along the balcony, his slippers reducing his footfalls to whispers, the men following. He tapped politely on a door.

Erzelle wanted to scream a warning. She dared not.

But when the door opened, she heard a greasy chuckle that made her stomach flip. The patriarch joined the men on the balcony, saggy flesh visible through the gap in his bathrobe. He intended to watch the capture.

Then a cabin door opened on the first floor, and Olyssa strode into the atrium. Everyone on the balcony except for the Chef stared with wide eyes.

Erzelle held her breath. The scene had gone off script.

Olyssa had removed her opera coat, fully revealing her riveting blue blouse and a gold-hemmed indigo skirt suited for summer dances. She'd braided her hair into a coil, held in place by a flat ivory pick that glittered at either end with bejeweled knobs. She walked to one of the mesh tables that dotted the courtyard, set down her mandolin case and opened it without even looking up at the men on the balcony.

From the case she lifted a long steel-grey tube. Etchings dimpled the surface, drew strange patterns of reflected light down its length.

One end had a notch in its rim. Over that she fitted a tiny wooden object that Erzelle recognized after a moment as the mouthpiece of a hand-carved reed. Then Olyssa took what looked like a small flared bell and fitted it over grooves at the other end.

Settling on a bench, Olyssa held the bizarre instrument against her chest, put the reed to her lips and began to play. She blew across the reed while her free hand fluttered at the mouth of the bell, covering and uncovering the opening with two fingers, three, four, or her flattened palm. Notes fluttered and trilled, faster than Erzelle could ever play on her harp.

The etchings on Olyssa's pipe began to glow soft blue. The Chef made a move toward the stairs, but the old man put a hand on his arm to stop him.

The tune soared quick and haunting, like a child's ghost singing from the bottom of a well. Other doors opened, heads blonde and brunette appeared, blue eyes watched, enraptured. When she stopped, wistful sighs echoed in the narrow space.

She addressed the patriarch on the balcony with a coy smile. "I had thought, after that wonderful meal, that I should repay your kindness. Perhaps tomorrow, when we eat again, I could accompany your harp player. Her music, though lovely, is unrefined, but if I accompany her, I can promise you the experience will be something truly transcendent."

Oh, how the old man's eyes twinkled. The Chef began to speak, but stopped mid-syllable as his patron raised a hand. "My clan and I had imagined leaving in the morning," he lied, "but what's one more night to the likes of us? It would please me immensely to see such lovely pairs of hands create something beautiful together."

With a slight bow of her head, Olyssa replied, "It would be my honor."

A smirk curled across the Chef's long jaw. "Splendid, then. It shall be so." Then he descended the stairs and approached her table, while his men looked on unblinking. He spoke more softly as he reached her. "Madame, as one who knows of ghoul flesh you will surely understand. May I examine this fascinating instrument?"

She raised her eyebrows. "Of course." And handed it to him.

Erzelle's pulse pounded in her ears as the Chef's meaty hand closed around the pipe. She knew the glowing knife would slide out of his sleeve at any moment. But instead he held the pipe up to the light and stared down its full length. As he did the blue glow reappeared. It grew brighter as he turned the tube over. Erzelle realized he was reading the symbols.

"It will always be true to its purpose," Olyssa said. She sounded, for the first time, tense.

At last the Chef handed it back to her. "An intriguing trinket. When we're all rested, I'd love to know more about its make."

Olyssa smiled, showing teeth. "Perhaps."

The Chef smirked and nodded, then gestured to his men, who followed as he left the guest quarters. Olyssa settled and began to play again — this time there was no tune, merely practice scales, though even those were breathtaking, executed at perfect pitch with incredible speed. The old man regarded her for an uncomfortably long time. Erzelle wondered if he would join her at the table, but finally he grinned, displaying long yellow teeth, and withdrew. The other doors had long since shut.

Olyssa took a breath, placed the reed to her lips, and beside Erzelle a voice whispered. "Quiet, girl."

Erzelle gasped. The voice — Olyssa's — continued. "I know you're under there. Wait until I've gone back to my room. Wait a count of one thousand. Then come inside. My door will be unlocked." She wasn't looking Erzelle's way, nor were her lips moving. She removed the reed and bell from the pipe and replaced them in the case, which she tucked under an arm, keeping the pipe in her hand. She retired, and Erzelle was once again alone.

She followed the instructions she'd been given. An eternity later, she slipped into Olyssa's room. Its interior was opulent and plush as such a cramped, windowless space could be made, with carpeting, bedding and wallpaper all red as a womb. A mirror glinted from atop a wooden dresser, and Erzelle glimpsed herself in it, a gaunt ghost of a girl with eyes huge in their hollow sockets, her once tawny skin now moon pale, her sandy hair tangled in an unkempt nest, her mint green blouse threadbare. She averted her eyes, resisted any urge to take another glance.

Olyssa perched on the edge of the bed, looking more giantess than ever in her blue and gold, cleaning the bore of her pipe with a long, thin brush. The pipe's case lay open, exposing custom-fitted felt-lined padding, with a long compartment carved out to hold the pipe. There were notches too for the bell and the reed. A panel gaped open in this layer of padding, revealing it to be hollow, with even more parts for the instrument contained inside.

"Who made that for you?" Erzelle asked.

Olyssa regarded her coolly. "What makes you think someone else made this?"

She sounded angry. Erzelle didn't answer.

"I'm looking for a woman tall as I am. Her hair is long and wavy like mine, her skin brown like mine. But her eyes are like yours. Green. Have you seen anyone like that here?"

"No."

Her mouth thinned to a grim line. "How long have you been here?"

"I think ... two years? Three?"

"What's your name?"

Erzelle told her.

Cold and business-like, "Why are you here?"

Erzelle started to cry.

A tender hand against her cheek surprised her. "I'm sorry if this is difficult," Olyssa said. "I need to know. It'll help us both."

She had no reason to trust this stranger, but perhaps because of that single word, "Help," Erzelle gave in to a treacherous surge of hope. She told her story, all of it. Her parents, her father an accountant and amateur flautist, her mother a concert harpist frequently sought after by the tenement lords who ruled what was left of the world. The invitation from the Gaults, one of the wealthiest clan in Minnepaul, far wealthier than her parents could ever dream, rich enough to employ their own militia against ghouls and other clans. Her father's eagerness, her mother's worry, the small jet that took them out of the walled city and down the length of the Great River. The descent through the riverboat's vault door.

She described the crowd that had boarded, many rich clans, and the Family themselves — Erzelle didn't know their real names — to whom all the rest kowtowed. The meal, the awful taste of that spiced and spoiled meat. How even with head reeling and stomach boiling she'd been made to play her harp at the insistence of the patriarch.

How the Chef and his men came for them afterward, overpowered her father and mother and dragged them away. How the patriarch had leered as he told the Chef she wasn't ripe enough yet, that she could enhance the meals with her talents until ready for the table herself.

"They were going to do it to you," she said. "Take you down to the ghouls. Let them bite you. Make you change. Then bring you back, all carved up, like those ghouls you saw today, all chopped up except your head ... like they did ... like they did ..." Erzelle no longer saw the cabin. She saw the dining hall, scene after scene that she'd fought to wall away with the notes from her harp. "Sometimes when it's someone young, older than me but still young, they bring them out without cooking them first, snarling and howling and snapping their teeth like dogs. They're strapped down and the Family will cut away pieces. Eat them right from the body. The old man loves to do that. With the girls. Sometimes the boys. Sometimes—"

Olyssa's touch on her shoulder startled her, but she didn't scream. Nor was she crying any longer. Her words came from a hollow space where tears and screams no longer mattered.

The piper's question startled her even more. "Where do they keep the ghouls?"

Erzelle blinked, couldn't for a few moments form an answer. "I think they're in the below deck."

"The cargo hold? Where is that?"

"I think ... you can only get to it through the kitchen."

"I see." Olyssa pulled out the brush, then wiped the outside of the pipe with a cloth.

Erzelle stared at the inscriptions along its grey-blue length. She couldn't bring herself to ask what Olyssa planned to do, so she asked, "How does your pipe work?"

"It works because of the same magic that made the Storms and ghouls. That's all you need to know." She put the pipe away and took Erzelle by the shoulders. "Go back to where you sleep. If anyone asks, you were with me, practicing for tomorrow." Her grip tightened. "Don't let anyone know what we talked about."

Now the words burst out. "What are you going to do?"

Olyssa's fingers dug in. "This conversation didn't happen."

Erzelle wrenched herself away. She wanted to shout at this insane woman that no plan she had could ever work, she had to get out, get out, get out — but Olyssa's unblinking stare silenced her as roughly as a cloth stuffed in her mouth.

She hefted her harp and left. As soon as she stepped outside, the door shut and locked.

Hours passed before Erzelle finally slept. When she did, yet again she dreamed of thrashing on a table, the old man leaning over her, candlelight glinting off the knives clutched in both his hands.

The second dinner was unlike any Erzelle had ever witnessed in her time aboard the *Red Empress*. For the first time, the Family's guest joined them alive and intact for the next day's meal. Had events unfolded as normal, the patrons would have returned to the hall wearing ritual black and amulets that glowed the same red as the Chef's knives. And the guest would have returned through the kitchen doors.

But here they came once again in tuxedos and gowns, Olyssa in her opera coat. As she had last night, she wore her hair up, held in place with the jeweled pick.

Exhausted, Erzelle dreaded what lay ahead, but her fingers moved without her conscious direction down the octaves of the harp. They understood what survival required.

Rogiers offered Olyssa a chair, but she surprised him and everyone else by gliding straight to the stage. As she set down the mandolin case, the patriarch chuckled at some private amusement, his belly jiggling.

The Chef, who stood at his usual post before the stage, raised an eyebrow as she passed.

"Tell your man to bring that chair here," Olyssa said, imperious. Erzelle cringed — but the Chef did as commanded. Soon the tall woman sat beside her, back straight and proper as she assembled pipe, reed and bell.

Erzelle's fingers faltered at the strings.

"Just play what comes to you," Olyssa said. "I'll follow along."

So she plucked out yet another variation on a too-familiar melody. And Olyssa's pipe sang, filling in the spaces between Erzelle's notes, fluttering around and above them, washing over Erzelle as if the roof of the *Red Empress* had cracked to allow in cool breezes and warm sunlight. Her heartbeat sped, and her hands began to move with new energy. She altered the melody, improvised, and the pipe harmonized without pause. She created new phrases, not from fear but exhilaration, and Olyssa matched her measure for measure. Their audience appeared to share in Erzelle's fugue, still and silent, all eyes fixed on the players.

Even the help seemed paralyzed until barked orders from the Chef sent them scurrying. He followed after his men through the saloon doors. None of the Family paid them any mind.

The runes on the pipe started to glow, shining brighter and brighter blue.

Erzelle's fingers summoned an exquisite tempest of sound. She hardly noticed when Olyssa spun the bell off the end of the pipe and palmed it. Even then the pipe's notes still quivered inside her head, accompanied by a whisper. "Play, Erzelle, like your blood's on fire. Play!"

Her hands scaled the octaves fast as a waterfall, not once missing a string, while Olyssa reached inside the mandolin case. She found dual melodies, built a harmony from nothing, but broke out in sweat, because without the pipe it was abruptly hard work, the hardest thing she'd ever done. And her concentration began to slip, because from the corner of her eye she noticed Olyssa had attached a black rectangular device to the end of the pipe that had held the bell.

The piper sat up, holding an oddly shaped column of wood that she levered against the black attachment and locked into place. An instant later she clicked the open end of a thin metal box into the rectangular device.

The patriarch's oldest son realized what Olyssa was doing and lunged from his chair.

Olyssa put the butt of the carved wooden piece against her muscular shoulder, and Erzelle's fingers abandoned the strings as she recognized Olyssa now, impossibly, held a rifle. The runes along what was now the rifle's barrel flared in a blaze of hungry red.

A dark pinhole appeared in the oldest son's forehead, just below the point of his widow's peak. Blood sprayed from the back of his head as he bulled forward, and at the table directly behind him an aunt loosed a gurgling scream as the bullet's trajectory ended in her throat. She collapsed, dragging the tablecloth with her.

Olyssa's voice boomed in Erzelle's head. "BEHIND ME! DOWN!"

A shell casing bounced and clattered on the stage planks. When it came to rest, runes etched in its brass wormed matchstick orange, then extinguished.

Rogiers stood stunned at the saloon doors, a gurney stalled in front of him. He started fumbling for something, Erzelle never learned what. In one motion Olyssa stood, swiveled and twitched her finger at the trigger. Her shoulder jerked. Rogiers dropped like a sack.

The patriarch stood up, astonishingly all smiles, his hands raised to placate. "There is no need—"

And dropped to the carpet, the hole in his forehead a twin to his son's. Another trigger pull, and his wife's grey head snapped back, a look of surprise frozen on her craggy face.

Gasps and shrieks from the remaining Family members quickly fell quiet. Peering down the barrel, Olyssa stage-projected, her voice merry. "So much more merciful than what they deserved. See the runes that burn on the casings of those bullets, good hosts? No matter how much flesh of the ghoul you've consumed, take my word that this weapon will kill you. And take my word that it doesn't miss. It is always true to its purpose."

One of the blonde granddaughters screeched, "YOU MURDERED—"

The bullet took her in the eye.

"I'll kill the next one that makes a sound," Olyssa said. "Now leave." And she smiled. "Whoever is last to the door dies."

Silent chaos overtook the hall as the Family scrambled for the exit. Erzelle found herself fighting not to laugh, and terrified that if she began she'd never stop.

One of the granddaughter's husbands stood his ground as the others fled behind him — someone not of the blood, a pasty fellow with a weak chin and teeth that recalled a rodent's, his ill-fitting tux stretched by his girth. Sweat plastered his thinning hair to his pate.

The man's gaze was affixed to the business end of Olyssa's wickedly long gun.

"What a noble sacrifice," the piper said. "Carrion eater." And she delivered on her promise.

Then she apparently took complete leave of her senses, because she dashed straight for the kitchen door. She stopped beside it with back pressed against the wall, out of view of anyone on the other side.

She glanced back at Erzelle, who still lay on the stage beside her harp, gawping. And a gentle voice whispered in Erzelle's head, "Hide yourself."

Olyssa pivoted to dash past the gurney and through the swinging doors, and as she did, the Chef's bulk smashed into her and sent her stumbling back. He wrenched the rifle out of her grip and flung it aside, slammed her to the floor and crouched atop her, one huge hand crushing her throat, the other raising a meat cleaver that glowed as as fierce a red as her discarded rifle.

Her rifle.

Erzelle started to crawl toward it.

The cleaver swung down.

She sprang into a run.

Olyssa blocked the blow with both hands, the bright blade suspended inches from her face, as the Chef squeezed her neck. She gasped, face reddening as he angled the blade, forcing it down, his smirk widening. She was strong but no match for his sheer mass.

They stayed that way a moment, eyes locked, as he bore down slowly and the cleaver descended to Olyssa's throat. Then she broke from his gaze and turned her head, pushed his arm just a fraction to the side, let go of his wrist with one hand. He laughed at her maneuver, and didn't notice as her free hand grabbed the end of her hair pick.

Then he reared back with a roar, clutching his face, a jade knob jutting half an inch out of his left eye. The pick remained in Olyssa's hair, an empty sheath, one jeweled end now missing.

Erzelle almost forgot to pick up the rifle. Almost.

She didn't know how to use it, but as she lifted the rifle, her enemy saw the glowing barrel and scrambled. He ran into the kitchen, howling, stiletto still protruding from his face.

Olyssa coughed and swore. "I need that knife back." She saw Erzelle, and loosed a long sigh. "Thank you." She held out an arm. "Give."

Erzelle hesitated. "We can leave now."

Olyssa's voice grew steely. "I can't go yet."

"Why?" Erzelle pleaded. She hated how frightened she sounded.

Olyssa used the gurney to pull herself to her feet. She could easily have wrested the rifle away, but instead replied, "There's no time to tell now. Give."

Erzelle obeyed. Without another word Olyssa charged into the kitchen. The rifle discharged, then again. Three more of the kitchen crewmen dashed out and kept running, none giving Erzelle a second glance. She watched them throw open the bronze dragon doors, thought about slipping out after them, thought about the armed guards at the vault door that led to the outside world, wondered if they'd gotten word, were on the way here.

The Chef's abandoned cleaver glinted from the floor. She picked it up. Though an ember glow still pulsed in the symbols etched along its blade, it felt no different in her hand than an ordinary knife. It was heavy, suited to its usual wielder.

She followed Olyssa.

Rogiers' body and that of another crewman lay just inside the doorway. Another lay dead between two long steel counters, face down in the mess spewed from two overturned gurneys, colorful sprays of vegetables, broken tubs of spreads and dips, a brown pool of soup, scattered slabs and strips of grey meat. Withered arms and legs strewn among them, severed from their owners, browned and glazed. In the center of it all, an upended four-layer cake stanched the flow from bleeding wine bottles. The remains of the ghouls who'd given their limbs to the feast were arranged on a countertop in neatly severed pieces, glistening bones chopped apart and stripped of all meat. Split ribs yawned like shutters, the black muck inside mostly scooped out.

The main course was arranged on the other counter, naked, immobile except for its uncooked head. One lidless eye twitched, the other hidden beneath a droop of loose skin. A wormy remnant of tongue flapped at Erzelle as it snapped its jaws. Click, click, click.

Her shoes splashed through spilled stew as she ran past it.

She passed a steaming oven that she didn't dare glance at, reached an opening in the far wall, darted into a narrow passage leading out of the kitchen and drew up short as a huge figure strode toward her out of the dark. She lifted the cleaver above her head, but the figure grabbed her wrist.

Olyssa's laughter held no humor. "Is that for me? Really?"

When Erzelle shook her head, Olyssa let go. She had undone her opera coat, exposing a vest made of thick leather. She was using a handkerchief to wipe off the jeweled stiletto.

Erzelle stared. "Is he—?"

"No, alas, he pulled it out himself. That one has partaken so much of the undead even one of my bullets might not kill him." She replaced the needle-thin blade in its sheath, still bound in her hair. "Help me. Hold this." She handed Erzelle the stock and chamber of her rifle assembly.

A groan emanated from the darkened passage. Olyssa paid it no mind. She produced the reed and bell from a coat pocket and reattached them to the pipe. Another moan, higher pitched, sounded behind her, then another.

"What are you doing?" Erzelle demanded.

Olyssa scowled at her. Or — it wasn't a scowl. The piper's eyes were moist. She ground her teeth. "I have to see if my sister's down there." Her mouth wasn't moving. "You asked who made this pipe for me. My sister did. She foresaw I would need it but her magic didn't tell her why." She took the rifle assembly back from Erzelle, tucked it in an inside coat pocket. "She ran afoul of sorcery even worse than this lot's perversions. But it doesn't have complete hold." She put a hand on Erzelle's shoulder. The words in her head sound plaintive, as if Olyssa needed to convince herself just as much as her new companion. "Because notes still play. Something remains. Enough that if I find her—" She squeezed her eyes shut. "When I find her, I'll undo what was done to her." She rebuttoned her opera coat, turned, and for the first time Erzelle saw the open hatch in the floor behind her. Beyond its black depths the corridor dead-ended. "And if I can't undo it, I'll end her suffering."

Erzelle asked, "You think she's there? Why?"

The top of a metal ladder protruded above the lip of the hatch. Olyssa sat with her boots over the edge. She wasn't looking at Erzelle. "Wait here. Once I'm done, we'll leave."

She lowered herself onto the rungs and vanished into the pitch dark. And in that darkness, a chorus of groans and hisses, rising in volume as more and more voices joined in. Something let out a shrill giggle.

Then notes began to ascend from the hole, a sweet flutter amidst the growls and moans of the ghouls. Erzelle crept closer, peered over the edge. Deep below, blue phosphorescence glimmered as somewhere out of her view Olyssa blew across her reed.

The metal cavern of the cargo hold echoed with throat-tearing screams. Howls, shrieks, splatters of sprayed vomit, the cries of men and women and things too decayed to be called either, coming from mouths stretched inhumanly wide. Moist flesh slithered, hands pounded cage bars, or seized those bars and shook them.

Still Olyssa played, her melody fragile as butterflies. In the pitch, the pipe flared bright blue.

And the ghouls fell silent. The pipe's glow dimmed as Olyssa moved further away from the ladder, the notes she blew repeated with such speed and complexity it sounded like the piping of three musicians, or four.

Erzelle leaned over the hatch until she feared falling, trying to see. She could count each heartbeat over the trill of the music.

She began to descend the ladder, mouse-quiet. Each time she took her foot from a rung, she imagined a slimy hand closing around her ankle, and felt no safer once she reached the slanted floor.

Then her eyes adjusted, and when she saw what was happening a kind of wonder took over.

The ladder had deposited her against one wall of the hold, which stretched further to either side than the light from Olyssa's pipe could reach. Iron cages large enough to hold lions lined the opposite wall, each crammed full of ghouls, faces melting with rot, muscles animated by magic, soft and ravenous things that had once been living people, who'd been brought here struggling and screaming and locked in the cages. The sorcery that kept the ghouls alive compelled them to bite and pass on their terrible curse, spread the living death, keep the larder packed for the customers of the *Red Empress*.

The monsters pressed against the bars of their cages, watching Olyssa as she played. She walked slowly past them, so close, close enough for claws to seize, and looked each creature in the face, searching, her light revealing mouths that oozed drool, dipping to illuminate the legless ones crouched at the feet of their fellows. She stared into every suppurating eye.

Olyssa's sister — a ghoul? As Erzelle watched, her own urgent pulse raced in her neck, her temples. She wanted to go to her rescuer but she couldn't bring herself to move. She kept her back against the wall, its solidity providing at least an illusion of security. The darkness growing between her and the piper could have been another wall, built from terror.

No light reached into the hold's opposite side. In that void, a red flicker, so faint Erzelle wondered if she actually saw anything.

But there it was again. An ember glow, disembodied in the darkness. A thin line of symbols, curved like the edge of a knife.

The ghouls across from her were no more than vague shapes, their wet surfaces reflecting the barest hints of the piper's light. Something huge and black moved between them and Erzelle, striding silently toward Olyssa. She glimpsed again a cobweb-slender glow from runes etched on a blade.

Erzelle's knees went weak. *No, no, no, NO!*

The first step took so much effort she might well have been bound to the wall by magic. She made herself take another, another. She floated in the dark, a mere arm's length from the motionless ghouls in their cages, the cleaver barbell-heavy in her hand.

Then she was running.

The Chef's black form eclipsed Olyssa's light. He spun at the sound of Erzelle's footfalls.

She swung wildly, struck solid flesh.

The Chef bellowed, a wounded animal. The cleaver's handle ripped from her fingers. A mountain collapsed on her, crushed her under its brutal weight as the ghouls erupted in pandemonium.

Unable to move or breathe, she faded. She heard Olyssa's shouts, one more voice in the chaos. And the sound of a hammer striking metal. Fading, fading, her awareness reduced to the pain swelling in her chest, building, building, threatening to burst her.

She thought the pain was the Chef's knife stabbing in until he flopped away and air rushed into her lungs. The shrieks of the ghouls were deafening as Olyssa dragged her away from the cages.

The splotches cleared from Erzelle's vision. Olyssa stood over her, holding the glowing pipe lengthwise in her teeth. In her hand she held the meat cleaver. That too glowed, where the blade wasn't black with blood.

The Chef was pinned against the bars of the cage, suspended lengthwise three feet above the ground, straining against grey-green arms wrapped around his shoulders, his waist, his hips, his biceps and elbows, his legs. One ghoul tore at a long wound gaping just above his left knee. With a flip of her stomach Erzelle recognized it as the result of her cleaver swing.

Another monster gnawed at the stump of the Chef's ankle. Erzelle stared uncomprehending until she noticed what lay in the blood pooled in the dented floor. Two slippered feet. Two hands, one still clutching the ceremonial knife.

One of the ghouls, a shriveled woman with bulging yellow eyes, extended a bone-thin arm, snatched that hand, dragged it into the cage. A moment later she stabbed the blade into the Chef's neck and began to saw.

His mouth twisted in a snarl.

Erzelle wanted to take the cleaver from Olyssa, to aid the ghouls in their task. In her mind she sat on the stage, harp balanced between her knees, as the covers were lifted off the gurneys and the things that once had been her mother and father grimaced without tongues.

Olyssa's voice in her head. "He won't die, whatever they do to him. Go back up, Erzelle. Stay hidden and wait till I'm done."

Her words brooked no argument. Erzelle turned at the ladder, foot on the first rung, to see Olyssa toss the cleaver so it fell within the ghouls' reach.

An eternity passed, it seemed, before the music of the pipe began again and the ghouls went quiet. When the song stopped at last, the creatures in the hold remained subdued.

Olyssa emerged from the hatch. Her eyes glistened. She said only, "She's not there."

Without terror of the Chef to spur them on, the crew of the *Red Empress* proved that keeping their lives mattered more than any loyalty to their cult, though even cowering obeisance didn't save them if they failed to follow Olyssa's orders with sufficient speed. Olyssa's wrath frightened Erzelle, and at the same time her heart rejoiced at every death.

When she and Olyssa reached the gangway, the black powerboat used to ferry guests to the *Empress* was pulling away from the wharf with a deafening roar. Figures moved in the cabin, silver ghosts above waters turned to ink by the moonlight.

Olyssa fired four shots, yanked out the magazine, took another from her opera coat, fired two more. The boat slowed, and the engine stalled.

Her voice carried clear as a chime. "Bring that boat back."

Sounds of whispers and weeping. A high voice shrieked, "No! Start the boat—"

The rifle reported, silenced the protester mid-scream. A man called, "We're coming back!"

"I'm watching," Olyssa said.

A black uniformed crewman had to lean over another one slumped at the wheel in order to steer. A child's sobs grew louder as the boat pulled alongside the dock.

Olyssa strode down the gangway, unbuttoned opera coat sweeping behind her, the barrel of her weapon trained on the boat's occupants. She spoke in a conversational tone. "Come off of there. Bring your dead with you."

When the remaining members of the Family hauled the last corpse off the boat — the twelve-year-old boy that Erzelle had noticed before, his twin sister wailing beside him — Olyssa addressed the clan. "You brought me here to feed me to ghouls and dine on my living corpse because you thought it would keep Old Man Death away. I think the results are fair trade.

"Do what I tell you, and when I leave, I promise, it will be the last time you ever see me."

A dark-haired, blue-eyed youth spat, face swollen with anger and grief. "We still have business with you." One of the others raised a staying hand, too late. "We'll find you. There's nowhere you can go where you'll be out of our reach."

Olyssa raised her eyebrows. "Is that so?"

And didn't wait for an answer. She killed the youth who spoke, the elder who tried to shush him. Two more crewmen who groped for weapons fell. Mayhem erupted as the Family scattered into the dark, but Olyssa didn't stop, her rifle blazing with every shot. She emptied her clip and loaded another one to shoot those who'd dived into the water.

At the end, two crewmen who'd sat petrified in the boat during the massacre were the only ones left alive. Olyssa ordered them back onto the *Red Empress*, to aid in the tasks she'd already set for their fellows. She had the harp and pipe case brought to the wharf, and vegetables from the kitchen stores, the best stuff, not the slop Erzelle had been forced to eat all through her captivity.

Erzelle sat on a pylon and dined over the bodies of her enemies, feeling both sick and elated.

Olyssa spoke in her mind. "Spare yourself only a little. We'll starve later if you don't."

The deck of the *Empress* had once sported tiers of glorious windows, since paneled over with black metal. Olyssa watched the crewmen scurry there, laboring to undo moorings that had rusted in place years ago.

At last one of the men shouted, "All done! I swear!"

As if cued, the wharf shook, and the gangway creaked as the current started to push the *Red Empress* out of place. Wood split, and one of the banisters snapped and fell into the river.

"Swim," Olyssa called. "You'll regret it if you stay." But she was disassembling her rifle again, exchanging stock and chamber for bell and reed.

"You asked me why I believed my sister could be here," came a new whisper. "She is being used for her magic. By vermin like these. I know this in my heart, even if I don't yet know how or where."

She began to play.

"But one day, I will."

Before Olyssa left the ghoul cages, she had unlocked them. Erzelle didn't know she'd done so until she heard the noises coming from the *Red Empress*. As it drifted toward the middle of the river, the undead boiled from its hatch.

"Don't worry, young one. They won't harm us. Nor will they be of any more use to carrion eaters."

The runes on Olyssa's pipe shone brighter than the moon. She called to the ghouls, drew them off the floating fortress and into the water. They fell like fruit from an overturned basket, and the current tumbled them away.

Erzelle had balanced her harp between her knees even before the piper whispered, "Join me."

Beneath the red moon, she plucked new melodies in the spaces Olyssa left for her.

So began the first of many lessons.

PART TWO: BONE MOSAICS

"Mind the thorns at the corners of the leaves," Olyssa commanded, "and stay still."

A half an hour passed as Erzelle and her teacher crouched in the crook of this immense white-barked tree, peering out into the forest.

Growing up first in the caste layers of Minnepaul, then in the black passages of the *Red Empress*, Erzelle still hadn't completely acclimated to wilderness, its dizzying sky, its openness in all directions, its lack of symmetry. Other aspects of freedom she'd embraced with glee — bathing in the river, Olyssa's comb straightening her hair, the way her ragged clothes, once cleaned, no longer itched against her skin — but the openness of the world could still give her vertigo. Especially when viewed from a height.

Their perch overlooked one of the rare patches of pure green in these desolate hills. New growth cluttered the glade, saplings with leaves like flattened hands rising from bushes with red-veined foliage, all of it wound through with bright-flowered vines that Olyssa warned Erzelle repeatedly not to touch. Past the burst of greenery a spring trickled from a deep split in a rock and bubbled down an incline through the grove its waters had carved, weaving between older trees that displayed the bewildering symptoms of the blight induced by the Storms.

Some trees, blackened as if by fire, continued to unfurl sickly grey leaves. Others raised proud canopies to the sun, yet oozed black slime that Olyssa warned was both poisonous and acidic. Still others twisted in agonized contortions, branches stabbing the ground like roots, while their roots groped up from between them, producing unnatural leaves. Rarer, but impossible not to notice, some trees stood inexplicably lush and hale, grown to tremendous size, their outsized leaves hogging the sunlight, their growth still spurred by the residue of the long-gone Storms. The tree they waited in, a mutant birch, was one of these.

Erzelle hadn't been born when the Storms erupted, raw tempests of magic that roared across the world, destructive as cyclones or typhoons. Olyssa had once shared that she'd been a child when the Storms started, which Erzelle had trouble reconciling, as her teacher could only be in her thirties at most and the Storms devastated the world decades ago. She'd hoped to hear more of what the Storms were like, but Olyssa seemed disinclined to share more and Erzelle lacked the nerve to breach that silence. Much of their travels took place in silence — Olyssa wasn't prone to casual conversation.

Tall and broad-shouldered, in her leather jacket and brown trousers, Olyssa seemed to meld into the tree, motionless as she observed the glade, her rifle nestled in the crook of her arm, poised in line with her gaze, the ruby glow of its runes dormant. She'd told Erzelle she expected the spring would attract game — they were nearly out of food — yet so far they'd seen nothing larger than a lizard. A sheet of ocher clouds veiled the lowering sun.

The crook of branch that supported Erzelle made for an uncomfortable chair. Some unseen beast resumed its high-pitched cries, sounding like a child under torture.

She didn't realize how much she fidgeted until Olyssa softly spoke. "You have no patience for this sort of thing. My sister, she's the same way."

Erzelle willed her teacher to share more. Three months together and Olyssa had hardly breathed a word about her ill-fated sibling, though the possibility of finding her motivated everything they did. "You once said I looked like her?"

"Shhhhhhh."

Erzelle bristled. After all, Olyssa had broken the silence first. Yet she obeyed, and chided herself for being ungrateful.

Olyssa returned to scanning the woods. Her next words were not spoken aloud. After weeks of traveling together, Erzelle no longer mistook Olyssa's mindspeech for her physical voice. For one thing, her teacher seemed more at ease sharing her thoughts directly, and she'd go on at much greater length. *She looks like me, but more slender, though I'm only a little taller, if you can believe that.* She glanced Erzelle's way. *Your eyes, though, they're almost the same. Both in color and in the hint of mischief that invades when you're happy. We wondered where she got those eyes. Both my mother and father had eyes dark as mine.*

Erzelle tried to imagine her green eyes in Olyssa's face. She started to say so when Olyssa raised the rifle. She pulled the trigger, agile as ever despite the bindings on her hands, and the runes along the barrel flared red.

A deer took two steps and toppled to the grass.

Olyssa was out of the tree in an instant, reaching up to help Erzelle down. *We'll cook it tonight.*

Unbidden, the dining hall of the *Red Empress* flashed within Erzelle's mind, with its walls and tables the color of raw meat, and she couldn't suppress a shudder.

Erzelle helped lug the deer carcass back to their campsite, a not-quite clearing where trees were sparse, with a rock jutting up on one side like a giant's lost tooth and a swath of low-growing cedar on the other. She also helped Olyssa skin and clean the deer, though to be truthful her teacher hardly needed any help. She'd lived as a nomad for many years. Once again Erzelle couldn't stop herself from wondering how her teacher knew the customs of lavish city life so well that she'd been able to trick the Family into taking her in.

They dug a shallow fire pit and soon the deer roasted over it. The smell was maddeningly good, the taste even better. Afterward they watched the fire, their backs to the rock.

"Fetch your harp," Olyssa finally said, as she opened her mandolin case and exchanged the rifle assembly for the reed and bell. "I think we'll risk another lesson."

A man's voice chimed in from the dark. "And what lesson would that be, my lady?"

Erzelle shrieked in surprise.

Olyssa sprang to her feet, letting the detached reed bounce in the dirt as she grabbed up the rifle assembly, trying to attach it before realizing she still needed to spin off the bell. She was up, rifle aimed, with astonishing speed, yet visibly flustered. Erzelle had never seen anyone get the drop on her. The man stepping out from the cedars with his hands raised most certainly had.

"No closer," barked Olyssa, as the barrel flared red.

He lifted his empty hands to shoulder level. "As you can see, I didn't bring a gun."

"What do you want?"

Amusement coiled through the silky tenor of his voice. "My people's due."

The man's smile didn't articulate across his face the way a typical human's would. The corners pulled up toward his cheekbones, while the center of his lower lip pulled down to a point. His eyes were tilted at a startling angle above his streamlined nose, not slanted slightly upwards like Olyssa's but nearly vertical, and their orbs were huge. His irises glinted red in the firelight, and his pupils were slitted like cat's eyes. His thick hair was also red, as if he wore a crown of flame. His dark clothes clung snug to his frame: a long sleeve jersey, black jeans and black boots. His slender body tapered gracefully from chest to waist, and just like Olyssa, he wasted no movement.

Olyssa replied, "No riddles, vulpine."

Erzelle started. Growing up in Minnepaul, she'd heard of the vulpines, but such stories had all the exaggerated character of tall tales. As had stories of the ghouls. Mere phantoms to frighten children at night, they seemed then.

She'd occasionally heard whispers of the vulpines among the guests at the *Red Empress*: turns of phrase, "clever as a vulpine," or more often, "hungry as a vulpine." Remembering that made her own stomach boil. But she'd never once thought of the creatures as real.

More alarming was the fact that though he was without question something other than human, the man half-revealed in the flicker of their fire had a beauty to him, an allure, that defied all better intuition. Erzelle found his fanged smile repellant but at the same time thrilling. She didn't want to look away.

"There's no riddle," he said. "You've poached on our land."

"The deer?" Olyssa's voice rose, incredulous.

Her off-kilter reaction startled Erzelle. She's seen her teacher calmly inform armed men of their impending death multiple times.

Was she now rattled at being caught off-guard, or did the vulpine's peculiar beauty unnerve her as much as it did Erzelle?

Olyssa went on, "This scrawny thing will barely feed the two of us for a week!"

"It was kind of me to even let you have any. It belongs to us by right."

"How about I give you a bullet instead?"

The vulpine's eyes went almost round before narrowing, the fire's glow reflected in near-vertical slivers. "You might fell me, but you don't have enough bullets to fend off all of us."

He spread his arms to indicate the woods behind him.

Last night, after they'd found shelter from a light rain splatter beneath an outcrop of shale, Olyssa had confided that she needed to make more bullets, which meant buying or scavenging more of the right kind and inscribing them with runes, a prospect that seemed unlikely in the wilderness. She'd used half of her supply in the *Red Empress,* and a quarter more in the riverside village of hardscrabble fisher-folk where they'd taken shelter after abandoning the powerboat stolen from the ghoul-eating cultists.

The vulpine must have been spying on them and overheard their conversation. Erzelle's skin goose-pimpled. What else had he heard, what had he made of it? Had he seen Olyssa's hands unbandaged? They'd almost completely healed from the burns that had seared the runes from the pipe into her palms. In another night or so, she'd no longer need the medicines Erzelle kept helping her prepare.

Olyssa was a woman of amazing strength and power, but Erzelle had no inking of the extent of that power until the night at the fisher-folk's village, when they had been besieged by cultists seeking vengeance for the destruction of the *Red Empress.*

—❦·⟨❦⟩·❦—

"Come out, witch," called a mocking male voice from the lot outside the hostel.

This dowdy building where they'd played music to pay for their lodging had once been some sort of administrative office, its cinder block shell erected nearly a century before the Storms. The large family that lived in it now, and occasionally let rooms to those passing through, had rebuilt its shattered wings as best they could. The old couple heading this clan had broad, crinkled faces rendered adorable by their smiles, and when earlier in the day they'd requested news of other places, Olyssa politely rattled off a number of things about Minnepaul, Millwalk and other cities that meant little to Erzelle. Despite Olyssa's evident lack of enthusiasm, the couple attended every word with eager nods. Erzelle went outside and ended up playing hopscotch with a pair of twin girls two years her junior. Her and Olyssa's arrival in this shantytown clinging to life on the riverbank seemed to have stirred a lot of interest among the residents, but Erzelle abandoned herself to the game, ignoring the stares of the twins' older siblings and the other children who gathered to watch.

It was one of the twins who warned her just after dark that a man dressed head-to-toe in black had come through the village earlier that day asking after a piper and harpist and left quickly upon getting an affirmative.

Olyssa had gone downstairs to urge the old couple to gather their family and leave, and seen the cultists coming up the street from the wharf. At least thirty, all armed with rifles. When she returned to their room on the second story, with its single shade-drawn window and its stained wooden paneling and its pair of cots, she told Erzelle that there might well be more cultists covering the other exits.

After that brief announcement she sat lotus-style on the floor between their cots with her rifle in her lap and began to chant as the rough voice outside taunted.

"Come out and know our mercy. Come out or you'll wish you had been eaten."

She held the rifle up with both hands as if presenting it for an offering. Its red runes glowed brighter and brighter, her chant unceasing. Huddled under a cot, Erzelle made out the words, uttered fast and sing-song: "Find my enemies. Find my enemies. Find my enemies."

Glowing brighter still, the rifle shuddered and lifted into the air.

Sweat glistened on Olyssa's brow, beaded on her arms, where there'd been none a moment before. And the rifle, with runes blinding bright, tilted toward the floor like a dowsing rod and fired through it, sending splinters of wood flying. Erzelle clapped her hands over her ears. The rifle pivoted and tilted up toward their window, swept back and forth as it fired five times in a row. Glass shattered as bullets ricocheted off the top of the window frame. The taunting voice cried out and fell silent. Other men screamed. The rifle turned back to the floor again, shot four more times through it, the impacts vibrating the boards so Erzelle felt them through her shins and elbows. It lifted and blasted the wall beside the door. Olyssa chanted non-stop. "Find my enemies."

Erzelle could hardly sort out the cacophony. The crack of wood splintering, pings like pans striking stone, split-second high-pitched whines. The sounds of bullets ricocheting, terminating in surprised, anguished cries.

The rifle moved on its own, firing at nothing. Yet it never missed.

Shell casings clattered on the floor as the shouts below cut short. The barrel grew even brighter, intensifying from red to gold, an effect Erzelle had never seen before. Olyssa paused for breath, long enough to spit out a word: "Clip!" In that instant the runes dimmed and the rifle dipped in the air. It slowly rose again as its owner resumed her chant.

The barrel continued to swivel, though it had ceased firing. Erzelle scrambled for the mandolin case.

"Find my enemies. Find my enemies."

"Where the hell is she?" whispered one of the cultists, his voice carried through the new holes in the floor. "Those bullets came from everywhere." Speaking from the room immediately below them.

Elsewhere in the building, heavy boots ascended stairs.

She dug through the case in a panic, grabbed one of the clips and tossed it back in before she realized what it was. Olyssa never stopped her chant.

The footsteps reached the hall outside their room. Although she wasn't loud, they heard Olyssa's constant mutter.

"Shhh! What's that?"

Olyssa held her hand out. Sweat dripped from her fingers. Erzelle nearly dropped the clip again before her teacher snatched it from her.

Gunfire shredded her eardrums. Erzelle threw herself to the floor before she realized the men were emptying their weapons into the unoccupied room next door. Glass shattered, wood fragmented, paneling flew apart.

Olyssa's strained mantra filled the silence that followed as she loaded the new clip into the floating gun. "Find my enemies. Find my enemies."

"Not in here!" one of the hunters yelled.

The symbols etched in the pipe flashed white as the rifle spun like a compass needle, fired nine times into the adjacent room, trigger moving of its own accord. A chorus of heavy thuds followed.

But a thunder of footsteps did too. Olyssa's rifle pivoted to the door and discharged over and over again. More bodies fell, leaving nothing but the patter of a single person running back down the hall. The rifle fired. A bullet ricocheted. The fleeing man collapsed.

Though it wasn't out of bullets, the rifle hung motionless, then fell. The dingy mat it landed on began to smolder. Its barrel continued to glow white.

Outside, nothing but silence, as if no one in the whole village dared breathe.

Olyssa took in a great gasp of air and wheezed for several breaths, her hair plastered to her scalp, her blouse soaked through. She remained in lotus position, the blazing barrel just inches from her knee. "The reed," she rasped.

Bewildered, Erzelle scrambled to find it. She could smell smoke rising from the mat.

She spotted the reed beside the mandolin case and brought it to Olyssa, whose dark eyes bored into hers. "Your harp. I need you to play it. Now!"

Erzelle obeyed, wondering if her teacher's mind had been broken by the terrifying spell she'd cast. She jerked her harp from its case and plopped it between her knees. As Olyssa had given her no instructions she plucked the longest strings to sound the first notes of "The Mountain King," a simple tune her mother had taught her.

Olyssa held the reed in her lips, and picked up the pipe. She didn't flinch. At the hiss of searing skin Erzelle almost let the harp spill from her lap.

However, she knew not to stop playing until told. As much as she wanted to grab the pipe from Olyssa and fling it away, she stayed put.

Olyssa brought the end of the white-glowing length of metal to the reed at her lips and attached it. Erzelle's heart fluttered as she imagined the little wooden piece bursting into flames. But Olyssa blew around it, producing a note more piercing than a kettle whistle. It descended in register, and when it did the pipe's runes changed instantly from white to blue.

She added harmony to Erzelle's melody until the pipe no longer glowed torch bright. Then she set it down, flexed her fingers, winced and asked Erzelle to bring her medicine pouch. Her palms and fingertips were red and bloody. Yet Erzelle noticed those burns were nowhere near as severe as they should have been.

Her ears rang, her pulse thumped in her neck and the smell of smoke and white-hot metal hung in the air. Olyssa calmly instructed her in how to mix the poultice, how to soak and apply the dressings. This short-term supply of purpose made for a welcome distraction.

There came a timid knock on the door. Erzelle jumped, losing her grip on the bandage she was winding around her teacher's right hand.

"Miss?" It was the matriarch who ran the hostel. Her voice quavered. "Please. We want you to leave."

Olyssa's response was loud as a gong. "Are you prepared to make me?"

Erzelle cringed, recalling the old woman's sweet smile, but she held her tongue. No answer came from outside. Soft footsteps eventually stole away, following an odd rhythm, as if stepping over many objects that blocked the way.

Indeed, at least a dozen black-clad bodies of the cultists blocked the hall when the pair emerged.

Though she shook with exhaustion, Olyssa observed the carnage without expression, her mandolin case slung over her shoulder beside her pack. She turned to Erzelle and said "I'm sorry we had to give up our beds tonight," as if they'd had a mild dispute with the hoteliers and nothing more.

"Again," Olyssa said to the vulpine, "the remains of this animal will hardly last the two of us a week. I'm sure there are many others in the forest. Why does this one concern you?"

"Because it's rightfully ours," he said.

Every night since the attack in the village, Erzelle had helped Olyssa re-bandage her hands. There was no way to know how many other vulpine might be waiting in the forest, especially if they were all as silent as this one. Even if Olyssa could steal enough time to chant her rifle aloft, arm it to kill all her unseen enemies with ricochets that never miss — Erzelle never wanted to watch her teacher torture herself that way again.

She took a deep breath and in a voice much less steady than she'd intended said, "Maybe we can offer you something else?"

The vulpine's red gaze flicked to Erzelle. She went on, "If you've heard us talk then you've heard us play."

Olyssa's voice in her head: ***Don't bother bargaining with it.***

But Erzelle had already opened her mouth again. "Surely if we played for … all of you, it would be a fair trade?"

Erzelle, stop!

"Why? You heard what he said! What good will scaring him do? I don't want you to hurt yourself again. I spent years in that ship where they were fattening me up to be eaten. I'm not going to volunteer for it now!"

It took Erzelle a beat to realize she's retorted to Olyssa aloud. She must have sounded like someone hallucinating. Olyssa wasn't looking at her, but the vulpine was staring, his eyes almost round, his mouth working, flashing fangs.

Finally his tenor thrummed indignant. "Young miss, what tales have you heard? We're not cannibals. We're not ghouls. I assure you I'm just as human as you are."

The way he glared, the way his face drew up in a snarl, the flesh folding to either side of his nose into an expression furious as a shaken fist, Erzelle might well have doubted his word, had he not sounded so genuinely appalled.

"I'm sorry," she said.

When Erzelle apologized the vulpine's expression softened, a spectrum of emotion playing across his features: confusion, sadness, resolve. Then he replaced his disconcerting smile as if it were a mask. He stepped backward into the trees, calling: "'T'will be a delight to hear you play. Please do. Then we'll decide."

It was as if he'd never been there. No further noise came from the trees.

Olyssa hadn't budged. Neither had the barrel of her gun. As the fire crackled, she waited, eying the forest. At last she tipped her weapon up. Erzelle removed her harp from its case, expecting Olyssa to project rebukes into her head at any moment. Yet none came.

Finally, her teacher sat to dismantle her rifle. *We'll practice the concerto again.*

Olyssa had been leading her through a three-movement concerto that accommodated flute and harp. Erzelle didn't know which instruments the composition had originally been written for, but she marveled both at how well it worked and at the astonishing depth of Olyssa's memory, how she could keep all that music in her head despite years without a score to review. Even more astonishing, this concerto was just one of many Olyssa could call to her fingers at will.

When the pipe was assembled to play, Erzelle plucked the shortest strings to begin the long descent of the opening notes. Once Olyssa joined in Erzelle found it easy to lose herself in the challenge of negotiating this complex dance of melody and harmony without any missteps. She took comfort in the fact that when she did make mistakes their unseen audience was likely none the wiser.

—◎·(◉◗◉)·◎—

Once the last notes died away, the vulpine returned.

"Splendid! Splendid!" he said, clapping in wide-eyed delight, aquiver with buoyant energy, like a child looking forward to a favorite game.

Olyssa watched him with a predator's unblinking focus but allowed him to sit at the fire across from them. No others came out to join him, and Erzelle wondered if his statement about outnumbering Olyssa's bullets had been all bluff.

If so, Olyssa hadn't called him on it. Instead, she asked, "So do we have a bargain now?"

"After such an enchanting performance? I'm ashamed you felt you even had to ask. Of course, you may keep that stringy thing. Though I confess, it smells so good, I'd love a taste if you cared to share a small portion?"

Olyssa blinked, then betrayed the slightest of smiles. "Will we, from now on, be left in peace?"

The vulpine inclined his head, only slightly disappointed that his question had gone ignored. "Play each evening, madame, with the beauty I've just heard, so long as you roam our lands, and I promise no harm will come to you."

"Well, then. How far does your land extend?"

"East to the river, south to the ruins of the old rocky city, west to the Violet Bluffs."

Olyssa had said little about the Violet Bluffs — only that it was another place of sorcery where her sister might be found. How she knew this, she had not yet divulged. Erzelle remained too grateful for her rescue and too intimidated by Olyssa's might to demand such answers. Still, her desire to know more and her resentment at not having it sated had been growing without her even realizing it, until tonight, when she undermined her teacher in front of this bewitching fox-man.

In a rare display of intense interest, even eagerness, Olyssa said, "We're looking for the Violet Bluffs. Can you tell us where they are?"

The vulpine's astonished expression dissolved into another odd smile. "I can't help but confess that makes me curious. It doesn't surprise me that the foul place has a reputation outside our hollows, but I've never imagined I'd meet someone who actually wanted to go there."

"Why? What's there?"

"Some very strange people … If the way I look bothers you, I have to imagine the folks at Violet Bluffs will have you in fidgets."

Erzelle sensed an edge of hurt beneath his jocular tone.

Olyssa didn't rise to his bait. "Why?"

He again regarded Erzelle. "My people didn't ask for what the Storms did to us. How they changed us." And she again said "I'm sorry" but he talked right over her. "The folk who live in the Bluff, they've been changed, too. But not in the same way that we have. We bleed. They don't."

"Ghouls?" Olyssa asked.

He laughed, a delightfully wicked cackle that warmed the cooling night. "I know what a ghoul is, my lady. Ghouls don't dress themselves in robes. Ghouls don't converse. Ghouls don't farm, though what the Grey Ones plant by their temple is something no one in their right mind would want to harvest."

"What is it they farm, then?"

"I've never been there myself, and I wouldn't want to go there. I've only heard stories, that they collect the bodies of the dead … for many dead remain from the Storms when they rampaged through these mountains, entire towns destroyed, their bodies never claimed, no one to claim them. What business the people of the Bluff have with the dead, I can't tell you."

"So you've never seen any of these people yourself?"

"Oh no. I have." His ever-present smile faltered, and he grew quiet.

Olyssa let her impatience show. "There's no need for games."

He spread his hands. "There's no need for rebukes, lovely miss. I'm not playing a game. I'm genuinely flummoxed, trying to figure out how to describe these Grey Ones to you. They're not a subject I'm ever asked to expound on much." His grin returned. "It's not as if you can just sit down and share good moonshine with them. Their faces are like plaster masks, and they look at you as if you're a tree they'd rather saw down than acknowledge. You think they're mute, and then one speaks, and it's as if its words were pre-recorded." Again he regarded Erzelle. "You do know what I mean by that?"

"Yes, she does," Olyssa said, before Erzelle could respond. "So you've spoken to them?"

"On occasion."

"Tell me more."

He shifted, crossed his arms, bemused. Erzelle noticed thick red hair where his wrists emerged from his sleeves, not quite dense enough to be dubbed a pelt. "They dress the same regardless of the weather. Wrap themselves head to foot in coarse cloth and keep hoods pulled down to shade their faces, even at night. Maybe to hide their skin. Their faces are blotched like they've been splattered with ink."

"You said they harvest the dead. Do they harvest ghouls as well?"

"Now that's an interesting question." He stared into the fire. His jaw clenched.

"Is there any reason why you can't just answer it?"

His eyes narrowed. He shook his head. "So rude!" The knowing grin he shot Erzelle's way betokened sympathy. Despite herself she had to suppress an answering smile.

"We have an arrangement with the people of the Bluff," he explained. "Should we spy a ghoul anywhere within our territory, we're to let them know."

Olyssa leaned forward. "Does that arrangement extend to living people?"

He raised exquisitely tapered hands as if to ward her off. "We truck no business with them unless we absolutely have to. The ghouls, though, we're willing to let them handle." He made a show of shuddering. "Those things. They wander in from anywhere. And we're as vulnerable to them as you are." Again, the emphasis, the hurt. "The Grey Ones make them vanish."

"What do they do with them?"

He laughed. "Turn them into frogs, for all I know."

Erzelle curled tight and hugged her knees, remembering the hold in the *Red Empress*. The Violet Bluffs might harbor another cult. And Olyssa wanted to go to them.

Her teacher's voice grew cold. "I said no games."

"There's no need to be so demanding. They have a temple atop the Bluff, a building I've heard used to be a monastery by a parkway. I assure you the road's long gone. There is no line to see inside the temple and if there was one I wouldn't be in it." And now he glared. "And you shouldn't be either. These are men and women who don't hunt, don't cook, don't drink, don't yawn, and as far as we can tell don't ever sleep. It's certainly no place to bring her." He pointed at Erzelle.

For a second, Olyssa pursed her lips. Apparently his words had struck a nerve. Yet she didn't relent. "How many are there?"

"Hard to know, they look so much alike."

"Surely, as effective at spying as you are, there have been attempts?"

He bared teeth in response. "We learned a long time ago not to spy on them." Rage contorted his face. Both Olyssa and Erzelle recoiled. But just as quickly he redrew his smile. "We've talked for a long time without any introduction, and that just doesn't seem right to me, especially as thoroughly as you've worked me over." He stood and executed a rakish bow. "I'm Reneer. And I'm pleased to make your acquaintance." He cocked his head at Erzelle. "And you?"

"I'm Erzelle Cardona," she blurted, her full name sounding so strange to her — it had been years since she'd spoken it or heard it spoken.

Don't let your guard so far down, Olyssa chided. She offered only her first name when the vulpine turned to her. She stood and offered a hand, which Reneer quickly squeezed, muttering, "Charmed."

Erzelle realized even she didn't know the rest of her teacher's name.

Reneer remained standing. "Now, Olyssa, I don't suppose you'll tell me why you want to go to the Violet Bluffs? Or why you'd risk bringing a girl her age there?"

Olyssa's voice often sounded most musical when she was at her most sarcastic. "I'll wager my apprentice could tie you in knots single-handed, Mr. Reneer."

Reneer's lip curled up wryly. "No doubt she could."

Erzelle realized she was blushing, and looked away.

"As for your question," Olyssa said, "no, you can't know the why. It's best that you don't."

"Hmm." Reneer flashed his grin once more. "Well, seeing as we've enjoyed so much small talk this evening, perhaps I should take my leave of you beauties?"

Olyssa actually seemed caught off guard for a fraction of an instant before she straightened the smile that dimpled her cheeks. "How far to this temple you mentioned?"

Sighing, the vulpine clasped his hands together. "If you started walking now you could be there at this hour tomorrow."

For a moment, Erzelle thought Olyssa was actually going to tell her to pack the camp so they could start out. Instead, she just said, "Thank you. And my thanks to your people for being so reasonable in allowing us to trade."

"Oh, yes," he said, eyes twinkling, "I'll tell them."

"Oh, really?" Her eyes narrowed. "I thought they were watching us."

"And perhaps they are," he retorted with a grin, the mischievous glint never leaving his eye.

"I see."

His expression turned serious. "Are you sure you won't perhaps rethink this journey you've chosen to undertake? The music I heard tonight — it'd be a shame for it to vanish from the world."

Olyssa blinked. "It won't."

"My lady, I hope you speak truth." He nodded to Erzelle. "Good night." He turned to the cedars, merged into their shadows and was gone.

Say nothing else unless you must. That one may well hear our every word.

Yet later that night, lying by the still-warm embers, thoughts of the ghoul-collecting Grey Ones so badgered Erzelle that she could no longer keep quiet. "Why do we need to go to this place?"

My sister.

"What makes you so sure your sister is a ghoul?"

Mind your tongue.

"Is she?"

It's hard to explain. What was done to her, it's as if she died, the way a ghoul is dead. And yet she lives. Some part of her remains here. I know she's alive because the pipe she made for me still plays. That much I've told you before.

"Why do you think she's there? At the temple?"

Keep your voice down.

"Why? I want to know why!" She rolled over to face Olyssa, whose eyes glistened in the moonlight. "I just escaped from a terrible place. And this sounds even worse. Why are we going there?"

I won't make you go. You don't have to. But I do.

Such a long time went by that Erzelle thought Olyssa wouldn't answer, and as her anger lost steam she found she didn't have the will to push her teacher further. By and by a sensation like a long sigh wound through her mind, a breath drawn in before singing.

Many years ago, before I started my search, I wove a spell. I tapped the darkness, for the first and only time in my life. Something I'd sworn I would never do. I did it for my sister.

Tapped the darkness. Erzelle didn't recognize the term but couldn't bring herself to interrupt.

I played the pipe my sister made for me for a full day, never stopping. I wove a spell that created a thinking entity, a being made of light and energy. I ordered it to tell me where my sister was. But the thing I made, its mind was rough clay, crumbling from the moment I shaped it. It wouldn't answer the way I wished it to. It told me all the places where she could be, and it did so in riddles that took me long months to decipher.

I had quite the ugly surprise in store when I arrived at the first place the spell had mapped for me. An entire island infested with ghouls.

Their minders were a sect of warlocks not unlike the ones who held you captive. They kept the ghouls limbless and buried up to their necks in the sands of the island. Luckily for me, the ruse I put on — the unsuspecting minstrel hoping for food and lodging — served me just as well there as when I found you.

The next place was like that, too, another nest of sorcerers. Those seeking the mastery of this new magic and the prolonged life it brings recognize that those mindless creatures can serve as a power source. Dangerous as they are, they're easy to capture and control if you have the right knowledge.

Once I understood what this pattern told me, that my sister has been enslaved the way these ghouls have been enslaved, I learned as much as I could about every single cell of carrion eaters: Who and what I would find in each place. How best to get there and get out. I knew for many years that I would visit the Red Empress. And if I didn't find Lilla there, I'd seek her next at the place called Violet Bluffs, though about that place I've learned little.

I plotted this route years ago based on the riddles I deciphered. Erzelle, if she's not at this temple the vulpine spoke of, assuming he didn't lie for the fun of it, I know already where I'll head next. But it's too soon to talk about that.

Never had Olyssa said so much at once. Erzelle kept her gaze fixed on the wisps of clouds shrouding the moon. The blanket her teacher provided cocooned her in warmth, but the things Olyssa hinted at stretched jaws open wider than the world, a hungry abyss that had dined on millions.

She thought Olyssa had finished. Until more words came, demure and muted.

Finding you was a surprise. It's been a delight, having you to talk to and teach. But if you don't want to follow me on this path, I won't make you.

Erzelle couldn't imagine what horrors Olyssa had already endured. Or how deep her love for her sister must run, that it kept her going forward, not knowing what she'd ultimately find. Erzelle wanted to be that brave. She wanted to see Olyssa's sister freed the way Olyssa had freed her.

"I want to go where you go," she said.

After another long silence: *Thank you.*

—⊙·(☉)₀(☉)·⊙—

A figure strode through the forest, like a man but twice as tall, a deer's antlers growing from his head, not a pair of them but at least a dozen, so many that he should have staggered under their weight even if they weren't each as long he was tall — and yet he didn't.

From every fork and crook of those antlers hung a severed human head, each one still alive, eyes rolling in terror, mouths moving silent.

It stooped to pick up a new head that lay on the forest floor. Olyssa's. Her head fit easily in the creature's palm. Her dark hair cascaded through its fingers.

The creature's shoulders shook, and it loosed a terrible sob of grief.

Erzelle woke with a start, to find the figure standing over her, its horns bisecting the moon.

She gasped, only to start awake again, and turn to see Olyssa's face sketched in the gloom by the last of the embers, her breathing soft, sleeping with her eyes open as she often did.

—⊙·(☉)₀(☉)·⊙—

They hiked one more day and camped one more night. The next morning, they spied the cliff Reneer had spoken of and the temple squatting atop it, its layers of pale stone blocks evoking in Erzelle's mind the scales of an immense lizard, buttresses splayed out from its walls like crooked legs. The ledge itself rose out of the forest floor like a giant's tombstone, a sheer edifice of raw earth banded with sediment layers. Above the temple the slopes of a mountain stretched toward the sky. The flowers that swathed those slopes gave the mountain its name — purple flowers, each with two large petals spreading to either side of a golden core with a red center. They peered like an infestation of crazed eyes from between the leaves of the trees and bushes that covered the mountain's face. Even well below, an acrid scent of sweet pepper reached the travelers.

They couldn't approach the temple directly. Instead, they angled north, away from the bluff, until they found a gentler incline leading up into the foothills. Cutting their way through this long detour involved impasses and backtracking, and instances where the ground tipped so steeply they had to pull themselves up by clinging to the brush that stubbled the slopes. After just minutes of this, Erzelle's joints ached and her arms and neck stung from scratches. The awe she felt for her teacher also grew, as Olyssa wasn't the least bit encumbered by the mandolin case on her back — Erzelle, having lifted it a few times, knew how heavy it was. Erzelle wished she could have left her harp behind, but Olyssa believed they could need it. In fact, incredibly, she'd offered to shoulder it as well it, but given her own burden, Erzelle had insisted she could handle it. She refused to voice her after-the-fact misgivings.

Olyssa did her best to guide them so they kept out of sight of the stone monstrosity, and allowed frequent pauses for rest. At first Erzelle's chest tightened in shame, because it seemed these were for her benefit only. By the fourth time she'd become too winded for such thoughts, yet she vowed not to be a hindrance. She'd nod to indicate when she could continue, whether or not she was truly ready.

During one of those stops, puffing for breath, she murmured, "I wish we'd asked Reneer if there was a path. I bet he'd have told us."

So our little fox-man is a friend now? Olyssa's tone wasn't at all amused. *Don't be fooled, Erzelle. There's no one we can trust, least of all him.*

Erzelle had never before believed so whole-heartedly that her teacher was wrong. But she kept that thought to herself, instead saying, "I'm ready. Let's go."

They'd been climbing for hours, the sun high in a dizzying blue sky, the sweet-sour odor from the flowers overwhelming her sinuses, when Olyssa told her they needed to start back down. At first she was confused, until she looked out through the shade of the ugly purple flowers all around them and understood they'd ascended above the ledge where the temple stood, and now had to clamber down to it. The flowers sprouted from vines that choked all the other growth and made the going even slower than the ascent had been, as the straps of their packs were constantly getting hooked and had to be yanked free.

The vines had pink tendrils growing from them like beans or peas, that curled and contracted around whatever touched them. Though Olyssa went first and did her best with the long knife she kept in her boot to clear the way, more than once Erzelle had to rip her ankles free, and the noise it made caused her heart to leap.

Slowly, Olyssa cautioned. ***Calculate every move you make. We're getting close.***

Not long after, she pointed out through a gap in the flowers that afforded a full view of the former monastery. To Erzelle it resembled a fortress far more than a place of worship, despite the pair of circular stained glass windows set high the facade, mounted to either side of an arched gate sealed by outsized iron double doors. The gate and windows together created the impression of a frowning piscine face.

The top of the bluff had been cleared of all wild vegetation. A field of turned earth in the shape of an eight-pointed star marred the grounds before the temple entrance. No crops grew in the brown expanse, yet three figures clad head-to-toe in grey toiled in it nonetheless. One held a sack, while the others meticulously prodded the soil with small spades. The diggers unearthed pale rocks which they picked up and placed in the bag.

Then one of the stooping Grey Ones pulled a head from the earth. The head wasn't severed, but plainly attached to a neck and shoulders. The other Grey One involved in the digging set down the spade and produced a small scythe from the folds of its ragged robe. One stroke freed the head up for the sack. The rest they left as they continued their probing search.

Olyssa and Erzelle watched in silence. Erzelle's muscles grew sore from staying still so long. She recognized now that the pale stones the Grey Ones collected were human bones. Sometimes they found more intact bodies, and would amputate pieces from them seemingly at random. A hand here, a shin here, an unrecognizable tangle of gristle here.

Erzelle wanted to ask, *What are they doing?* but was afraid even to breathe too loud. If the Grey Ones buried the bodies there to begin with, why did they search so meticulously, as if unsure what would be found beneath the dirt?

A bell chimed once. The low, moaning note didn't come from the temple's tower, but from somewhere deep inside it. The Grey Ones at once stopped in their tasks and huddled toward the huge door, dragging their bag of bones and body parts with them. The doors swung inward and the warped figures shuffled into darkness.

Erzelle didn't notice when Olyssa drew her pipe from its case, but she had it in her hands when she stood.

Stay back. I have a hunch.

She started to play. Erzelle recognized the tune immediately — it was the same one Olyssa had woven as she'd looked into the eyes of the ghouls in the hold of the *Red Empress*. Yet it wasn't precisely the same; this was slower, more complex.

The doors had started to swing closed, but they stopped as Olyssa emerged from the thicket and strode into the clearing.

The three wrapped figures reappeared in the entrance. Another appeared behind them. And another.

The one in front, the tallest, came forward, oddly hesitant, moving as if underwater. Olyssa faced the lot of them from directly across the star-shaped field, as three, then four, then more of them staggered out into the light. Like the ghouls drawn from the *Red Empress* after it drifted away from the dock.

But these Grey Ones weren't ghouls, not if Reneer were to be believed. They could talk. They had minds of their own.

Erzelle, come out. I need your harp.

More than a dozen of the creatures clustered outside the temple now. They all looked human in some way. A couple of stooped-over women mingled in with the men. Olyssa's playing appeared to hold them entranced. Hoods shrouded all their faces.

Erzelle, I need you!

Erzelle pushed against her fear-induced inertia, and bulled her way out through the grasping, choking vines. She sat by Olyssa's feet and put her harp in her lap, averting her eyes from their bizarre audience.

Play the melody.

Erzelle shot a worried look at her teacher. Runes shimmered blue along the pipe's length as her fingers fluttered at the bell. Erzelle's harp held no magic.

Still, she followed the processions of notes, plucked them out along the octaves with little difficulty, and couldn't help but take pride as she played along in perfect synchronicity for several bars.

Keep that going. Don't stop until I ask.

Olyssa began improvising through variation after variation. Half-notes became trills of eighth notes, became runs of thirty-second notes, and faster. A heartbeat-like rhythm of surprisingly deep tones appeared in the spaces between the trills. Erzelle couldn't tell how Olyssa was breathing to sustain it all.

The horde across from them, numbering almost two dozen, shifted uneasily with each change, and Erzelle pieced together what was happening. Somehow Olyssa had deduced that the Grey Ones shared enough in common with the ghouls that her pipe could control them, and she was searching for the variant on her spell that would make the control complete, her hold secure. These creatures wrapped head-to-toe in wide strips of a leathery fabric that looked unnervingly like tanned skin were immobilized but no more than that, perhaps even fighting to break free from the music's power.

A movement caught Erzelle's eye, closer than the crowd swaying outside the temple door. She glanced over and regretted it. All through the star of turned earth, bones and worse sprouted from the soil by the hundreds. She faltered in her playing.

Ignore it! Concentrate!

She closed her eyes, focused on the notes and shut out everything else, as she'd done for so long in the belly of the riverboat. She didn't consciously mark the moment when Olyssa's harmony stabilized into a repeating pattern, though the tension left the air and maintaining the melody became much easier.

Stop. Put your harp away. I need you to speak for me now.

The soil stopped birthing its grotesque crop. The Grey Ones now stood in ordered ranks. No doubt it was when they arranged themselves this way that Olyssa had known she'd achieved her aim. She continued to play this new variation, recognizably the same but faster and more complex, without stopping.

What I say to you next, repeat to them.

Erzelle obeyed. "Lower your hoods. Expose your faces."

The Grey Ones pulled back their hoods and tugged the leathery gauze from their heads.

All but three were men, and just as Reneer had said, they had ink-splotched faces. Their paper-dry skin crumpled around yellow eyes that were almost lost within the alternating blotches of bloodless white and ripe-fruit black, startling patterns that swirled and spattered across their features.

"What is the purpose of this place?"

The Grey Ones stared, unmoving. The only sound came from Olyssa's pipe.

Erzelle almost didn't hear the answer when it came. A female in the back rasped in a voice like a dried creek speaking. "We … serve … this place. Its purpose … we are … not told."

"Who made you?"

Again, a long pause. "We … are born … in this … place. It … makes us … as it … needs us."

"Who is buried in this grave?"

The woman took a step forward, a dark patch swirling up from her chin, covering her mouth, curling up her right cheek and across her forehead to finally spiral around her left eye. The socket there was empty.

"No one … buried … they are brought up … from below."

"What do you mean, from below?"

The woman didn't answer. A couple of the men fidgeted, as if resisting the compulsion to talk. Finally the tallest, his face split vertically by a mottled stripe, opened his mouth to reveal a withered tongue flapping. His words were almost unintelligible. "Drawn … earth … mountain … calls … to purpose."

Olyssa played on several more seconds, then asked Erzelle to follow a different tack.

"Who else dwells here?"

"There … is … no one."

"Are all of you here?"

The tall man again spoke. "Some … deep … low."

"Are there ghouls kept here?"

The first woman spoke again. "Under … temple."

Erzelle swallowed before uttering Olyssa's next command. "Take us there."

She almost laughed as the Grey Ones all spun, leathery clockwork dolls, and moved in lockstep through the frowning mouth of the doorway.

Inside the vaulted entrance hall dust and dull heat weighted the air. The stained glass windows filtered the light dark blue and burgundy, obscuring at first the walls that were bricked with bones —thousands of them, arranged in elaborate designs, starbursts formed from thighs, pentacles from forearms, jaws in clover-like quartets, ribs ringed in concentric circles, all underscored with deep shadow.

Ask where the bones come from.

Erzelle, wide-eyed and open-mouthed, recovered and relayed the question.

The grey spokeswoman rasped, "From … the dead … and the … undead … all through … these hills."

At the opposite end of the chamber a second frowning mouth led into complete darkness.

Erzelle repeated Olyssa's next question. "What's back there?"

A different woman, a pattern of teardrop blotches staining her face, said with startling clarity, "The mosaics and the tunnels."

"Are the other ghouls you tend back there?"

"It is the way to them."

Then we'll go that way. Take us. The tempo of Olyssa's melody intensified.

But Erzelle peered into the dark doorway and couldn't bring herself to repeat her teacher's command. Nor could she step any further into the bone-lined sanctuary.

Without pausing in her playing, Olyssa turned to Erzelle, eyes widening.

"I need light," Erzelle said. In the hold of the *Red Empress*, the light from Olyssa's pipe had not reached far. She didn't want to be alone in the dark with these motleys who were not people.

One of the Grey Ones produced a scythe from the folds of cloth around his torso. The first spokeswoman extended a thin arm as if gesturing for Erzelle to stay still. The scythe came down and severed the woman's arm quick and neat as if it were a stalk of wheat. She made no cry. No blood oozed from her wound.

Erzelle stepped backward, another step, another.

Be calm. They're trying to obey.

Another of the men picked up the hand, tightened the wrappings around it. He also produced a scythe. The two scythe-wielders then hooked their blades together and scraped the edges against one another in a blur of speed. Sparks flew. The cloth around the hand flickered and caught fire.

Another pried the bowl of a split skull from the wall. The burning hand was tossed into the hollow that had once held a brain, and the entire improbable torch offered to Erzelle to take.

She wanted to roll on the floor, laughing. To howl in hysterics.

Take it. I'm sorry I didn't think to provide you with light.

Reluctantly, Erzelle did. The bone felt cool and smooth against her palms.

Now please, ask them to lead us.

Erzelle did. They filed into the darkness and Erzelle walked after as if pulled along in a dream. Behind her, Olyssa played.

The skull-and-hand torch revealed more bones ribbing the passageway. The Grey Ones moved through it, silent; presumably they had no need of sight to find their way. Hunched in close, Erzelle could no longer ignore the baked-flesh stench they radiated.

Lightless rooms branched off to either side of the hall, but their guides ignored these. Instead they reached a stair that spiraled down. Every brick in its well was a bone: a length of leg or arm, a plate of hip or shoulder, a square of fingers, an interlocked row of eye sockets and sinus cavities. How could there possibly be so many? Who could have taken the time to set it all in mortar?

Some of the rare whole skulls she spotted were further distorted: teeth too long, eye sockets too wide, nasal openings too tall and narrow. She couldn't even fathom what sort of creature they could have come from.

Each landing held exits leading off into corridors equally bone-lined, but the stairwell kept descending, Olyssa's notes doubling and redoubling as the spiral bored and bored. The fire in Erzelle's hands cast the Grey Ones in constantly shifting shadow.

Their escorts reached the bottom of this stair to nowhere and vanished into a raw wound in the earth. Erzelle hesitated, the skull bowl and its flames shaking in her grip.

Stay with them. We can't let them wander out of range of the music.

At that gentle shove, Erzelle lurched through the rip in the stone. She stumbled with her very first step, almost dropping her torch. The passage slanted downward, no longer paved or shored up with brick but scooped crudely out of the meat of the mountain. Yet here too were bones embedded in the walls. Not fitted together, not artistically arranged, with none of the unnerving beauty of what came before. Rather than carved and altered pieces, whole skulls, whole hands, whole forearms like violin bows, whole spines with ribs extended like wings were pressed into the soft stone like rocks in a river bank. A worm with what seemed a thousand legs slithered into hiding inside a broken stalk of vertebrae as the fire of Erzelle's torch revealed it.

She didn't let herself recoil, reminding herself, *You've seen worse. It's just a bug.*

The shroud-wrapped creatures ahead of her seemed gigantic in this claustrophobic space. She could only see about five feet in front of her, with the grotesque shapes of the Grey Ones blocking any further view. They continued the relentless descent, their collective movements emitting no more than a muted rustle. Where Olyssa's notes had echoed on the stairs, here they were muffled. The stale air had given way to moisture and an overwhelming smell and taste of loam. Erzelle felt as if she'd breathed in mud. An attempt to spit brought no relief.

Entrances to other tunnels yawed sudden darknesses, burrowing away left or right, angled up or down, never level. The pattern of embedded partial skeletons continued from the main passage into these rough-hewn shafts.

What had this place been? A mine? Erzelle couldn't fathom what these creatures could be digging for, if in fact they were the ones who made this awful place. The way the Grey Ones led them through curved gradually, first right than left in a long serpentine descent. Her grisly torch grew dimmer, and the deeper they went the more insects they disturbed. Erzelle couldn't see them but occasionally she heard one scuttling away. They were large enough to cause a racket that pierced through Olyssa's playing.

Erzelle knew she could never be the pillar of indomitable daring Olyssa was, to descend into a place like this and never take a false step or miss a note.

Ask them how much further, Olyssa commanded.

Erzelle did. The croaked reply, "An hour yet."

Erzelle's head went light. She knew she'd never see daylight again, that she'd escaped the *Red Empress* only to become trapped someplace worse.

Erzelle, don't slow.

She kept moving, her breathing growing ragged.

Olyssa continued as if Erzelle weren't on the verge of panic. *I've seen these barbarities before, but never on this scale. Sorcerers who harvest the ghouls to break them apart and drain the magic that makes them walk will sometimes keep the remains nearby, believing they still hold power. I believe that's what we're witnessing. Every bone we see once belonged to a ghoul. Yet I don't understand their aim. I see no runes etched in the bones. These shapes they've been made into aren't familiar to me.*

All shared without a hint that she found any of it frightening.

"It's horrible," Erzelle whispered.

Yes. Horrible and sad.

Those words in her head, not soothing but calm, helped Erzelle gain control again, though neither her heartbeat nor her breathing slowed.

Much as I hate to suggest it, you should tell our escorts to replenish the fire in your torch.

"Stop," Erzelle said, and the Grey Ones did, though none turned to face her.

They had paused by one of the side burrows, this one tunneling up to the left, and as Erzelle started to voice her demand, another loud scuttling distracted her.

She turned at the noise and beheld its source. Not an insect, not a creature like anything she'd ever seen. It clambered up the wall in a spidery fashion, though its legs were too pale and thick and its body too round and wet to be a spider. It climbed to a skull protruding gape-mouthed from the surface of the curving crawlway and wedged itself into an eye socket.

At that moment, Erzelle recognized what it was. An eye. A human eye, glistening and bruised, carried on a tripod of fingers. Animated somehow, moving on its own. The three fingers each hooked around the ridge of the eye socket to keep the eye in place as it swiveled. Its pupil contracted in its cobweb-pale iris as it oriented toward the torchlight.

The eye glared, not at Erzelle but behind her, at Olyssa and her pipe.

The skull's lower jaw shifted. Dirt crumbled away from it.

Erzelle tried to talk but no sound came out. More scuttling, deeper in the side tunnel.

What is it? Olyssa demanded. Erzelle tried to speak again but only managed a "Huh … huh …" and so she clutched the gruesome torch to her chest and pointed.

Still playing her hypnotic melody, Olyssa met the gaze of the eye on the tunnel wall.

A noise from far below, like a long, rasping sigh, but very loud and very distant.

The Grey Ones turned as one to face Olyssa and Erzelle. Olyssa reacted to their motion by playing faster. Urged on by her frenzied notes, they began to pull objects from their shrouds, scythes or short, pointed spades.

Erzelle wondered what Olyssa was trying to do, when her voice sounded in Erzelle's head. *They're not under my command any more. Run, Erzelle!*

At the same moment, all the Grey Ones opened their mouths. The skull with the eye mounted in it flexed its jawbone. As did all the other skulls in the walls that she could see, some of which now housed eye-creatures just like the one Erzelle had first seen, all looking at Olyssa.

And all those mouths moved in time with the distant rasp from somewhere deep below. "Ooooohh … Lyyssssss … Aaaaaaaah …"

Erzelle even felt the skull in her hands tremble, though it had no jaw.

A blast of darkness roared through the tunnel from below, too quick to avoid, a sudden gust carrying shadow instead of air, shadow that felt cold as sleet against Erzelle's skin. For an instant she was blind, but the gust kept traveling up the tunnel and, miraculously, the light returned as her bone torch flared.

She heard a cry. From Olyssa.

Her teacher was staring at her pipe, dark eyes wide with shock. Her instrument's runes no longer glowed.

The Grey Ones advanced, scythes gleaming in the torchlight. Erzelle threw the bowl of burning remains at the charging line of creatures. The hollowed skull overturned and the Grey One in the lead stepped into the flames, which surged up his dry-husk body. He made no sound as the fire consumed him. Behind him, his fellows drew up short — then started hacking him apart to clear the way.

Olyssa tried to play her pipe. Pitch black darkness flared in the runes where there should have been blue light. She wailed in anguish and tossed the pipe away. Erzelle's knees went weak, but then she straightened again immediately as she became so angry — angry at Olyssa for bringing her here, angry at herself for being frightened — and she turned to Olyssa determined to demand a weapon.

"Get out of here!" Olyssa shouted, but she didn't see what Erzelle did. Behind them in the tunnel, bony arms were reaching across to one another, grasping hands, blocking the way.

Olyssa pulled the long knife from her boot, roaring in wordless defiance.

The Grey Ones finished off their fallen comrade and stepped over his remains, which guttered out, making the darkness complete.

Erzelle stumbled backward and was shoved aside, she didn't know by whom or what.

She landed on her back. Her harp splintered beneath her. Then and only then did she scream.

Olyssa shouted in the dark. A chaos of noise. Scuttling all around. Cloth rustling. A clang and scrape of metal striking metal. The thump of something heavy falling.

Erzelle shrugged off the straps of her ruined harp's case. It made a plucking, clanging noise. She scrambled to her feet, used her hands to steady herself, felt cold bone under her hand, felt it move. Recoiled.

Olyssa's voice, both in her head and shouted aloud. "ERZELLE, RUN!"

Erzelle heard a thunk of metal striking flesh. And another. And another. Olyssa moaned, then went silent. The sound continued. *Thukk. Thukk.* The sound of a blade plunging into meat.

Disoriented, Erzelle retreated from the direction she thought the sound came from and tripped, falling face first. One of her outstretched hands came down on a cold metal bar.

Olyssa's pipe.

Something skittered over Erzelle's hand.

So deep below the earth, with no light. She remembered the arms reaching across the tunnel behind Olyssa, blocking the way. She had no hope. She would die down here.

She began to crawl. Faster. Things moved beneath her in the dirt. She got to her feet, groping blindly, one hand at the wall, the other holding the precious instrument that belonged to her teacher.

The sounds of struggle had ceased behind her.

A rustle of cloth, coming closer. She began to run.

She stumbled more than once but panic kept her moving forward. She held Olyssa's pipe in front of her as if it could somehow shield her, and didn't let herself think about the dirt and rock tumbling all around her or the soft, slimy things that scurried away as her arms brushed against them.

Then she felt nothing to her left or right. She'd reached a point where tunnels crossed. And it hit her that she had no idea how to find her way back to the stairway. Only that she couldn't double back. Much as it shamed her, she whimpered in the dark. Olyssa never would have done that.

Olyssa. What had happened to her? Had she been hearing the sounds of her teacher's murder when she fled?

She froze, lost and terrified. A sound of rustling cloth reached her, and she could no longer tell which direction it was coming from.

Then, a gleam of light caught her eye.

Impossible.

She blinked and blinked and there it was. A distinct shimmer of daylight, sunlight, to her right and up. Not enough to help her see what was in front of her, but enough to lead her on. She sprinted, tripped almost immediately, felt something claw feebly at her belly, scrambled to all fours and kept going.

And going, and going. The gleam stayed far ahead of her, her surroundings never lightening. She reached a switchback that hinged down at a steep slant and narrowed until barely shoulder-wide, the mud squeezing her as she forced her way forward. She had thought that past the sharp bend she'd at last see the source of the glow, but she found only a hint of it, still distant, far below.

Her mind was playing tricks. Even so, she had no other options but to wait in the dark for the scythes to find her. She descended, still holding Olyssa's pipe before her.

And the passage turned again, not right or left but sharply up, at an even steeper angle. She struck her head on the ledge of the ceiling before she understood this.

The phantom light now beckoned her up the precipitous climb, no closer than before.

"No," Erzelle said. "No, no, no." She was so tired. She wanted to wake up, wake up and be back in her family's apartment in Minnepaul, strands of music from her mother's harp lulling her out of nightmare, easing her re-entry into the waking world.

Behind her, the sound of rustling cloth. She thought of waiting for it to reach her.

She climbed. It was hard, but she was small enough to move and find places of purchase in the tight, twisting space. Dirt came loose and pelted her hair and her shoulders.

Once she dropped the pipe, and the light above her seemed to dim. Heart pounding, her tongue and throat gritty with mud, she fretted over what to do, and her pulse sped until it screamed through every limb, her breath coming short and fast, as she lowered herself to retrieve it.

Luckily, the pipe hadn't fallen far. It lay wedged across the tunnel, barring the way down. She grabbed it and she could have sworn the light above her grew brighter than ever. A trick of the eyes.

She was finally forced to crawl on her belly through a shaft barely two feet high. She imagined it simply coming to an end, the light revealing itself as illusion, and she, stuck like a rat in an ant hill, miles underground.

She had to turn another corner. It required a painful contortion of her body, and for a second that stretched into eternity she thought she'd be lodged like that forever, back bent the wrong way with jagged rocks pressed against her face.

Then the mud gave way, she was through, and the space around her widened.

She gasped.

She was no longer in the tunnel.

An immense man peered down at her from his throne formed of a bowed tree wrapped with bundles of straw. Bare-chested beneath his cloak, head lowered in a pose of majestic sadness. Except he wasn't a man. He had the long, tapered head of a buck, with a crown of antlers rising from his brow. Dozens of antlers, too many for one head, stretching up into a blood-hued sky where clouds rolled like fire in a downdraft. Gory fruit hung from every fork and crook in his forest of horns, heads of men, women, children, fat and gaunt, light-skinned and dark, some fleshless, some burned black, the ones in the lower reaches marred with ink-splotched, piebald skin.

Golden light, the aura of day, shimmered around the man-beast's body. That same light burst from his chest, pulsing with the rhythm of his heart. A sad sigh, and the vision vanished, leaving Erzelle dumbstruck.

She stood in a dead end, a tiny, rounded chamber scooped out of the rock, nowhere to go except back into the hole she crawled out of.

She could see.

Where the immense antlered being had been, a pinhole of light pierced through the wall, as big around as her fist.

She pressed her eye to the gap.

Outside, the sun hovered just above the horizon, robed in rose sunset, casting the treetops in amber.

She clawed at the gap, trying to widen it. She took the pipe and shoved it into the hole like a pry bar, wiggling it around, used the bell at its end to dig.

A noise, behind her. She looked back to see a dirt-covered, cloth-wrapped arm reach out of the shaft she'd emerged from, a wicked scythe clutched in its grey fingers.

In a frenzy, Erzelle gouged at the pinhole as the Grey One pulled itself into the tiny space with her. She threw herself against the barrier between her and the sky. Screamed as it gave way. Something hooked into her tunic as she tumbled out into open air.

She'd burst out of the side of the bluff.

Tumbling down the slope of sedimentary rock, a good thirty feet, she landed with a squelch in standing water and marshy grass. Up she came, bruised and scraped but still whole.

A splash beside her. The scythe of the Grey One, falling out from where it had hooked, right under her collar.

She grabbed it, glanced up at the opening she'd made in the cliff, saw a dark shape moving there.

She fled into the trees, with Olyssa's pipe clutched tight.

Without Olyssa she had no hope of finding her bearings in the forest, even in daylight. The sun had long since set, and the cold wormed into her skin. She had no notion if she'd managed anything close to retracing her steps. Yet she kept calling out.

"Reneer. Reneer. Please, Reneer. I know you can hear me." She knew in her heart he couldn't. Was it too much to hope that he had followed them, that he'd be spying on her now? She didn't believe anything was listening to her.

She was wrong.

One moment, she was alone in a copse of spiny evergreens. The next, a Grey One stepped from around a tree as if he'd been standing there all along. At least two heads taller than she, hands held out to snatch: it was the same one that had tried to plant its scythe in her back.

She hadn't lost that scythe. She swung it at the creature's blotchy, warped-checkerboard face. It caught her wrist with ease. She wailed as its grip ground the bones of her forearm together. With its free hand it plucked the scythe from her grip, raised it to sever her arm. A snarl, and a blade flashed, and the Grey One's hand flipped away into the air, still clutching the scythe. A second snarl, and the creature's head tumbled away. It still didn't let go of Erzelle's arm.

Reneer's bared teeth and wild red eyes appeared abruptly behind the decapitated Grey One's shoulder. He brought a long, paper-thin dagger up under the arm that clutched Erzelle, sawed up through it. He heaved the body to the side.

Still, it didn't let go, the crushing pressure unceasing. She slid to the ground. Reneer loomed over her. "Give me your hand, and hold very still."

She was too paralyzed with pain to comply. He took her wrist, the Grey One's hand still squeezing, and used his dagger to cut into its thumb. Then he broke it loose and flung the hand away. He went to the place where the head had rolled and stomped it under his boots until it was dust.

Then he returned and looked her over. The scrapes, the bruises, the torn clothes, the pipe she clutched. The bell remained in place, but the wooden reed was gone. "I have to get you away from here," he said. She was too dazed to protest as he lifted her in a fireman's carry.

His eyes remained wide and wild. "I told her so," he said. "I told her so."

"Help ..." whispered Erzelle.

He leaned his head closer. He smelled of salt and lavender.

"Help me find her," she finished.

"You're as crazy as she was," he snapped, and started walking.

"Not ... she's not dead." Yet she'd heard the scythes striking. "You have to help me find her."

"We have miles to go before I can hide you somewhere safe. There's no need to exhaust ourselves with chit-chat." He didn't sound angry so much as deeply upset, as if his voice would at any moment break.

"We have to find her." And she started to struggle in his arms.

He was much stronger than she, and he didn't slow down. "If I go in there I will break the truce. And if we survived it and actually made it back, my own people would gladly kill us both to set things right with those creatures."

"Then let me go back alone!" Erzelle punched him in the mouth.

Reneer let her fall. When she sat up he had a hand over his mouth and blood between his fingers that stained black under the starry sky. The moon reflected red in his eyes.

"Stupid child! Would you rather I let you die?"

"Yes! Then I wouldn't have to look at you. You coward. Coward! Coward!"

He stared, a membrane sliding down over the orbs of his tilted eyes and up again. When at last he spoke his tone was soft and sad. "How do you even know she's alive?"

"I ... I ..."

She had no answer. She didn't know what to say, other than that her brave, merciless, invincible teacher couldn't possibly be dead.

I know she's alive because the pipe she made for me still plays.

The pipe her sister had made for her. Surely her life force was entwined in it at least as much. And no, she told herself, this wasn't a desperate clutch at a useless straw. She could not, would not accept that.

She had never tried to play Olyssa's pipe, had never even asked if she could be allowed to, had assumed if she did the answer would be no.

Erzelle held it before her, stared down its length. She'd watched Olyssa play it so many times over. She could even guess how to make certain notes. She knew this without having to dig consciously for the knowledge.

But the pipe's reed was gone.

She blew across the opening where the mouthpiece usually fit. Nothing happened.

Reneer crouched to watch her as she tried again. "What are you doing?"

Olyssa always said her sister's life was tied to this magical wonder she wielded, but she never said anything about herself.

When she and Olyssa had played together, every night since the escape from the *Red Empress*, Erzelle had sensed something in Olyssa's music … Every musician who meant it let a bit of her soul leak into whatever she played, invested her own spirit in her art. Erzelle's mother had done that. Erzelle knew this, on a level deeper than conscious understanding, every time she'd heard her mother play, every time the strains from the harp had floated into her room from her mother's study.

Even when Olyssa used mindspeech it was always out of necessity, never for small talk, never for sharing anecdotes or random moments of joy. On the other hand, playing harmony with her, *that* was like talking with her, engaging in conversation, as if the real woman joked with her, laughed with her, embraced her, wept with her, in a way that seemed impossible interacting with her outside the music, that towering, taciturn, intimidating silence, speaking only when necessary, killing without warning.

She made the leap. "If the pipe can play, then she's alive," she said. "But I've lost the reed. It won't play without the reed she made."

She stood as if she intended to retrace her steps and hunt for it, even though she knew this was folly, even though she didn't know in truth what she would or could do if she found it.

Reneer stepped to intercept her. "Stop and think what you're doing."

"It needs a reed. I need to find it."

He knelt beside her, his head still level with hers. "*Erzelle*, listen to me. You can't stay out here. We can't stay here. These creatures have tunnels all over and even I can be snuck up on, believe it or not." His cocky grinned returned, and Erzelle noticed for the first time he was covered in mud. Because *she* was. "Now, then: in town there's someone who owes me a favor or two who might be able to help you with that instrument. Might even be able to get it to work herself."

"But …"

Erzelle wanted to protest, but Reneer caught her staring at the mud all over him, and added, "I know! My momma will have a fit!" And she couldn't help but laugh. He laughed with her and she felt such a tremendous, irrational surge of relief, that she had a friend and knew it.

Once they regained their composure he said, "If you can prove to me that Miss Olyssa is still alive … then maybe I'll see what I can do."

Her relief gave way to darkness. "But we can't wait. You need to help me *now*."

"If you go back now, even if she's alive, you won't save her."

Erzelle had no answer to that.

"Can you walk or do you need me to carry you?"

Erzelle glared into the fox-man's eyes. "I'll walk."

He shrugged and grinned so broadly she couldn't help but smile back.

The vulpine town melded so subtly with the forest that at first Erzelle didn't know they'd crossed its border. Her all-over ache from the ordeal underground had further layers added on, lactic acid in her legs from the unending hike, sore toes from rocks and roots tripped over. Her determination kept her silent, though the miles tempered any anger she still held. Reneer's own words to her held timbres of empathy. He chatted regardless of whether she answered. "Looks like the clouds have decided to share the moon. Perhaps they're not such greedy bastards after all." And then he said, "Turn here," and fell silent as they stepped out of thorny evergreens and into a brick-cobbled alley.

This street sliced level into the hillside like a groove carved out of a mound of marble. Bricks firmed up the alley walls. As they continued down the street Erzelle spotted doors and windows, some shuttered closed, some with lanterns burning behind curtains. As the hill the city had been excavated from rose in elevation, the facades flush with the street grew taller, and Erzelle spied second story windows. One was open, and through it she heard snoring.

When they reached a cross-street, Erzelle realized her first impression wasn't quite correct. She again studied the tops of these walls that concealed houses nestled side by side, a dense and most civilized den.

The entire hill had to be artificial. These dwellings were built first and then sod and even trees placed above their roofs to camouflage them. She squinted, and saw there was netting strung above the narrow streets. The nets were covered with leaves yet allowed in many pinhole shafts of moonlight.

Downspouts descended the walls at regular intervals, plunging into gutters alongside the cobbles, punctured at regular intervals by drain holes.

Much to her shock she caught a whiff of petrol. A stoop they came upon had a little alcove beside it, and inside that inset space a motorcycle crouched, chained and padlocked.

She exclaimed, "You have fuel out here?"

"You're sharp, little miss," Reneer whispered. "We make our own."

Erzelle was about to ask where they were going when he hissed "Shhhh!" and grabbed her by the shoulder. "Down behind there, now," he said, pointing at the motorbike. She crammed herself into the tight space between its back wheel and the bricks as Reneer walked out into an intersection. Heart pounding in her ears, she thought about calling out after him, wiped the thought away when she heard him speak. "Happy midnight, Marshal Greegrim."

"What have you been wallowing in? You stink." The low snarl didn't mirror Reneer's joviality.

"Mud's good for the skin, don't you know?"

The Marshal talked over him. "I had not heard that you'd returned."

"I suppose you didn't! Curiously, sir, I met no patrol coming in."

Erzelle couldn't fathom how someone could make such an animal growl and speak at the same time. "You disrespectful rat! Someday you'll regret mocking me. You don't appreciate how much privilege your bloodline brings you."

"Oh, I appreciate it every day."

A huff, a spit. "So did those fools meet the Grey Ones?"

"Nothing's changed from before, Marshal. I spoke to them two days ago, they went their way, I haven't seen them since."

"I'm not pleased that you even spoke to that witch and her whelp."

"Too bad you weren't there to voice your objections. You know I'd have listened." She could hear the ear-to-ear grin in his inflection. After a long silence, Reneer added, "Are we done then?"

The reply came out half-snarled. "Get out of my sight."

Minutes passed. Erzelle began to wonder if she'd been abandoned when Reneer whispered to her.

"Sorry about that. We need to go a different way, and quickly."

He helped her clamber out and unbend her legs, which had fallen asleep. She winced with each step as needles pierced her feet. He said, "We are so lucky he didn't hear us coming. He's not as sharp as he was five years ago."

"Who was that? And why does he hate you?"

"I can't take the time to explain. Come on."

He helped her to walk as they hurried down an alley that had been practically invisible until they were right at its entrance. Garbage bins stood sentry along one side. They dashed through and kept going, pausing to hide in nooks and by corners until they wound their way back into the open.

Based on Olyssa's suspicious reactions, Erzelle certainly hadn't expected the vulpine city to turn out so genteel, yet more evidence of its sophistication confronted her at every turn. In places the streets became tunnels, earth and forest heaped above, and these structures proved square and clean, with cement ceilings dotted with blue strips of electric light. Reneer didn't like being in the tunnels with his charge, so he rushed through, which frustrated Erzelle because the artificial lighting afforded the best views of the curious facades of the house rows. All were riverstone, but the patterns, sizes and colors would alter from home to home. The front doors were narrow, adorned with brass knockers and usually rounded on top, while the windows were tiny and square. It reminded Erzelle of stage sets, as if all these fronts were props for show, and if you actually opened one of the doors you'd find nothing but dirt on the other side.

This fancy of hers fell to pieces as a door they approached opened from the inside.

"Stand behind me," Reneer hissed. "Keep your head down."

Erzelle complied just as a portly fox-woman in a nightgown emerged holding a flashlight, her hair a frightful red bush.

"Morning, ma'am," Reneer said, and tipped a non-existent hat.

"Reneer du Vreez," she said. "What are you doing on this street? At this hour? Looking like that? With a …" she sniffed the air, "… child? What on Earth—"

"Merely escorting the young miss home as a favor to a niece," he said. "Her friend here was sleeping over, but I'm afraid this particular uncle is a bit of a noisy drunk. Poor thing crawled through the garden-boxes to hide from him. He won't fall asleep, won't shut up. A bit like your Robert. Ma'am."

The woman's eyes, which were slanted steeper than Reneer's, bugged fit to burst from her head. She bared a lot of teeth, and her mane if anything grew bushier. With a "Well, I never!" she slammed the door.

"That was easier because I had an audience to embarrass her in front of," he said. "Now we'd better run."

They took off, feet slapping down the cobbled streets, out of one tunnel, around a curve and into another.

"Where are we going?" Erzelle finally asked when they slowed down.

"Shhhh. Almost there."

They ducked into an unlighted alley half as wide as usual. No doors or windows stood to either side. Reneer led them to a dead end where a single door stood, a radial pattern like flower petals carved in its center. Erzelle's breath caught as Reneer scaled the river rock wall easily as a monkey and tapped his claw-length nails against a tiny window high up and to one side. His taps made a pattern: clikclikclick-CLACK clikclikclick-CLACK clikclikclick-CLACK.

He put an eye to the window, then dropped to the street as the door creaked open.

"Finally," he muttered, almost to himself, "someone I want to see."

The woman standing ghost-like in the entrance, a candle in her hand, wasn't much taller than Erzelle, and slender as a sapling. Her hair was silver rather than red, just as the skin left uncovered by her robe was pale rather than tawny. Her canted eyes blinked behind spectacles that magnified them to enormous size. Gold irises reflected the candlelight.

Erzelle thought at first might she might be elderly, but when she spoke it was in a spry alto. "Reneer, though it's redundant, what the devil?" Then she spotted Erzelle. "Oh my. Is that …?"

"The harper girl," he said. "Who no longer has her harp."

Her voice lowered to a whisper. "Why'd you bring her here?"

"She needs the kind of help that only you have the touch for."

Did the fox-woman flinch? She did regard Erzelle for an uncomfortably long moment. Erzelle felt a strange tickling inside her skull, as if fingertips tentatively touched her mind, for just an instant.

"Inside," she said.

They stepped onto the landing of a wrought-iron stair illuminated by an overhead light. Erzelle had time to glimpse an oval woven rug of straw and a lumpy, cozy-looking sofa in an anteroom on the upper level before the woman shooed them downstairs, into what, Erzelle supposed, was the den. Warmth and woodsmoke greeted them in passing.

She heard Reneer ask, "How's your Mamaw doing?"

"Not well," the woman replied.

"I'm sorry."

"Now's not the time to talk about it. Young miss, this way please."

They turned away from the heat radiating from a wood stove and passed through a comically narrow side door into an apothecary little bigger than a master closet.

Erzelle had to duck to avoid all the bound herbs hanging to dry. The heady aromas overwhelmed her: mint, sage, thyme, basil, oregano, mustard, others she couldn't identify. It was too much in such close quarters.

"Since our rude mutual friend hasn't introduced us, I'm Braeca," the fox-woman said.

"I'm Erzelle."

"Please sit," and she gestured to the cushion-backed chair pressed against the desk with its hutch holding many, many small drawers. Then she did a double take. "My goodness! Do you want to wash up?"

Reneer chortled. "You'll note, she didn't ask me."

"Ignore him," said Braeca.

Erzelle wondered how that could be possible, before scolding herself to focus. "Later please. I need your help now."

"What do you think I can do for you?"

Erzelle held up Olyssa's pipe. "I need to play it. But it needs a special reed. He thought you might be able to make one."

"I'm not a musician." She aimed a sharp glance at Reneer, before turning to study the instrument in Erzelle's hands. Her eyes widened behind her glasses "That's ... you told me of that pipe. How ... where is the woman who plays it?"

"In the mountain behind the Violet Bluffs," Erzelle said.

Braeca swallowed. "... dead, then?"

"No!" Erzelle shouted.

Reneer intervened. "She tells me that if Olyssa is still alive, the pipe will play. But she needs a proper reed to play it. I thought you could at least look at the piece and the writing on it."

Braeca hadn't calmed. "You're not thinking of—"

He laughed. "When am I ever thinking? But I'd like to know if she's alive."

Braeca sighed.

"May I?" She extended a trembling hand.

Erzelle hesitated, her grip involuntary tightening as she pondered how unnerving it would be to see Olyssa's pipe in a stranger's hands.

What choice did she have? She relinquished the pipe.

The fox-woman took it, studied the notched end where the reed went, the bell at the other end, ran a finger along its length, tracing the symbols and the alien letters etched in its steel. Wonder brightened her face. "Sometimes, when an artifact like this is missing a piece, it wants that missing part, and that want can tell you what you need to do." She glanced again at Reneer, excited now. "We have nothing like this in Fabelford." She held it up, tilted it so it caught the light from her desk lamp. "It's not easy, but I think I can read it," she said. And Erzelle had a flash of chilling recognition, remembering how the Chef had studied Olyssa's pipe, how he had read it and the runes began to glow.

"I will always be true to my purpose," Braeca recited, as the symbols etched into the pipe started to glow.

And then they filled in black.

Braeca recoiled. She let go of the pipe, but it hung suspended beneath her hands, while smoky strands of darkness tangled like cobwebs around her fingers.

Erzelle tried to grab the pipe, but the darkness twined around Braeca's hands manipulated them like puppets, making her shove Erzelle to the floor.

"What's happening?" Reneer shouted. He too tried to grab the pipe but Braeca spun away from him, stumbled back into the shelves, smashing jars onto the floor as black smoke spouted from her eyes.

The darkness coiled throughout the apothecary, snarling around the bundles of drying herbs, the lattice of the chair, even twisting into Erzelle's hair. A mass congealed in its center like a spider's egg sac, the size of Erzelle's head.

Erzelle heard a word, repeated in her mind. *Lisch-te. Lisch-te. Lisch-te.* Faint. Growing louder.

An opening in the growing sphere leaked out a slow syllable. "Ooooohh ..."

Lisch-te. Lisch-te. Lisch-te. Now Braeca's mouth moved even as black motes swam in her gold eyes.

"Lyyssss ..."

And now Braeca spoke the words aloud. "Lisch-te. Lisch-te. Lisch-te."

"Aaaahhh ..."

"Lisch-te. Begone, fiend, die in the light, meur-te lisch-te!"

The desk lamp flared blinding bright, as did, for a moment, the runes of Olyssa's pipe, blazing blue.

The thing of smoke vanished. The pipe clattered to the floor.

Braeca leaned against the wall, gasping. Reneer grabbed the collar of Erzelle's blouse and pulled her to her feet. "What was that? Tell me!"

Upstairs, a woman moaned.

Reneer yelped in surprise as Braeca grabbed him by his ear. "Don't you hurt her, Reneer du Vreez. She didn't know."

Reneer let Erzelle go and raised an arm in surrender. "That thing spoke Olyssa's name," he said.

The words left Erzelle's mouth before she could catch them. "It did under the temple, too."

"What did?"

"There was a voice. Deep underground. Then it breathed. The breath was like black smoke. Like what we just saw. It killed the light from Olyssa's music. And those things … the Grey Ones … they attacked with their scythes …"

Braeca was staring in horror, but Reneer's eyes narrowed. "How did you get out?"

The man-beast, sad on his throne.

"I don't know," she said. "I got lucky. I thought I saw light. And there was a hole in the rock. That Grey One you killed chased me through it." Braeca clutched both hands to her mouth beneath her spectacle-magnified eyes. "I got a good ways ahead of him before he caught up. Before you found me."

Braeca looked back and forth between them. "What have you got into now?" Erzelle couldn't tell if she spoke to Reneer or to herself.

Upstairs, the woman moaned again. "Coming, Mamaw," she called, and said, "Both of you wait till I get back," and left the apothecary.

But Erzelle picked up the pipe. It felt different, lighter, more vibrant, now that it had been exorcised of the magic from under the mountain. Erzelle couldn't explain how she felt it, but she did. The metal hummed, somehow, though there was no physical vibration.

I am always true to my purpose.

Some musicians are born with their talent so innately rooted that they can pick up any instrument, and even if they've never touched its like before, they can in a few minutes cause it to produce notes and in a few minutes more make it sing.

Erzelle had seen her mother do it. Seen her pick up a trumpet, a strange kind of rounded guitar, a chime set struck with mallets, and in minutes produce one of the same melodies she plucked over and over from her harp.

Her mother's talent had made her jealous — a good jealousy, a combination of adoration and a kind of shame-faced avarice, *I hope one day to do that too, oh I hope I hope I hope* — but she had never tried her hand at any instrument other than the harp. Certainly nothing so impossible as Olyssa's pipe, which shouldn't by any logic play music at all.

How many times had she placed the little wooden reed in Olyssa's case for her? How often had she turned it over in her fingers? Studied each millimeter?

She held the pipe up, comparing its end to the thickness of the stalks hanging from the cords in the little room. Everything was too thin, too delicate. Except a long sprig of fireseed, with its blood-bright spray of burrs, fat at the base of the stem.

"I need your knife," she said.

"Why?"

"I think I can make what I need." She pulled the sprig from the pin it hung from.

"Use this one," Reneer suggested, unfolding a small knife from his pocket. "But do be careful. I never let it go dull."

She had never tried to whittle before. She made up for this with slow, precise movements. She concentrated. She cut. She nicked herself but kept going. A shape floated in her mind, its details more vivid each moment, and this vision wouldn't let go. She compared the tiny asymmetrical section of wood to the end of the pipe, the notches there. The hum of the metal in her hands grew more intense and at the same time more soothing each time she picked it up.

She proceeded as if in a trance. And it did, at the end, resemble at least a crude approximation of Olyssa's reed. She tried to hook it into the end of the pipe. It resisted, and color rose in her face as she realized she'd botched the job. But then it slid into the grooves and fit perfectly.

She looked up from the desk to see Braeca had rejoined them. Both of the fox-people had been watching her in silence.

Erzelle held the reed to her lips and blew.

It made a shrill whistling noise.

She cringed and held the piece a little further away. At times when Olyssa played she appeared to breathe across the reed rather than into the pipe — Erzelle always marveled when she witnessed this, because she knew it shouldn't work, and found it in some ways more magical than all spells it generated.

She cupped a hand under the pipe's bell, though it was hard as her arms were much shorter than Olyssa's. She tried again.

A low, uncertain note shook from the pipe. She blew with more force and the note grew louder.

Blue embers flickered in the writing on the steel.

She experimented with covering and uncovering and partially covering the bell, with leaving small gaps between her fingers, with pressing her lips against the reed, with barely breathing on it. She made the pipe descend a scale.

It shouldn't have been so simple. It was as if the pipe greeted her, recognized her as its partner, and longed to dance once again.

Her mind, shuffling rapidly through questions and options, found the concerto Olyssa had tried to teach her. On the pipe, she found the concerto's first note.

She played as she would have had Olyssa been with her. She got many notes wrong, but she didn't start over. She pushed on.

A scene formed of phantoms congealed around her. In it, she sat by a guttered-out fire pit, the sky above oscillating with a blood-red aurora that vanished and reappeared, vanished and reappeared. Long silhouettes of trees etched the horizon, yet these trees were arms with flesh withered to the bone, frozen in the act of clawing upward.

A figure stirred in the dark beside the fire-pit, bound hand and foot, struggling to lift her head.

Erzelle?

A vast writhing spiderweb. Olyssa at its center, unblinking, lips parted without shaping words. *Erzelle, is that you?*

Darkness fell and the scene vanished as if swept away by a descending blade.

Erzelle sat shaking, reed still pressed to her lips.

She stared up at Braeca and Reneer, who stared back wide-eyed.
"She *is* alive," she said.

"We saw," said Braeca, and Erzelle understood why they were so
shaken.

Reneer asked, "How do I know you didn't plant that in my head?"

Braeca put a hand on his shoulder. "You know because I know she
didn't."

"Well, then," he said, clenching his fists. Did the hair of his mane
stand on end? "Well, then. I don't understand what I saw, but I didn't
like it. I. Did. Not."

He quivered from head to toe. Braeca regarded him over her
spectacles. "You know you can't."

"Oh, my darling," and he said the word as if it were a pet name,
though his bared-tooth smile seemed dangerous, "I know no such
thing. You know very well how I feel about the Grey Ones and the
yoke they keep us under. We cower and kowtow when we should burn
them in their burrows."

His fists clenched again, but Braeca reached out and folded her
hands over his. "Enough of that, Reneer."

Her touch calmed his shaking, but not his voice. "I know you feel
the same way. After what happened to your father …"

"Shhh," she said. "Shhh." In a whisper, "Yes, I feel the same."

Erzelle was on her feet, looking from one to the other. "You'll help
me then?"

Reneer eyed her with his angular grin on full display. "Young miss,
you haven't rested for a day and a night. Exhaustion won't help you
with the Grey Ones."

Erzelle gave that temptation about a second's thought. "No. We
can't wait. I won't."

His smile widened. "So be it, then."

Braeca cleared her throat. "At least let me clean you up first."

Reneer huffed in perhaps-feigned outrage. "And what about me,
darling? I'm filthy all over."

"You know where the workroom sink is," replied Braeca without a
hint of humor. Yet Erzelle spied a smirk on her face as Reneer stomped
out of the room with an exaggerated sigh.

"Now then," Braeca said, "let's see what we can do for you."

The water closet proved narrow, like everything else in the house, and somewhat overstuffed with a heady potpourri odor. It held not only a working sink but a porcelain tub, chipped and faded to brown, but still a miracle to Erzelle, who hadn't seen one since she'd left Minnepaul. Doubly miraculous was the warm water that poured from the spigot.

"You go ahead," said Braeca. "Tap the door lightly when you're done — my poor mother doesn't need any more rude awakenings tonight."

Erzelle nodded, her cheeks coloring.

"In the meantime, I'll see what I can do for you for clothes."

She showed Erzelle the soaps, brushes, sponges and towels, shut off the spigot as the tub was now half-full, then left. Erzelle disrobed and lowered herself into the water. Her skin stung for a bit in the places where she'd been cut or scraped, but a pink lotion Braeca had shown her made those aches fade, and her sore muscles, too, relaxed. After that it was bliss. For a long time she simply lay there, not wanting it to end, a selfish part of her wishing time could stop. Yet the lavender scent of the soaps finally tempted her out of her lethargy. The water gradually turned black as she scrubbed, and it seemed no matter how hard she scoured she could never be clean, could never scrape off the filth of what she'd endured.

She did her best to put her troubles out of her mind a few minutes. At last she drained the water, much as she dreaded getting out — through some alchemy it had never gone chill against her skin. Swathed in a huge towel with tattered edges, she tapped the door. Immediately Braeca was there. "My mother never throws anything away. For once I'm grateful for that. Let's see if any of these fit you."

Erzelle ended up in a grey hooded sweatshirt and rugged coveralls repaired with many denim patches, and thick socks that felt warm as a hug.

"How old are you?" asked Braeca.

"Twelve, I think."

"Well, I was sixteen when I was wearing these. You're a tall girl." She picked up a hairbrush. "And a pretty one, though I wonder when you last ate? You're so thin."

Erzelle knew exactly when she'd last eaten. Reneer had shared sweet crackers and cheese with her about an hour before they'd come to Fabelford. Even so, the thought of food made her queasy.

She stared at her reflection, her tan skin newly clean, dark circles around her eyes. Braeca gathered a length of her sandy hair in a fist and dragged the brush through the curls, her gold eyes focused and her upper lip curling in an inadvertent sneer of concentration as she pulled the tangles free. She fussed over Erzelle, occasionally pausing in the grim task of detangling to playfully arrange a forelock. It was quite different from the many, many times her mother had purposely hovered by her side, primping her for one of those fancy dinners with potential patrons that required her to sit still and behave until she wanted to burst. And yet, on some deep level, it was much the same.

At one point Braeca plucked a flower from the potpourri jar and tucked it in her hair. "My, you clean up well," she said.

Abruptly Erzelle was crying.

Braeca hesitated, nonplussed. "Do you need me to leave?"

"No," Erzelle sobbed.

Braeca met her eyes in the mirror, one kind of sadness acknowledging another. Then she put her arms around Erzelle and simply held her until the sobs stopped.

"Maybe you need to rest," she said.

Erzelle shook her head. "No. I have to go back. I have to help her. I owe her so much."

Though Reneer had supposedly done nothing more than wipe himself down over the sink — and he wore the same all-black outfit Erzelle had seen him in before — he looked polished to a gleam and shiny-eyed, and for a second Erzelle hated him. But she needed him too much and he was too eager to help for that to last.

"Perhaps I should come too," Braeca said, but Reneer gently sighed. "If not you to take care of your Mamaw, then who?"

The sky had lightened in the east, foreshadowing full dawn. Reneer told Erzelle that if they made haste, they could be back at the Violet Bluffs before noon. He would rather enter the bone-lined tunnels by day, even if its light would not reach them once inside.

Sometime before Erzelle finished her bath, Reneer had left the house and returned with a backpack and two solar-paneled flashlights, leaving Erzelle amazed that such objects still existed. To hide the pipe,

Braeca gave Erzelle a tube she used to gather herbs, with straps that allowed it to be worn over one's back like a quiver.

While Erzelle waited in the den, with its dried floral arrangements mounted in hoops on the walls, and pondered where the ventilation took the smoke from the fireplace, Braeca took Reneer aside and the two talked quietly. She finished eating the bread Braeca had brought, cut in long slices and smeared with a sweet honey. Mounting impatience to start back toward the Bluffs made her tap a foot.

Then Braeca came to her, teary-eyed behind her spectacles, and held her once more. Her pale hair tickled, simultaneously silken and prickly. "You came out once. Do it again, this time with your friend."

Erzelle didn't answer, but hugged her back fiercely.

When they parted, Braeca punched Reneer's arm. "Don't screw up." And went upstairs.

"That one sure knows how to make a man feel brave," he muttered. To Erzelle he said, more loudly, "Now, let's get you out of here. Keep your hood up."

By day, Fabelford's streets bustled. Small electric cars and even a carriage drawn by a single horse wove among the pedestrians that in places trickled and in places thronged through the streets and tunnels. During the night Erzelle hadn't been able to make out the bright colors of the stone facades: gold, green, turquoise, pink. The leaves matted in the nets above let just enough light through while providing comfortable shade. The fox-people themselves dressed in a hodge-podge of fashions, a T-shirt here, a petticoat there, and all wore more layers than Erzelle would have expected given their light red pelts. She saw no others who were pale like Braeca.

Reneer maintained a brisk pace. The thought of Olyssa paralyzed in a web kept Erzelle from letting her attention linger on any new sights or smells no matter how curious they made her. They paused only once, when a grey-muzzled man recognized Reneer. "Hey, there, trouble. Since when are *you* up this early?"

"I have a long day's hunt ahead," Reneer replied with a grin and a comical half-bow. "Gathering mushrooms for my mother's soup. Her favorite patch is half a day way. I admit it's hard to sacrifice sleep, but if I'm to sleep in *tomorrow*, I must be off, old friend."

"Rascal," the fellow called behind him, and spared Erzelle a wink.

Before Erzelle knew it, they were back in the forest. Reneer knew all the paths, which made the going easier. Erzelle's nerves jangled at every unexpected sound even as her mind drifted and she kept wishing she could just lean against a tree for a minute and shut her eyes. Her companion began to ply her with questions —

"Young miss, where *are* you from?"

"How *did* you learn to play the harp so divinely?"

"Where *is* your harp?"

"How did you cross paths with this lady piper?"

— which at first so annoyed her that her answers were curt. He pressed on undeterred, and a little later, almost by accident, she had told him almost everything there was to know about her, growing up in Minnepaul, her captivity in the *Red Empress*, the surprise rescue by Olyssa. She hesitated before telling him that Olyssa sought her missing sister, herself a sorceress, and perhaps now among the undead.

"Mmm." He mulled over that bit of news, peering thoughtfully off past a stand of twisted, oozing tree trunks. "Mmmm."

He had a right to know, Erzelle reasoned. Even though Olyssa was a stranger, he was about to risk everything for her. He asked many more questions about her teacher, where she came from, who her family might be. She recognized he was doing it to keep her awake and engaged as they walked, but at some point his genuine curiosity took over. Each new thing he learned made the next question more intense.

"Merciless," he said to himself. "Yet driven by love. The stuff of epics." He threw back his head, barked a loud laugh and clapped his hands to together in delight.

"It's the truth," Erzelle said as they intersected into a vale crossed by a wide stream. She fought an impulse to join in his glee, because she had to admit it did, when he described it that way, sound so *made up*.

Reneer led her to a ford the vulpines had built, a sturdy bridge of stone and wooden boards, concealed within a cluster of thornleaves. Miles went by on paths between trees and around hills before Erzelle at last resolved it was her turn to ask questions. "Who are you, to Fabelford?"

He guffawed. "A troublemaker." After a moment, he shared more, unprompted. "I'm a lucky, lucky boy. Bastard son of the hereditary Mayor of Fabelford, and my daddy loathes me, but I'm my granddad's favorite, and no one's more scared of him than my daddy." When Reneer said "Granddad's favorite," he held up a long-nailed pinky and used his other hand to mime something wrapped around it. "We do fine, snuggled in our little dens. We've made wonders happen out here, Erzelle. You've not seen even a fraction of what we've made and remade here. The water powers our turbines. Fuel drips from our stills. We make our own light — we have farms in domes under the earth and we don't want for what we can't easily hunt. We've built a peaceful haven out of the chaos left by the Storms. We could be doing even better, without the Grey Ones infesting our land."

"What have they done to you?"

"They don't have to do anything, anymore," he spat. "Our fear of them is so woven into our lives that it's part of the mortar between our bricks, the carpets beneath our feet, the pepper on our food." He gnashed his long teeth. "Their price for leaving us in peace, Erzelle, is that they take our dead. Their mounds are filled with our family's remains. We don't even know what they do with them."

And Erzelle recalled the strange, long-toothed skulls she'd noticed among the mosaics. She felt humiliated and shamed that she hadn't realized what they were when she saw them.

She kept that memory to herself. Reneer was plenty upset already, unspooling a long pent-up rant as they trekked between the warped trunks of the trees and the sun rose higher.

"The children of Fabelford hear from the time we're kits about the Grey Ones and their supposed powers to make those who dared speak against them disappear. Our elders act like this is the way the world always has been, as if we've lived in this underground city forever and we're allowed to do so only by virtue of these monsters' supposedly generous tolerance. When I was your age there was serious talk of fighting back. But — too many cowards in the government. Those who spoke openly of defying the creatures began to disappear. They blamed the vanishings on the Grey Ones themselves. But my grandfather has other suspicions. Some of the cowards in the council have exploited our situation for their own ends. My grandfather keeps warning me to keep my mouth shut, but he knows I'm not the type." His grin grew even more feral. "Marshal Greegrim, damn him. He knows much more about those disappearances than he's ever told.

I'm sure of it." His bitter glare was meant for other surroundings than theirs. "He's gotten where he is based on his ability to witness atrocity after atrocity and say nothing unless it's convenient for blackmail." He spat, and when Erzelle said nothing, shot her an apologetic glance. "I'm so sorry to trouble you with this. But I can't help it. I've seen the joy in his eyes when his constables move in on someone who dares speak up in the council chambers. He loves those grimaces of pain when his men twist an arm to shut someone up."

Sighing, Reneer clenched a fist, a gesture Erzelle was coming to recognize. "Braeca's father, poor man, he voiced the loudest objections. When she was born that color, they said it was because of *him*, because he defied the Grey Ones. Ignorant worms! As if no one remembers what any of us were before the Storms wreaked their changes, when we looked like you and could be all colors."

Erzelle didn't know how to respond to that, but Reneer didn't wait for her. Braeca's talents, too, he said, were regarded as a curse of the Grey Ones — though plenty of other vulpines could sense and even use the magic in their veins. By virtue of the unwanted attention focused on her silvery hide, Braeca was the only one who couldn't keep it private.

"Since her father disappeared, her poor mother's never recovered. The people — they shun her by day — visit her shop by night to avail themselves of her potions. She lives on thin ice." His voice remained sprightly, but it was a glee born out of malice. "I'll tell you how she and I met. I heard a girl cry for help and came upon a pair of whelps trying to drag her down the steps into one of the raingutter tunnels. One of them had a can of fuel in his hand. They spotted me and asked me if I wanted to help burn the witch." His lips peeled back in nothing like a smile. "I left them in no condition to ever explain what really happened to them. It was the only time I was happy to see the Grey Ones get credited for something they didn't do."

Erzelle remembered how she'd felt, watching Olyssa exterminate the Family, frightened and delighted all at once. She thought she understood what he meant.

Abruptly, he stopped talking and drew up short.

"And we're here," he said. And laughed, looking up at the bluff. "That's quite a hole you made."

Erzelle blinked. She felt no relief that they'd at last reached their destination. Listening to him with the other half of her mind focused on what they were heading toward, she hadn't recognized any familiar landmarks. She had to guiltily admit she'd happily have listened to more of Reneer's tales for days on end rather than face the mosaic tunnels again.

Yet Reneer seemed cheered. Eager, even. Without apparent difficulty, he scaled the cliff-face to the puncture Erzelle's body had made in the earth. Then he removed a thin but steel-strong rope from the pack slung over his shoulder and lowered it down to her, grunted only a little with the effort as he hauled her up.

No welcome party awaited them in the earthen chamber where she'd seen the antlered man.

Reneer regarded the hole in the floor, a tight squeeze even for him, while Erzelle scanned the room, a mere bubble in the dirt, for any trace of the vision she'd had there. Nothing.

"Clever, clever young miss," the fox-man said, and grinned his angular grin. "Bright-eyed, bushy-tailed, ready for another round?"

"Yes," she lied.

"In this case," he said, "ladies don't go first."

Soon enough, they were inside, the beams of their flashlights scraping valiantly at the dark.

They retraced Erzelle's flight through the tunnels. Again Erzelle felt as if her throat clogged with mud as the walls squeezed in. She didn't understand how Reneer could be so assured in the course he picked until he told her, "I'm following your scent. It's not hard to pinpoint. It's too wholesome for this place."

When they reached a nexus of intersecting shafts, he held up a hand. "Shhh!"

And Erzelle heard what had accompanied her all through her journey out: the noise of something small, scuttling.

Reneer cocked his head, then aimed his beam and revealed the offender.

Erzelle assumed she'd see another crawling eye, but it wasn't so. Four hands, all female, fused at the wrists, skittered blindly up one wall, attempted to gain purchase on a crude scapulae diamond protruding from the dirt, lost their grip and lay twitching like an overturned bug.

She and Reneer both watched it a minute, repelled and morbidly fascinated, before he finally grunted, "Come on."

More and more of these fused abominations revealed themselves as they continued. There were crawling eyes, like Erzelle had seen before, though they didn't react to the intruders' presence as the one who'd given away Olyssa had. They saw a long, flat worm made from ears that inched along on strips of contracting grey muscle. A hand by itself, fingers and thumb removed, all its severed stumps grafted with bulging tongues. Once something hopped past them, large and white, five legs joined at mid-thigh, a heart pulsing in the lattice of tendons and bone that joined them, jaws opening and closing beneath the crooks of their knees.

None took notice of the living pair in their midst.

"I have a hunch," Reneer whispered, "that if you played the pipe they would see us. So if you were planning that, I hope you'll nix it."

How was it that even now, here, he made her want to laugh?

She said, "I thought the same thing, but thank you."

"Did you now?"

She shone her light at his face. "You think I'm lying?"

Despite the glare in his eyes that made them flash red, he appeared unperturbed. "Of course you're not." The slight hint of a grin made the cramped dark less cramped.

The abominations flopping blindly under the cliff grew easier to ignore the further down and in they went. After negotiating another nexus, and another, Reneer turned to her in wonderment.

"You are one lucky little miss, Erzelle! You didn't miss a turn!"

Erzelle didn't know how to explain to him about the ghost-light and the vision of the man-beast, so she shrugged. "I guess. We haven't found the main tunnel yet."

Minutes later, they did. They also found the remains of Erzelle's harp, right where she'd fallen on it.

Reneer crouched, laid a gentle hand on its broken frame. "Perhaps we could …"

"No," Erzelle said. "Leave it." It had been her only companion, the thing that kept her alive, for so long. But it was wood and wire and she had no room for such thoughts just then.

Soon they found the signs of Olyssa's struggle. Ruts in the floor. Bones strewn everywhere, knocked from the walls. Erzelle shone her flashlight up the way she and Olyssa had come, but no bony arms stretched across to block the way.

Reneer sniffed. "There's blood." He knelt, put a hand in the mud, sniffed again, his flashlight beam reduced to a puddle of light, etching his face in white silhouette against the tunnel's darkness. "And this."

Solemnly he handed her Olyssa's dirt-caked hair pick.

Stuffing it in a pocket, she sealed it in tightly while Reneer went on searching. Slowly she dragged the glowing circle made by her flashlight over the scene but found no trace of the mandolin case.

Finally Reneer said, "It's not a lot of blood." He spoke as if it were a tremendous relief, the best news he'd heard in ages. "There's hope yet, Erzelle."

And she smiled. A crazy thing to do, at that time, in that place. Nonetheless, she did. And he returned it.

The way was clear now.

Down they went.

They heard the machine, then smelled it, long before they glimpsed any part of it.

A rhythmic clash and crash, at first no more than a distant drumbeat. A stench like a mass grave torn open, which Erzelle supposed was exactly what this place was, hundreds of mass graves violated and raided. The old Erzelle, the little girl who lived with her parents in Minnepaul, would have been rendered weak-kneed and sick by that smell. The Erzelle who had studied under Olyssa used Reneer's knife to cut a strip of cloth from Braeca's sweatshirt, which she tied behind her head to cover her mouth and nose. Reneer nodded in approval and they kept going.

More noises fleshed out the drumbeat. Shrieks of grinding metal, bellows-like whoomphs and hisses, rumbles of gears turning, a whine, crackles of electricity, low moans as of people in pain, though Erzelle knew those noises couldn't possibly be made by living people. At a place where the tunnel widened, Reneer told Erzelle to stay put so he could scout ahead.

"No," she said. "We go together."

He started to protest, but she brought the flashlight up under her chin so he could see her glare. "Ha!" he said. "All right then, as you wish."

The crude bone mosaics continued even down here, still not as dense or as artistic as they were in the temple proper. The way they were arranged end to end in pale stripes that flowed with the passageway put Erzelle in mind of lengths of cable, if cable could be formed from linked-together bone.

Reneer followed Erzelle's gaze with bewilderment, then paused to regard a vulpine skull. Finally he spoke. "They've been down here for decades, collecting the dead and the undead, making all of this. To what end?"

"On the boat … they ate the ghouls. It gave them immortality. Or that's what they thought, till Olyssa came on board." But Reneer was already shaking his head.

"Here there are no eaters. There's no one properly alive to enjoy a meal." He sighed. "I suppose there's no point in guessing." Baring his teeth in grim determination, he waved so that his light pierced further down the tunnel. "Let's find out the answer, Erzelle, before it finds us."

They at last reached a place where the passage ended and eight more branched off, four to either side, some angling down, some angling up, the conduit-lines made of bone spiraling around and funneling into these. If a spider's thorax could be hollowed out into a room and each of its legs into tunnels, it might have looked like this.

Reneer said through his cloth mask, "I would rather go up than down, how about you?"

Erzelle nodded. They took the route to the right that afforded the steepest ascent. It curved to the left, on and on, and after a bit they saw light, red and wavering. They shut their flashlights off and stowed them in Reneer's pack.

They came out onto a ledge that circled all the way around an oval chamber like the inside of an eggshell hundreds of feet high. The bone conduits tracked up to the central point of the ceiling, but it was the monstrosity that filled the bowl of the egg that captured their complete attention.

For that was made of flesh as well as bone.

Erzelle and Reneer crouched on all fours and leaned down. Erzelle's head swam, because the ledge wasn't level. It tilted slightly downward toward the bottom of the egg, and her mind kept insisting her perch was tipping out from underneath her.

Erzelle's parents had once taken her to visit a sad little curio museum in Minnepaul that kept lost and extinct animals from the world before the Storms preserved in jars of formaldehyde. She had seen a horseshoe crab with its underside full of spindly legs ending in claws.

Overturn that crab to find its nest of legs replaced with rotting human limbs and that would be the closest thing Erzelle could connect to what she saw below. Except this creation was hundreds of feet across, filling the bottom of the egg, every bit of it assembled from dismembered — still moving — pieces of ghouls, every surface a glistening, seething mass of contracting and extending flesh. Red energy like that Erzelle had seen from Olyssa's rifle and the Chef's knives flickered inside the works.

Within, every part of the machine convulsed and twitched, though what her eye had at first interpreted as pure chaos resolved as anything but. Every dismembered piece moved in repeated patterns: pistoning, rotating, spiraling, spinning, locking together and twisting apart. An incomprehensible clock. The sounds of metal clanking on metal rose from underneath the corpse-mechanisms, suggesting it had all been built on top of some more mundane machine. The patterns were hypnotic. Scanning them made Erzelle nauseous.

There was a central hub perhaps fifty yards across, its top sculpted into a round, concave basin. The limbs of the thing, eight in all, each thicker than the largest tree trunk Erzelle had ever seen, radiated out from the rim of the basin like spokes on a wheel. Within their girth, shelves made of bone jutted out and slid back in, gears of viscera spun and red light strobed. Each limb crooked up at an elbow bend to press an eight-fingered thumbless "hand" against the curve of the chamber wall. The fingers didn't rest on the smoothed-out earth but rather melded into it, with more conduits of bone branching upward from their tips.

Creatures like they'd seen in the tunnel crawled along the lip of the basin, or squirmed out from underneath it, or from inside it, scurrying blind until they randomly found their way into one of the access tunnels at the base of the egg.

One limb was quite different from the rest. It slanted like a long neck from the rim of the central pool at the point where the grotesque crab's "head" would be. It was even thicker, it didn't rise as high, and it terminated not in a hand but a face taller than a two story house. The face was formed like a mosaic, each piece a limbless, split open torso. Except for the eyes, which were empty holes, and the mouth, open in an exaggerated howl, baring rows of severed heads that substituted for teeth. As with the "fingers," the edges of the mask meshed into the wall.

Staring into the central basin, hoping for some clue as to what this charnel contraption did, Erzelle received the worst shock of all.

Black smoke pooled and churned in the heart of the basin, boiling with liquid consistency, but that wasn't what made her insides lurch. A sinewy net stretched over the basin, and a figure in a leather jacket was tangled in its center, spread-eagled over the tarry smoke. The webbing wrapped around her limbs, waist, neck, wound into her hair. Olyssa. She didn't appear conscious.

Erzelle pointed, and Reneer grabbed her wrist. "I saw. We have to get down there."

He turned back toward the passage they'd emerged from. A Grey One advanced toward them from the opening, scythe raised.

Reneer stepped forward with an arm extended as if inviting the Grey One to dance. It swung at him, but he was quicker, seized its forearm and spun, throwing himself against the wall and the Grey One off the ledge.

It fell between two of the great arms and smashed apart against the bone and stone floor of the egg.

"There's more coming," Reneer shouted. "C'mon!"

They ran clockwise around the ledge. The Grey Ones pursued, fanning out in both directions. Reneer stopped opposite the opening they'd come through, pulling his rope from his satchel. "Take my knife."

She snatched it as he held it up, nearly dropped it, shaking from adrenaline and vertigo.

He tied the rope through a piton and shoved the piton into the brittle rock of the ledge with all his strength. He shoved another piton in and twined the rope again around that, then tossed the remaining coil off the ledge.

Erzelle realized what he intended, and couldn't breathe.

"I don't know how you're going to do it," he said, "but you have to get her pipe to her." He gripped her arm, shook her. "I'm sorry I can't do better for you. Please don't fall." His eyes, ruby and urgent, snapped her stupor and she inhaled. Looked down. The rope reached almost to the crook of one of the arms. The face loomed just yards away.

The Grey Ones closed in. Twenty feet away. Ten. "Go!"

Breathing quickly, Erzelle stooped to grab the rope. Her fingers curled around it and she overbalanced, slipping off the ledge. She held on to the rope, though the drop itself scraped skin from her palms and agony wrenched her shoulders. She flailed with her legs, the chamber spinning around her in a chaos of mutilated corpses before she managed to catch the rope between her thighs. She looked up to see Reneer shoot a wide-eyed glance her way, though whether his terror was for her or for himself she couldn't know. He swung around, his long dagger in hand. A moment later another Grey One pitched off the ledge. It tried to snatch her as it fell past, but she was out of reach.

She dangled only a couple of feet below the ledge, breathing hard, too scared to move. There was another ledge beneath the one she hung from. It also circled the entire egg. There was another beneath that. She thought about trying to swing onto the nearest one, land and run. If she made it to the exit she could access from that level, how long before she met Grey Ones coming the other way?

She took in a deep breath, then another. She didn't look down. Slowly she straightened her legs, until she had the rope clenched between her boots rather than her knees. She clenched her feet hard together.

She let go with one hand, grabbed the rope again at waist level. Then did the same with the other hand. And again. More skin tore free from her palms, but in the rush of astonishment and terror she hardly noticed.

A head fell past her, and an arm, and the Grey One they'd belonged to. She wanted to laugh, some part of her wanting to declare it all a game, shut her eyes and wait for it to stop being real. She didn't dare listen to that impulse. She kept moving, hand over hand, slow, so slow.

Clangs of metal above her. Reneer shouted and another Grey One tumbled off, head attached to body by a thread of flesh, neck unhinged like an opened can. She wanted to lower faster, but had to fight her own shaking hands to release her grip on the rope.

She looked down. Her head went light. She was a mote several stories above the unforgiving floor. The great arm made of corpse parts, the only thing she could land on and survive, was still maybe sixty feet below her. The rope didn't reach all the way to it. She'd have to drop the last few feet.

Above her, Reneer cried out in pain.

She closed her eyes, moved one hand under the other, three, times, four, times, five, six. When she opened her eyes she was level with the second ledge down. Not enough, not far enough!

She loosened her hands, let herself slide several feet down. The pain was exquisite.

A tug on the rope, pulling her up.

"Erzelle!"

One of the Grey Ones had seized the rope, was using a sharp-edged spade to saw through it.

She let go.

Instinct made her draw her legs and arms together and roll. Her mind went blank.

She landed on her side atop the sloping arm of the corpse machine, in a spot where dozens of withered ghoul limbs were fused together in layers of oscillating shelves.

The panel she landed on splintered beneath her and she tumbled inside the machine.

The stench of it crammed into her nose and mouth. Ghoul limbs writhed all around her. Something hooked her leg and pinched it hard before she pulled herself loose. The shelf beneath her jerked and teetered, threatening to spill her even deeper into the works. Beside her head three interlocked gears spun together, all of them made of toes. A shinbone branched away from them to turn a hipbone disk, its edges corrugated with teeth, its surfaces etched with writing that shimmered red. Wet bundles of veins bound knobs of knuckles into chains. Above her the broken panel still tried to move, stabbing at nothing with jagged shards of bone.

Erzelle kicked at a thin support strut that held the smashed panel lodged in place, and as the support snapped the fastened-together shards tipped over and wedged into a nest of gears beside her. All the moving bits around her shuddered and froze. While the works stayed paralyzed she scrambled back to the surface. She'd inadvertently made a hole midway between the elbow and wrist of one of the huge crab-arms. She had a steep climb down to the level portion of the arm. Across that she'd reach the lattices of ribs that formed the rim of the basin where Olyssa hung suspended. Still well above the egg floor, she had no time to be choosy about her handholds. A slip to either side of the formation could kill her.

She groped, she skidded, she hopped.

Another of the fused-together creatures emerged from the black miasma in the basin, came scurrying around the rim and scrabbled onto the crab-arm-catwalk. Built from four arms joined at the shoulders to make a wobbling pyramid, the creature had a decayed, skinless head fixed at its center. As it approached it clicked its teeth.

Erzelle didn't shrink back. She laughed at the hopping monstrosity. This situation had gone so far beyond what she understood or imagined that she couldn't take the creature seriously, couldn't be frightened of it. She waited at the crook of the column's elbow, Reneer's knife in hand, and when the monster reached her she gripped it by an upper arm as if it were an unruly child. It spun to bite her. She stabbed it first in one eye, then the other, and kicked it away. It whirled off the side, flapping futilely.

She ran for the rim of the machine until, panting and wild-eyed, she balanced on a platform made of gristle-bound ribs and stared over at Olyssa. Her teacher's eyes were closed, yet her mouth was open, forming words, and she twitched against her bonds.

The webbing appeared fragile enough to snap as soon as Erzelle put her weight on it. It did, however, hold Olyssa fast.

The substance that roiled beneath the web was the same stuff that had attacked Olyssa in the tunnel and Braeca in the apothecary. It filled the entire basin. Though it resembled smoke, no smell rose from it to muffle the ever-present reek of spoiled flesh. Peering down into its flux and flow made Erzelle queasy.

So she looked instead at Olyssa. She pressed a hand on the netting. It bowed, rubbery, and it had an unpleasant feel, as if it were mildly electrified — the strands so thin they seemed unlikely to support her.

She pressed her forearm down across multiple threads. The wire-like threads bit into her skin but didn't cut and didn't break.

Erzelle crawled out onto the web on her forearms and shins. Contact with the black strands made her skin itch, and the itch spread, as if mites were seething up her body. She gritted her teeth and tried to move faster, but the web shook violently with each new push forward. She constantly had to stop and steady herself before advancing again.

The miasma below snagged the bottom of her vision, made her stomach twist. Erzelle refused to focus on it.

A shout behind her.

She glanced back to see a figure wrapped head-to-toe in grey gauze grasp the outside lip of the machine and pull itself onto the rim.

She lunged, no longer trying to be careful.

Her thrashing disturbed Olyssa, who winced as if in pain but did not wake. Staring at her teacher, Erzelle gasped. The strands of webbing didn't just wrap around Olyssa. They melded into her the way the bone conduits fused into the walls, piercing her skin and tracking underneath, drawing seams along her brow, her neck, her hands.

Had she time to think, Erzelle would have despaired at ever getting Olyssa free. The net vibrated behind her and she plunged on. Another shout, much louder. She risked another glance and saw Reneer standing on the basin's lip, his dagger skewering the head of the Grey One who'd tried to follow her.

"Don't stop!" he said. "There's more coming."

As if determined to verify his accounting, three more Grey Ones appeared at the lip. She redoubled her pace.

She reached forward, missed her target altogether and put her right arm completely through the web. Now she couldn't help but look down.

Shapes moved inside the black fog, pushing and pulling and swinging at each other with tremendous energy, tearing each other apart and reforming. Something that wasn't quite a complete head opened a silently shrieking hole that turned its entire form inside out as it vomited a thrashing humanoid shape that immediately engaged in the melee.

Seeming to sense her gaze, it turned, started swimming up toward her. Others followed.

"Erzelle! Move!"

Spurred by Reneer's shout, Erzelle tore herself free and scurried the remaining yards to Olyssa. Glimpsed at the bottom of her vision, the shapes in the miasma tracked her.

"Olyssa!" she shouted, then louder, "*OLYSSA!*" Her teacher continued to twitch and shudder. Erzelle leaned against Olyssa's ice-box cold body, tried shaking her shoulders. The entire web shook with her effort. "Olyssa!"

Still her eyes didn't open. About a dozen of the black threads wound into her head, under her skin, even through her eyelids.

For a terrible half-second Erzelle feared she'd dropped Reneer's knife, but she found it in the pocket of her coveralls where she must have tucked it. She climbed onto her teacher, gripped one of the black threads winding into her brow, and pressed the edge of the blade to it.

The strand stretched, tugging at Olyssa's skin. Then it broke.

Olyssa's eyes squinched tight and she moaned. The end left beneath her skin quivered and faded. Her eyes still didn't open. Erzelle started on another thread, and it produced the same response when it broke. At the third, Olyssa's eyelids fluttered.

A bright flare distracted her.

All of the heads that comprised the teeth of the enormous mask opened their mouths in unison, every gaping maw glowing flame-red as if stuffed with hot coals.

Erzelle started cutting faster. As the last threads broke, Olyssa opened her eyes. She stared about her, lips still moving wordlessly, until she focused on her rescuer. Erzelle had already started sawing at the threads that bound Olyssa's right hand. When Olyssa didn't say anything she said, "I have to give you your pipe. This is all magic. You can fight it with magic."

Olyssa's bewildered gaze flickered to where Reneer was fending off the Grey Ones.

"He helped me," Erzelle said.

With each strand cut Olyssa winced, though not as sharply as she had when Erzelle severed the cords binding her head. Erzelle wondered if she even understood what was happening.

The red glow from the mask spread outward from its gruesome teeth to fill the entire distended mouth.

With Olyssa's hand and forearm freed, Erzelle slid gingerly off of her to kneel with precarious balance on the webbing. She pulled Braeca's herb case from her shoulder and took out the pipe. "I had to make a reed for it. I don't know how well it will work, but it played for me." She held the instrument out. Olyssa simply stared at it.

Had something been done to her memory? Was she still even Olyssa? "Take it!" she shouted.

"Oh, child, you should have left her there," said a woman, her voice musical and bright with amusement. "All her worries were over. Forever."

The voice sounded so much like Olyssa's that Erzelle did a double take — was this mindspeech? — before she spotted the figure standing in the mouth of the mask.

Imposingly tall, though not quite as tall or broad-shouldered as Olyssa, she wore a simple robe that shimmered indigo, cinched at the waist with a red cord. She had Olyssa's long, dark, wavy hair, the same tawny skin and wide face. But the smile beneath her bright green eyes distended wide enough to reveal every tooth. The flesh of her face was smooth, waxy smooth, stretched so tight over the bone it looked as if a touch would peel it away like tissue paper, as if her very grin could tear her skin at the creases.

Even so, there was a terrible beauty about her, simultaneously riveting and repugnant, her large eyes vibrant in their jutting sockets. She had a mark on her forehead, a symbol too complicated for Erzelle to decipher from a distance

She was looking past Erzelle. "I see the vulpines of Fabelford have violated their pact." She sounded exactly like Olyssa did when delivering an ultimatum.

Erzelle hardly noticed her teacher taking the pipe from her hand. The other woman raised two fingers to her lips in a V-sign — her hands as fleshless and withered as her face — and puffed her lips between them as if blowing a kiss.

A cannon-shot of red fire hurtled across the width of the web, and Reneer howled mid-dagger-swing as he was blasted off the edge of the machine, flames engulfing him.

Erzelle screamed Reneer's name.

Olyssa's voice, at the edge of her hearing. "Find my enemies. Find my enemies." But she had no bullets, no access to her gun assembly.

The witch turned her eyes to Erzelle, brought her fingers to her lips. Erzelle scrambled backward.

The fire enveloped her, intimate as a mother's embrace.

Before her nerve endings had time to report their agonies to her, the witch's burning breath seared through the threads of webbing she crouched on, and she plummeted through.

As her body became an all-over shriek of charred flesh, the things in the fog seized her and tore her apart.

Her world went black.

She sat in cool grass. Above her the sky churned red. Before her a titanic, rope-muscled man with the head of a deer sat on a throne comprised of straw mats bound to the trunk and branches of a warped and unnaturally doubled-over tree. A forest of antlers rose from his brow to the sky, severed yet still-living heads dangling from every crook.

With eyes closed, he rubbed his palms together, engaged in some strange prayer.

She didn't see his mouth move, but he spoke, like stone shaping words. *I'm sorry that it's come to this.*

She held up her hands, studied them. They were untouched by fire. At the edge of her vision she perceived outlines of other trees, growing from a plain of sere scrub, and yet they were no more than that, vague forms sketched on air. The setting grew indistinct mere feet from where she sat. Squinting did nothing to resolve its details.

Terrifying though the antlered man looked, Erzelle sensed no danger from him. "Who are you?" she asked.

You have done so much more already than I could have asked for. But it's all coming to ruin. I cannot stay away. I cannot allow another mistake. I failed them too many times already.

Disconcerting, that this fearsome being spoke with such sadness. She asked, "Failed who?"

His eyes glittered like polished onyx. *You were not born to tap the dark, but yet you've touched it. It's shared its song with you. This gives me hope.*

Erzelle blinked. "I don't understand."

He opened his hands. A loop of black cord lay there. *Take it.*

Erzelle didn't obey. The loop appeared to be made from the same substance that held Olyssa trapped in webbing.

He extended his hand. *You will die if you don't wear it. It's the only way I can protect you.*

She stood, and picked the loop from his palm, gasping as she did so. His flesh was blizzard-cold.

The cord had a clasp. She undid it. It barely fit around her neck. She started to fumble with the clasp but the choker squirmed in her grip, fastened itself and tightened, ending up flush against her skin, but not uncomfortably so.

Thank you, child, he said. *I am sorry.*

And he pressed the tip of a thumb to Erzelle's forehead. An icicle of cold pierced her skull.

Help her, he said. *Help them.*

She felt as if her brain had frozen and cracks were spreading through it. Through those cracks leaked in rays of darkness, an energy that shone like light but drove light away. It flickered like fire and yearned like hunger.

You have a moment to yourself outside the flow of time. Learn fast, little one.

He faded, as Erzelle blazed, every neuron consumed by black fire.

She saw, not with her eyes.

She hovered, frozen, her mind liberated from the constraints of time, moving outside it, as the beast on his throne vanished altogether.

Ghost words followed her back into the world. *Never stray from her music. Never.*

She hovered in the pool, enveloped by the witch's fire and the black mist. She experienced both things, not as a tissue-destroying chemical reaction or a smoky congeal of animated malice, but as a latticework of energy akin to the forces unfolding through her mind and body from the touch to her brow. She reached out without using her hands, undid a link like yanking out a loose thread, and the fire was gone.

She remembered Reneer, and her consciousness expanded to envelop the full cavity of the egg without any need to will it so — her desire doubled as immediate command.

He lay on the floor, burning, all the tongues of flame trapped unmoving in this frozen moment.

She undid the fire, saw the ways the patterns of his body had been distorted, tried her best to restore them, at first unsure if she could.

In that same interval, unstuck in time, free to act in as many ways as she wished, she wrapped her mind around the dark energy in the basin and the rotting machine that pooled it there. For she could now discern its structures, too.

It wasn't like the flames she'd just banished. She couldn't comprehend it with such ease. Its conduits of energy encompassed the fused-together parts and the bodies and bones embedded in the passageways, funneled up from the point of the egg to the weird garden far above where the Grey Ones harvested. The boundaries of its network extended hundreds and even thousands of miles away, connecting to other structures similar and stranger. All of them formed letters in a word, each letter not quite complete, though what the word meant or what would happen to the world when it could finally be spoken, Erzelle couldn't fathom.

Each machine in the chain was working to complete itself, to find the right combination to activate all of its brethren to their full potential.

Olyssa had been made a living part of the letter and the word. The machine's creator had adjusted it to hold her soul and drain power from it. Even as she fought to flood magic through her pipe, the machine was still wound through her, muting her. Erzelle could undo the webbing with a flick from her mind, but then Olyssa would fall into this reserve of dark energy, black breath to be used to voice the word once it was completed.

Erzelle no longer found the miasma fearsome and alien. Or rather, no more alien than the antlered man's gift coursing through her blood. Around her the dark energy had an undersea quality, living ribbons like kelp, all snagged in the folds of the same net.

A shadow fell around her. Coming toward her from all sides. She perceived an implacable barrier shrinking closer, knew in her hyper-altered state what it had to be, the bubble of no-time that the antlered man had created for her, collapsing.

She finished restitching Reneer's patterns — she'd fixed them as much as she dared — and took hold of the ribbons of dark energy, gathered them and drew them into her, as the bubble of frozen time shrank to nothing and burst.

Inside her body, black smoke became black fire. The darkness swelled inside her, more exhilarating than any adrenaline rush, a thousand times more powerful, blazing so strong her body felt as if it could rip itself apart.

"Find my enemies," Olyssa whispered.

The witch was speaking, but Erzelle ignored her words. She floated beneath her teacher within the emptied basin. All the dark energy was gone. All the dark energy was in her.

The pipe hovered in the air, just like she did, its runes a faint red. It was seeking, Olyssa was seeking through it, a bullet, a pebble, a pin, anything to seize upon to allow it to be true to the purpose Olyssa willed upon it.

Erzelle ascended. And extended her arm. Streamers of black flowed from her fingers. Toward Olyssa. *Use me,* she told the pipe, told her teacher, without speaking. *Let me be your bullet.*

Her teacher's magic hooked into hers. The pipe spun, and black fire fountained from its bell.

The witch's green eyes bulged. She raised her hands, black smoke blasting from her fingertips a beat too late. Then she screamed, her cry drowned out as the flames enveloped her.

Erzelle's surge of triumph converted to a surge of power and the jet of flame gushing from the pipe expanded to a cone, completely consuming the great mask and the canted arm of corpse parts that connected to it.

"Stop!" Olyssa cried.

With a flick of her mind the web twining her teacher dissolved. Olyssa started to fall, but Erzelle caught her, without using her arms or moving from the spot where she hung in the air.

"Find my enemies," Erzelle said, and when she spoke tongues of black flame rolled from her mouth and streamed from her eyes.

Vines of fire poured into the machine, washed through its spaces and over its parts, torrented out through the cores of the eight-fold arms and from there into the walls of the egg. The embedded conduits of bone splintered as Erzelle's fury roared through them.

Olyssa stared about wide-eyed as the basin of ghoul parts beneath her transmuted into a blue-black inferno.

Erzelle reached further, past the egg, into the tunnels, into the surrounding earth. *Find my enemies.* Snakes of fire burrowed, divided, extended. They found thousands of remains. They found ghouls buried underground for the harvest. Erzelle burned them all to ash and kept going.

She experienced this constant surge of power as a swelling and pulling beneath her skin, as a tidal force, strong enough to rip her to pieces, yet she held together — she could feel the pressure of an external force pitted against her flesh, keeping her from flying apart.

She had no thought to spare for what it might be.

Her energy exploded out through the ground beside the temple, as she wound flaming limbs through the temple itself and pulled it down. She burst open a dozen cracks in the Violet Bluffs and forced them wider, and she stretched further yet, following all the secret tunnels bored by the Grey Ones over the decades and filling them with flame—

Olyssa, on her third try, put both hands around the pipe even though it was blacksmith-forge hot. "Stop now!"

The spigot closed. The fire shut off.

The backblast tossed Erzelle from the air.

She and Olyssa both landed in a mound of ash several feet deep.

Erzelle could hardly open her eyes. A weight like tons of rock immobilized her, except the compression came from outside, squeezing with equal force against the fire. The choker around her neck pulsed as the black fire started to subside.

She hardly noticed where she was or what was happening until Olyssa dragged her out of the mound and hugged her fiercely.

A few yards away, Reneer lay on his back, staring up into the tunnel Erzelle had blasted through the top of the egg chamber, which led up through a hundred feet of rock and out to open sky. Blisters covered his face. He tried to sit up, groaned, slouched back to the floor.

"Your pipe," Erzelle said, wanting to ask if Olyssa was all right, wanting to ask who the green-eyed witch was, though she thought she knew now and hoped she was wrong. But Olyssa shushed her, and pushed her hair back from her forehead.

And inhaled sharply. "The same mark. The same damned mark."

Erzelle managed to shape words. "What mark?"

Olyssa touched the spot on her brow where the antlered man had pressed his thumb. "You have the same mark my sister has."

"Your sis—"

"Yes, Erzelle — that witch was my sister." To a stranger, Olyssa's voice might have sounded completely devoid of emotion, but Erzelle had never heard her so sorrowful. "Much as I didn't want to believe she could become such a thing. That was she."

"Did I—"

"No you didn't." Olyssa answered her unfinished question, sounding both rueful and relieved. "You didn't kill her. The magic would have gone from the pipe. But it still works." She held Erzelle tight. "Oh, what has he done to you?" Tears streaked her cheeks.

"What has who done to me?"

Olyssa turned her gaze to the hole bored through the ceiling, where sunlight cascaded in. "My father."

Erzelle's jaw worked. "Your ... but ... he wasn't ... human?"

"That's who it was, Erzelle. Damn him forever."

At that moment Reneer groaned and propped himself up on his elbows. His black tunic and trousers were scorched. "Ow," he said. "This is an adventure in pain like no other! But I'm certainly glad to see *you* again, my lady."

"Reneer." Olyssa nodded diffidently. "I am grateful that you helped us." Her voice cracked. "But you'll wish you hadn't."

He started, then flashed his usual charming grin. "Nonsense."

His forced cheer faded as he took in her expression.

Erzelle remembered a name Olyssa had only said once in her presence. "Lilla."

Olyssa swallowed.

"But you thought your sister was a ghoul."

"Wait a minute!" exclaimed the fox-man. "That fire-breathing witch was your sister?"

Olyssa bit her lip and didn't answer him. From the way his eyes widened, Erzelle could tell the silence had sufficed.

Olyssa pointedly avoided Reneer's gaze. She asked Erzelle, "Can you stand?"

Erzelle tried and couldn't.

Reneer sat all the way up. "Looks like you were maybe about a quarter right. That witch was not the most alive lady I've ever seen, but no ghoul could do that."

"How much do you remember?" Olyssa asked him.

"What?"

"How much do you remember of her?"

"After she torched me, nothing. And then I wake up and all is ash, and she's gone, and here you two are. A good thing this young miss is so devoted to you, to go through all that to give you a pipe with a reed that doesn't quite fit." He laughed, a short, sharp bark, and winced. "Ow. And here they say laughter heals ... You know, I could've guessed she was your sister, but for the skin stretched tight as leather over her skull. And that rune on her ..."

His eyes focused on Erzelle. He touched his own forehead as if wondering if he might find yet another mark there. "What ... how ...?"

So many conflicting images tumbled through Erzelle's head, made more confusing by the fires, receded now but flickering at her mind's edges, just out of reach. "A man gave it to me. A giant. With the head of a deer. And antlers. So many and so tall I don't know how he held his head up. There were heads in the antlers, hanging like fruit."

"What are you talking about?" Reneer interjected.

But then Olyssa's legs went out from under her. Erzelle tried to prevent her fall but ended up on the ground herself. Her teacher sat down hard, both hands over her mouth, her brow a thunderstorm of anguish. "He's still ... he's still pretending ..."

Reneer called, "Are you okay?" He tried to stand and failed, slipping back to the ground in strange slow-motion, as if time itself lost momentum.

Can you see me, Erzelle?

A second Olyssa stood in the chamber of ruins with them.

She might have been thirteen or fourteen. She was taller than Erzelle, though still not as tall as she would be when she was grown. Her flow of dark hair reached her waist, and huge blue flowers were tucked behind each ear. She wore an airy green dress that flowed to the floor. *This is how I looked at my father's second wedding.*

I see you, Erzelle said.

Then we can make the most of what my father's done to you. I need to tell you what he's done, quickly, and I don't want to spill my entire life story in front of the vulpine.

Erzelle bristled. *He's a good man.*

I don't dispute that. The younger Olyssa's mouth didn't move, but her eyes smiled. *It's as much for his protection as it is mine. Perhaps more so for him.*

Erzelle sounded a bit resentful, even to herself, expressing her next thought. *I can do magic now, just like you. I can help you, like I haven't been able to before.*

One instant the young Olyssa was several feet away, the next leaning beside Erzelle. Her older self, her physical self, still hadn't moved, still held her hands over her mouth. A tear hung at her cheekbone without falling, frozen in place.

My father forced his magic on you without telling you the consequences, just as he did Lilla, the young Olyssa said. Erzelle thought she could smell the flowers, a faint vanilla scent.

Olyssa's distress still baffled Erzelle. *He saved me from dying. He said he didn't want another mistake.*

Well, he made one. Did he tell you how long you have to live, with that much power channeling through you?

Erzelle touched the choker around her neck, though not with her physical hands. In this conversation, in this mindspace, she could move without ties to her body. *He said I'd die without this.*

Because that much power should have burned you alive from inside out! He made that thing to hold you together. Who knows how long it will last?

Erzelle shook her head. *How can that monster I saw be your father? He seemed so sad.*

Olyssa was unmoved. *It's easiest to show you.*

What are you going to do?

Show you everything. I should warn you, once we start, it might feel as if hours or even years are going by. I promise you though, when we're done, you'll find no time has passed at all, and our friend will be none the wiser.

She held out a hand. Erzelle took it.

They were no longer inside the egg.

PART THREE: BURNING HORSES

"*I* made this for you," Lilla said.

Olyssa stopped rehearsing mid-note and set down her flute, balancing it precariously on the music stand. She did not turn to face her sister. Rather, she made a show of sighing and staring out the conservatory's west windows at the concentric tiers of her stepmother's garden. Snapdragons, tiger lilies and the last of the summer daffodils all wagged their pretty heads, encouraged by a breeze she had shut out so that her sheet music wouldn't be disturbed.

She avoided looking at Lilla because she had been interrupted, she told herself, not because the tangled, lopsided star etched into her sister's forehead unnerved her. Nor was it because of the dark intensity in her sister's eyes since she acquired that mark — a darkness that made Olyssa queasy. At times she could swear it was animate, shifting in the depths of Lilla's pupils.

"That's nice, but can't it wait? My recital's in two days—"

Lilla's hand touched her shoulder. "Just look. Please."

Peering out through Olyssa's eyes from inside this memory, Erzelle took in the octagonal chamber's sleek elegance, glass panels rising from the polished pine floor to the peak of the ceiling. Umber-stained chairs with backs that curled like ocean waves stood in a half-circle on a carpet plush as a bed. As Olyssa turned away from the garden a building came into view unlike anything Erzelle had ever seen before. Bricked with white marble, riddled with hundreds of arched windows, it towered six stories and stretched horizontally for at least a half-mile in either direction, its corners decorated by rounded towers topped with peaked turrets. A walkway glittering with blue pebbles led from the conservatory through another walled garden, bordered with rainbow-colored peppers like miniature candles, filled with zinnias and sunflowers. The walk ended at a pair of ornate doors tall enough to let an elephant through.

Yet Olyssa's attention wasn't on any of this. She regarded her sister, whose dark hair was yanked out of the way in an afterthought of a ponytail, her green eyes solemn as she presented an object. Erzelle recognized it immediately: the rune-inscribed pipe, gleaming silver. It had no bell, no reed, and no rifle assembly, but all the notches and grooves that allowed those attachments were there.

This was the first time the younger Olyssa had ever laid eyes on it. Her mouth hung open several seconds before she could even ask, "What is it?"

"I don't know."

Olyssa laughed. "You said you made it. How can you not know what it is?"

Erzelle's focus stayed on Olyssa's sister. Hard to reconcile her breathtaking beauty with the emaciated, grey creature who'd appeared in the mouth of the skull portal, though her height and her startling green eyes made the connection undeniable, as did the mark on her forehead. She could have been Olyssa's twin, only more slender. She wore jeans and a loose-fitting sweatshirt, ratty sneakers, no makeup. No effort made to render herself so lovely. She seemed as bewildered and awestruck as her sister by the magnificence of the object she held.

"I had a level of the labs to myself," Lilla said. "I conducted an experiment."

"Does father know you did that?"

"I logged it," Lilla said, dismissively. Olyssa's gaze flitted to the symbol on Lilla's brow. Every time her sister spoke so flippantly of tapping the darkness it made her want to grind her teeth.

Father insisted that both sisters had been born with abilities. The tests he ran showed they manifested slightly stronger in Lilla — though both had the potential, he loved to say, to "move mountains." Their father always doted on them: whatever his daughters wanted, from horses to airguns to VR simulators, he made sure they had it.

Sometimes Olyssa believed it wasn't just her imagination that he doted on Lilla more.

Erzelle, startled, was experiencing a rapid-fire string of mental associations as young Olyssa contemplated Lilla's forehead. The symbol there was a concentric series of seven-pointed stars, all connected, none closed. It wasn't a tattoo, wasn't inked on her skin, seemed to have no physical presence and yet was clearly visible.

The stirred-up memories from Olyssa's past ran even deeper, to things her father never spoke of: how he and their birth mother had learned to tap the darkness in their twenties, when such practices were newly "discovered," and how this learned behavior, these perceptions developed through long practice, became things she and Lilla were simply born with. How Olyssa'd never let any of it trouble her until this past year, when father had invited both of them to join in his experiments. His fleeting frown of disappointment when she rejected his offer. Her own frown when Lilla accepted.

That had been the first time, too, Olyssa'd begun to wonder about the source of their father's wealth. Had she the inclination she could wander through their palatial home for a full day — with all its priceless art, designer furniture, game rooms with every possible computerized interface imaginable, toy rooms piled with treasures arranged by theme at the sisters' whim, swimming pools and handball courts and a multi-storied library — and still not see the whole of what it offered. The cursory inventory didn't even include the levels underground, where father did his work, or the hangar on the roof for his private jets. Their house, constructed with at least thirty mock castle towers to keep the girls entertained when they were younger, squatted at the center of a range of fields and woods large enough, Lilla and Olyssa liked to joke, to be its own small country. They'd named it after their family surname: Hunterland.

The butterflies of Hunterland fluttered amid their stepmother's snapdragons as Olyssa took the pipe from Lilla and turned it over, studying the runes along its length. Cold against her fingers, the metal thrummed as if it already sounded out unheard notes. It had to be a musical instrument, but she couldn't fathom how to play it.

"It's beautiful," she said, and felt an impish thrill that she and Lilla had a new secret. She ran a finger along the pipe's length, felt the ridges and depressions of the strange letters against her skin. "These markings … what do they mean?"

"They're from the texts that father's shown me. I don't recognize every one of them. To be honest, I'm not sure what they mean."

Olyssa frowned. "How did you make it?"

"It's hard to explain."

"You think I won't understand?" Irritation made her flash a smile she didn't quite mean. "Try me."

"If you tapped the darkness just once you'd know." Lilla returned a smile that mirrored her own. They met each others' glares, but Olyssa broke first, because she hated how the darkness in Lilla's pupils seemed thicker than mere shadow.

"Sorry," Lilla muttered. "Okay. When you're tapping the darkness, it's like you're reaching out into a place that doesn't exist in this world and drawing on the energies that live there. You can see them, almost. They look like fire, though the flames are black. The stronger they are, the deeper the darkness. Father calls it *prana*, which he says means life energy. I think it should just be black fire."

She noticed Olyssa's puzzled frown. "Anyway, I guess you could say this place isn't subject to the laws of time and mass that govern our reality. In fact it lies outside time altogether. Our minds have all kinds of trouble perceiving it without additional guidance made from these same forces."

She tapped the mark on her forehead. Studying it, Olyssa pondered what on Earth perception of time had to do with metalwork. It simmered in her, a little, how eerily Lilla sounded like father when he slipped into lecture mode.

"When you've had enough practice, sometimes you can extend your awareness way out into this space. And sometimes ... 'hearing' isn't the right word, but I don't know how else to explain it ... you can hear echoes. Noises. Disturbances. Describing it in terms of sound isn't quite right, it's not literally sound, but that's the closest thing. Some of these echoes have to come from different points in time as well as space. They could even be from the far future."

Erzelle shared Olyssa's mix of elation and uneasiness — elation at the chance to talk with Lilla uninterrupted, unease over the topic. She'd rather have chatted about anything other than this. She wished she'd opened the windows after all, called in fresh air to alleviate the suddenly stuffy room.

"It's really hard to tell what they could mean, these echoes," Lilla went on, her green eyes meeting Olyssa's as she waved her hands in an imitation of sound bouncing. "I look at the numbers we translate from my electroencephalographs and it's like the data's in code. You know how we used to make codes by shifting the letters thirteen places so M meant A? It's like that, if I could just figure out how many places to shift it, and what direction, it would make sense. There've been times I think I might be on to something. Dad never agrees with my hunches."

Olyssa kept nodding, cringing inwardly when Lilla said "dad" instead of father. That hadn't started until six months ago, the same evening she'd come upstairs with that mark.

"So I set up an experiment of my own. On my own. I tapped the darkness and pulled the energy through the right lines and configurations and I asked the construct I'd made a question. I asked it to give me the thing my sister needs most of anything."

Olyssa's eyes stung, her breath caught. Lilla watched her in silence as she turned the pipe again, let its runes catch the sunlight. "This?"

"I …" Lilla shrugged and raised her hands, groping to find the right words as they floated, hidden, in front of her. "I don't understand it either. When the black fire left me and my mind cleared, I was holding it. And …" She swallowed. "The machine that records my patterns, it was gone. Just completely gone. Consumed by the spell, I think, to make that for you."

Olyssa let a laugh escape. "Right."

Lilla shook her head. "It doesn't matter if you believe me. The object had to start from something." She smiled sheepishly. "I opened my eyes, and there it was. No time had passed at all. Then I put my head back on the pillow, because I felt so tired, and fell asleep right on the exam table. I lost half the day."

"Oh, my." Out of long habit Olyssa reached to place her hand on Lilla's forehead, that universal unspoken question of *Are you sick?* She caught herself before she touched the tangled star, instead touched her cheek. "Are you okay? Did you … hurt yourself?"

Lilla tried to shake her head, but Olyssa sucked in a breath. "You're burning up."

"No, no, no, it's okay. I'm not sick." Her wide grin shocked with its brilliance.

Erzelle, remembering how Lilla's grin looked now, felt a chill completely out of sync with the scene.

"I've never felt better. My muscles ache, but it's a good ache, like from exercise, from whatever it was I did." She stared past Olyssa, out through the conservatory glass. Whatever it was she saw, it had nothing to do with the garden outside. "It took something out of me. I think that's why I was so tired. Usually I'm not tired after tapping the dark. I feel like I can go for weeks without sleep.

"Today it's a little different. As if I'm lighter somehow. That hasn't happened before."

Olyssa blinked. What had she just seen? Tongues of fire flickering in the corners of her sister's eyes. Black, like a photographic negative. Lilla continued, oblivious, her laughter a breathy, uncertain sound, and Olyssa couldn't be sure that what she glimpsed was real.

"It's a part of me. I gave a small part of my life, to make this." Abruptly she folded her hands over Olyssa's, which were clutching the pipe. "I asked what you needed and this is what the spell made. I want you to be okay. Always. That's what this is for." Her gaze became intense, imploring. "Don't ever lose it. Please. Tell me you won't."

Olyssa had to speak past a lump in her throat. "I'm going to figure out how to play it. And I'll never let it out of my sight."

Erzelle had a sense of days flowing by like leaves in a river. Time's passage slowed, and she peered out into a dining hall larger than the apartment she grew up in: all of its narrow rooms — her bedroom, her parents' room, combined living room and kitchen and the tiny extra bedroom where her parents had propped up padding on the walls so her mother could practice — would fit within this octagonal chamber with space to spare.

Olyssa, through whose eyes Erzelle watched, had *her* attention wholly fixed on the boy seated at the far end of the table. Father hadn't told them there would be a guest at dinner.

The boy lounged arrogantly as if all belonged to him. Father's smile widened just a fraction as he looked the boy's way. His eyes lit up the way they did when Olyssa mastered a difficult passage on the flute or when Lilla's horse took the lead in a steeplechase. The recognition of the look left Olyssa off-balance as father stood up to acknowledge his daughters.

Peering through the memory, Erzelle couldn't help but continue to be astonished by the opulence of the room, riches that put the Family of the *Red Empress* to shame. The table they approached was a sinuous ellipse, polished black. Off-white chairs surrounded it, each slightly different in shape so that the entire ensemble served both as practical furniture and avant-garde sculpture. Two chandeliers, blue glass anemones, hung low above the table, brushing the octagonal porcelain china with sapphire highlights. Large diagrams of labyrinths decorated seven of the room's walls, while the eighth was glass, overlooking the conservatory, and the gardens surrounding it, arranged in an elaborate star shape. Beyond the gardens lay a rolling field, and woods beyond that. An artificial breeze cooled the room. The boy and Olyssa's father both had salads by their plates, untouched, and wine goblets, each half-full.

Erzelle had expected the man who sired Olyssa and Lilla to be a giant, and he was. He shared his daughters' dark complexion and almond eyes, his scalp and lantern jaw smooth-shaven. Above his faded jeans his snug black turtleneck stretched over streamlined muscle. His smile was as radiant as Olyssa's, and Erzelle could easily imagine it filling with the same dark threat, though at the moment he radiated only warmth.

He had a tangled star on his forehead. As did the boy.

Pale all over with a shock of black hair — not just uncombed but unwashed, Olyssa guessed — his torso and arms painfully slender in a white mesh shirt with the sleeves torn off. While father appeared imperial even while relaxed, the boy slouched like any ill-bred teen. The only things striking about him were his eyes, a cold, calculating blue, amplified by the chandelier light. Olyssa disliked him on sight. She looked forward to the conversation she and Lilla would certainly be having later this evening, dissecting and mocking his every aspect.

"Your mother couldn't join us tonight," father announced. This prompted the sisters to share the look they did whenever he referred to their stepmother as their mother. Of late, their stepmother *never* joined them for dinner. "But there's someone I want both of you to meet."

When the boy stood his expression changed. His crooked grin portrayed nervous excitement and a dose of bashfulness, as if he

understood the surprise was awkward and wanted the sisters to know
he felt the same way. His demeanor seemed scripted to Olyssa, and the
way he looked from her to Lilla as if measuring their reactions set her
further on edge.

"This is Noffreid," father continued. "He works for me at the corporate
lab, and he's done such a good job with the projects he's been entrusted
with that I've brought him here for the next few months, to help me with
the tricky stuff. Noffreid, here are my treasures, Olyssa and Lilla."

Olyssa took his hand, which was cold, gave it a squeeze she hoped
would make him wince, and proffered her best fake smile. "Pleased to
meet you."

"Likewise," he said, not obliging her with a reaction. Instead he
turned to Lilla, and when he took her hand volunteered, "I hear you're
the real star researcher."

Father laughed, booming and indulgent.

Olyssa fully expected Lilla to toss the idiot's hand away and shrivel
him with a glare. Instead she put her other hand to her mouth in an
uncharacteristic show of bashfulness.

"Hardly."

Lilla permitted him to hold her hand for another beat until he let
go of his own accord.

It only grew worse from there. Lilla and Noffreid were already
talking to each other about work, most of it completely over Olyssa's
head, before the staff brought in dinner. Olyssa's distress and the black
garb the servants wore reminded Erzelle uncomfortably of the *Red
Empress*, yet the food made the difference. Brightly colored sweet
potatoes, seasoned greens and a beef au jus provided Erzelle with
the bizarre experience of savoring this remembered meal as Olyssa
absently pecked at it, fretting about her sister's surprise rapport with
the intruder. She enjoyed neither the leers he shot at Lilla nor the
pitiless look she caught him levying at her, like a cobra sizing up a
mongoose. Why didn't anyone else notice this? Father said little but
watched Noffreid and Lilla chatter with a satisfied smirk that Olyssa
wanted to stab with her fork.

She was the only one at the table without one of those marks on
the forehead. She had never been more aware of that than she was this
evening.

Olyssa excused herself early. When she nudged Lilla, her sister didn't get up. "Oh, I'll be a little longer," she said. "I'll catch up with you."

Noffreid smiled, and offered Olyssa his hand again. "This dinner was wonderful." His smile didn't touch his eyes. "I look forward to many more."

Time poured in a cataract of accumulated moments lived and gone. Olyssa chose to have her dinners in her rooms as Noffreid became a regular fixture at the table. She said nothing to her sister, who seemed unperturbed by the growing distance between them, and used every excuse she could make, every classical music retreat and symposium her father's money could wedge her into, to fly out from Hunterland and stay away for weeks at a time.

She returned from her latest trip at the height of summer, when the dry heat best suited the grounds. She meant to take a horseback ride alone through the forest trails, but much to her surprise, Lilla intercepted her on the garden path that led to the stables. Lilla's ponytail hung even more slapdash than usual, her sweatshirt rumpled, her complexion blemished, skin dark around her reddened eyes.

"Why didn't you tell me you were here? I've missed you."

In that instant, the ice thawed. They embraced.

A half an hour later, in the gaudy confines of Lilla's audio room, with its imposing multideck floor-to-ceiling sound system and wallpapering of posters — tattooed, bare-chested rap stars, horses in full gallop, gorgeous ice skaters, howling wolves — Olyssa shared a breakthrough with her sister that she'd kept to herself for nearly a month. "I can play the pipe you made."

Lilla's face brightened in delight.

Olyssa had made the pipe's first reed and bell out of plastic, designing the shapes on her computer, borrowing her father's personal three-dimensional printer to build each piece layer by layer out of quick-hardening molten polymer. If she wanted the instrument to sing with the same range and subtlety she could elicit from her flute, she'd have to remake the pieces from material of much better quality. She'd known she'd found the right track, though, when those runes shone blue. She hadn't mastered the pipe by any means, but she'd determined it required both breath-work and hand-work, akin to a recorder or ocarina and yet not at all like either. The pipe continued to surprise her with the things it could do that by rights it shouldn't have been able to.

She had often been tempted to ask Lilla what the blue glow of the runes meant, but she couldn't bring herself to do it when her sister was acting like it didn't matter if they ever saw each other.

Lilla examined the reed and bell with puzzlement, then watched and listened in gape-mouthed admiration as Olyssa played the melody of a simple folk song and the runes along the length of the pipe began to glow blue.

Olyssa stopped. "What does that glow mean?"

"I don't know, but maybe later I can figure it out." Lilla put a hand on Olyssa's arm. "I want to show you something, too, but to do it we've got to go to the Walking Tree."

The Walking Tree was the capsized trunk of an oak long ago felled by lightning near the border of the forest. Ten feet thick and over eighty feet long, it had often provided a base of imaginary operations for the sisters, as they'd clambered through the stumps of its branches and pretended to tightrope atop it.

Lilla's fingers radiated an unhealthy warmth.

"What's happening to you?"

Lilla frowned. "It's nothing. Please. I have to show you this. You won't believe it."

She seemed to have lost all interest in the pipe. The fervor in her gaze projected a heat all its own that drove Olyssa back a step. Lilla's eyes widened, and she let go. "Sorry ... I just ... I wanted to share this with you."

Remorse flooded Olyssa's heart despite the unnerving darkness of her sister's dilated pupils. They were together in a way they hadn't been in months. If anything further were to come of this, if Olyssa could be of any help to her sister — if there was any chance of Lilla allowing her to help — then she couldn't let it come to ruin now.

"Okay, let's go."

Erzelle, passenger on these starts and stops through memory, wondered what it could mean that Lilla had no knowledge of what the runes on the pipes said or what it signified when they glowed.

The Walking Tree lay across their path in the shadow of its many brethren who spread their leaves to hide the sky. Wind blew from behind as if the forest drew in breath. Loosened from her afterthought of a ponytail during the ride in the electric cart, Lilla's hair whipped over her eyes as she said, "Check this out."

Footsteps rustled through the underbrush.

A woman clad in green camouflage emerged from behind the Walking Tree and circled around its exposed roots, striding toward the sisters, accompanied by a rhythmic rustling.

Olyssa stared at Lilla. "How'd she get onto the grounds?"

Father's temper, she thought, was sure to reach volcanic scale when he found out.

"Look again," Lilla said.

Olyssa did, and put both hands over her mouth.

The rustling noise came from the woman herself, whose body was formed of leaves. Hair of willow and fern fronds, skin of layered birch, oak, and poplar, a laurel face with red berries for eyes. Wherever any gaps appeared in her foliage as she moved, wisps of black mist drifted out, sucked back in again. Strands of the same smoke swirled around her joints as they bent.

The fear and bewilderment that quickened Olyssa's pulse in the memory intensified Erzelle's jolt of recognition. The same substance that filled this leaf-woman's body had been pooled in the basin of the corpse-machine.

Olyssa whirled to find Lilla's eyes had filled in with black, the same wispy substance wavering at the corners of her eyes like seaweed in miniature. She raised her hands as if manipulating a marionette, and darkness pooled in the lines of her palms, the whorls of her fingertips, leaked from underneath her nails.

The leaf-woman changed shape. There came a noise like all of autumn churned in a gale as wings erupted from her back: maple and sycamore leaves feathering frames like the bones of bat wings drawn with smoke. The wings flexed with thunderous volume as the woman took to the air.

Lilla grinned. Smoke wriggled in the spaces between her teeth. "Isn't she beautiful?"

Olyssa's head swam and nausea poured through her. The knowledge that Lilla could shape such a creature, control it like a puppet, made her feel small. It dizzied her. It slammed home that her beloved little sister had stepped through a barrier that Olyssa herself could never cross. She would never again be able to look at Lilla without seeing this leaf-woman with red-berry eyes.

The creature alighted on top of the Walking Tree, straddled it as if it were a steed. Her legs lengthened, extending around the fallen trunk like pincers. She beat her wings faster, summoning more thunder. Olyssa covered her ears as the blast of air shoved her back. It felt cold. It felt *wrong.*

Snaps of vines and roots breaking. The immense trunk shook. It began to rise from the ground, wood cracking at gunshot volume as half-buried branches thick as a man's torso splintered and broke off.

Lilla squeezed her eyes shut as tentacles of smoke unfurled from between her eyelids, poured like dissolving dry ice over her lower lip as she clenched her teeth in apparent agony. A hum surrounded her. Olyssa felt its vibrations in her flesh.

"Stop it!" Olyssa screamed, grabbing Lilla's shoulders.

Next thing she knew she lay in the grass, head throbbing, her entire body racked with pain as if it were a single bruise. She sat up.

Lilla stood ten yards away, still staring into the forest. The Walking Tree had crashed back to earth, in a place different from where it had lain all the sisters' lives. Hundreds of leaves drifted slowly to the ground, tossed up and spun by unnatural winds.

"He was right," Lilla said.

Olyssa's ached for more reasons than the impact. Had her sister just tossed her like a doll? Was Lilla really standing there trembling with excitement, completely unconcerned with what had just happened?

Even worse, when Lilla turned her way, rather than running to her, rather than asking if she was okay, she stared somewhere distant, touching the fingertips of both hands to the mark on her head.

"I wish you could feel this," she said. "I wish you could see it!"

Something warm that wasn't sweat trickled down the back of Olyssa's neck. She touched it and brought back blood.

Olyssa rose unsteadily to her feet, unsure whether to demand an explanation from Lilla or to run from her. The pounding in her skull, the stench of copper, made it hard to think. Finally, she said, "Who was right? Father?"

Lilla shook her head and finally looked at her. "Noffreid."

That night the Hunter house shook to its foundations, flinging Olyssa awake.

She had only a second to convince herself it was a dream before explosions from below proved it wasn't and set off new, deeper tremors. Her bed bucked and slid underneath her. Her bed frame collapsed. Her armoire toppled, all the fairy figures arranged atop it spilling off and shattering. Her bedside table capsized, the dainty lamp that had assisted so much forbidden night reading smashed in half.

The sounds of stone cracking, wood splintering, shattering glass, crumbling plaster, continued after the shaking stopped. Dust choked the air. Olyssa coughed but remained where she lay, heart hammering, breath coming shallow, until minutes passed. The tremors didn't return.

The house was equipped with emergency lights that should have flicked on at every corner, wiping away the darkness. They didn't come on.

Her first coherent thought was of Lilla and her canopy bed. What if that collapsed on her?

She hadn't seen Lilla since she'd fled on the cart after their argument and left Olyssa to limp back to the house all the way from the Walking Tree. She didn't know where to find Lilla now. But the thought that she could be trapped — could she? — drove Olyssa to search for the flashlight she kept in the bedside table drawer. Groping in the dark among disheveled and broken furniture, she barked her knuckles against the table's underside before righting it, snatching the light and breathing a sigh of relief that it held working batteries.

She sprinted across the hall, waving the dust from away her face.

Lilla's four-poster had collapsed. Olyssa's frantic scramble to pull off the canopy revealed no one underneath. Like her own bedroom, her sister's room had tumbled into chaos, but there was no sign Lilla had been sleeping there.

Olyssa dashed into her father's office, the room she despised most in the house. His big game trophies had fallen off the walls in a heap of antlers, fangs and glass eyes. No sign of him, nor was he in his bedchamber. She didn't call for her stepmother, who'd been gone from the house for months.

Her world became whatever her fluctuating circle of light revealed. Walls and floors fissured, paintings and photographs thrown off their hooks, nothing in its right place, her home become an unfamiliar labyrinth. Her journey reminded Erzelle so vividly of her own clambers through the Grey One's tunnels that she half-expected to see bones embedded everywhere.

Olyssa hurried through endless halls, shouting Lilla's name, but no cry came back. She encountered no one — not even the household staff. There should have been dozens of them, fanning through the house, trying to find her and Lilla. Where were they? What had caused those explosions?

They'd come from below. From the labs.

The scanner and keypad for the lift no longer worked, but the door sealing the emergency stairs had bowed open from the pressure placed on it by whatever force had been unleashed. Her father had the palace constructed to survive bomb blasts, yet Olyssa still found rips through the concrete as she made her way down.

The vault door sealing the first level of the labs had been torn completely off its hinges. A burning smell tarred the air and dust danced thick in her flashlight beam.

She steeled herself and stepped inside.

Olyssa had never taken much interest in her father's work, so she didn't know the names of the pristine white machines that loomed throughout the lower levels, except in instances where they duplicated some easily identifiable medical device, such as the ominous upright ring of an MRI machine. Others copied an iron lung's coffin-sized horizontal cylinder, and others were vertical with sliding-door entrances. She and Lilla had often joked that their father used those to change into his superhero costumes.

All the machines were tossed out of place like dice from a cup, many crumpled or twisted into wreckage as if their metal shells were no stronger than cardboard. The observation windows of the test chambers snarled at her, their five-inch-thick tinted panes blown out to leave tooth-like shards.

Her father made no noise. She had no warning. She screamed as her flashlight beam found him, pinned under one of the bulky machines, only his head, left arm and right shoulder visible. He didn't acknowledge her, didn't lift his head, but stared at the ceiling, eyes glistening, utterly silent.

"Daddy!" she wailed and knelt beside him.

He whispered. She leaned in closer.

"Get away."

She shook her head, refusing to acknowledge what she'd heard. "I'm going to help you."

She couldn't possibly lift that huge machine off of him, but maybe she could brace it and relieve the pressure it must be placing on his body. Then she could find help. Could he tell her where everyone was?

"Lilla … he killed her."

"What?"

Her legs went out from under her.

"Wha …" She tried to get back up. She needed to help him. She ended up crouched over him as he wheezed.

"He used her. He got her to tap the darkness beyond what her body could take. She's dead, Olyssa, but she still walks. I tried to stop her …"

Dead? Still walks? Her father was ranting. "Stop her from what? What happened?"

"She's been dying. Ever since she started listening to that boy. And now, so many are going to die. So many." His eyes rolled. "I can see them. So many, because of what we did here."

"Daddy." She couldn't waste any more time. She needed to tell him to stop talking, but she had to know. "I don't understand. Where is Lilla?"

"He killed her. He made her open a portal directly into the darkness, a physical portal, and it killed her. I tried to close it. She fought me with every bit of the power channeling through her. I couldn't." His voice broke and he sobbed. "I couldn't stop what she was doing." His eyes shone with tears not born from pain. "She wouldn't reverse it, Olyssa. She wouldn't listen to me! Only to him." He gnashed his teeth in a grimace as he sucked in another breath. "I tried to shut him up. Forever. I nearly got the bastard. Then she let loose everything she had at me. At me! It filled her like water in a shell. She tossed me around like one of her dolls—"

Olyssa almost voiced the absurd objection that Lilla hadn't played with dolls in years. Instead she grasped that straw as proof his words were babble.

"I'm going to find something to wedge under there. Then I'm going to call for help. But I need you to tell me where everyone is."

"No!"

She ignored his groans and started hunting for an object to brace the machine. In the dark, he kept ranting, his voice at times so thick with rage or sorrow that she barely understood him.

"They went through the portal and closed it. Where they'll come out, there will be no one to stop them. It's never going to close again. I can feel the echoes ... of what it's going to do. So many going to die, Olyssa ... so many going to change ... going to wish they'd never been born ... I'll be father to them all ... all the dead that walk ... all the monsters who never asked to become monsters ... I birthed them all. I'm father and mother to the death of the world."

She dragged a heavy chair back to where he lay trapped, intending to tip it on its back and wedge it into the gap next to him. But when her beam illuminated his face again she gasped and dropped the flashlight. It rolled and came to rest aimed at the side of his head, where it found nothing but roiling darkness. From the neck up he crawled with tongues of black flame, sinuous as snakes.

"Daddy!"

From the black blaze his distorted words stretched. "I ... deserve ... THISSSSSS ..."

The fireball of darkness uncurled tendril after tendril like a flower opening infinite layers of petals. Olyssa recoiled, tripped on debris, was thrown to the floor as the tendrils stretched out, up to the ceiling, somehow flowed through it, as if the concrete were a mirage and only the substance pouring up from her father was real. His prolonged scream distorted past all semblance to the human.

The wobbling flashlight illuminated empty floor. He was gone.

But then the light rolled, revealing her father's headless body, the stump of his neck smoldering, emitting noises like logs popping in a fire.

The machine atop him crashed down and grey dust spewed from beneath it, smothering the light, clotting in her eyes, clogging her throat.

She groped for the flashlight and found it but couldn't open her eyes. Her father's remains filled the air as she stumbled out of the room. From everywhere and nowhere came the sound of her father weeping.

They were back in the egg-shaped chamber. Ashen rubble surrounded them. Reneer remained frozen exactly as Erzelle had last seen him. The tear still beaded motionless on Olyssa's cheek.

He abandoned me, Olyssa whispered in her mind. *I was alone. I thought at first he'd committed suicide, but after many years ... after seeing him in dreams in that ridiculous disguise he wears ... I figured out he'd done something different. He took himself out of this world that he ruined.*

In dreams. Erzelle remembered the first dream, the antlered man stooping to retrieve Olyssa's head.

Right after that, the Storms began. It took me a while to understand that was what he meant, about an open portal that would never shut.

For the longest time, though, I didn't understand what he had told me about Lilla. That she was dead, yet still walking. It made me sick to think of it, but when the first ghoul epidemics broke out, I thought that could be what he meant. When I came across the first sorcerers' enclave I became sure of it. I thought Noffreid had her in his possession, was using her somehow, as the sorcerers use the ghouls. I never thought ... never thought ... this. That for all these decades I've chased a lie.

The world moved again. Olyssa closed her eyes, her face a mask of grief. Erzelle hugged her tight around the neck. When her teacher didn't respond in kind, she let go and uncertainly stood up.

Reneer regarded them both with bewilderment. "What happened just now?"

Erzelle's mind reeled. Olyssa remained seated on the floor.

All too much. The idea that the antlered man was Olyssa's father, the witch was her sister, that her family had a connection to the Storms, to the creation of ghouls, were even responsible for the existence of a whole people like the vulpines. That Olyssa, who looked to be in her thirties, had been a teenager before the Storms erupted all those decades ago.

Erzelle wanted to ask so many questions, and that was exactly what she couldn't take time to do, not there, not now. She took those pieces of information with all their implications, folded them up in her mind as small as she could, and shoved them aside.

"We need to find a way out," she said.

Reneer looked Olyssa over. It warmed Erzelle's heart to see his genuine worry.

Her teacher sat so long that Reneer finally asked, "Can she walk?"

"I can stand," Olyssa said, but didn't until her companions helped her. Erzelle handed her the hair pick. She started at it as if she didn't know what it was, then quickly and absently wound it in her hair without a word of thanks.

Olyssa's distracted state plucked at Erzelle's nerves. She tried to start her teacher talking. *What will we do now?*

I don't know. Olyssa seemed to look everywhere but at her. *Maybe we do nothing.*

Erzelle blinked and swallowed. *Nothing?*

It doesn't matter, Erzelle. None of it ever did.

Unbidden, words from the argument by the Walking Tree surfaced in Erzelle's mind, a memory of Olyssa's that was now hers too. *You look disgusting. Like a monster! ... That smoke looks like poison. I hope it is! I hope it rots you inside out!*

Olyssa met Erzelle's eyes with a hollow stare. *I got my wish.*

"Are we leaving?" asked Reneer, who'd watched the silent exchange in puzzlement.

Erzelle felt as if she were at the edge of an inward precipice, beyond which lay rage or tears. She forced herself to back away from it. She spoke over Olyssa's silence. "Yes."

As Reneer took them back into the tunnels, where the bones were now ash and a burnt stench accompanied them everywhere, Olyssa moved like a blind woman: Erzelle needed to hold her hand to guide her even though they had light to illuminate the way. She kept hoping her teacher would snap out of it, revert back to the leader rather than the led.

It took them twice as long to find a way out as it had to make their way in. The burrows had collapsed in places. They relied mainly on Reneer's sense of smell and direction and often ended up doubling back to try new tunnels. Olyssa didn't offer advice, or show any signs of coming back from the broken place her mind had gone.

Still, the sun hadn't set when they emerged from the Violet Bluffs through an entirely new passage made, apparently, when Erzelle purged the Grey Ones.

Blinking in the sunlight, Olyssa listless beside her, no joy buoyed Erzelle at the sight of the sky. They'd emerged in a glade surrounded by blackened fir trees that dripped foul sap.

"Um …" Reneer seemed unsure how to address the woman who'd brazenly aimed a rifle at him just days ago. "I have a friend in town. Your apprentice has met her. She knows medicine and magic. She could look you over if you need … looking over."

Olyssa said, "It doesn't matter."

Vulpines in dark green uniforms stepped out from behind every tree in sight, at least twenty of them, their rifles aimed in even distribution at Erzelle, Olyssa, and Reneer, who uttered a single, sheepish laugh.

"I should have smelled them coming," he said. "Sorry."

"Congratulations, Reneer," snarled a gravelly voice from behind them. "You dung-eating maggot. You've doomed us all. It's too bad for you the law prevents me from shooting you like you deserve."

Erzelle started to turn her head and a cold metal gun barrel stabbed her in the cheek.

"Be still or die, witch-girl."

Reneer put his hands in the air. "Evening to you too, Marshal Greegrim."

The Marshal circled around them. Short but thick with muscle, a mane of rust and silver ringed his square, squat face. His frown sliced too wide for his flattened features and his near-vertical eyes sat too high and too tiny in his face. He wore a black-billed cap and a unisuit that alternated dark grey and dark green on his stocky frame. A black pistol gleamed in his fist, pointed at Reneer's brow.

"I don't care about your babble," he said, "and neither will the Bear Trap."

"The Bear Trap? What are you talking about?" Reneer waved a hand toward Olyssa and Erzelle as a dozen rifles cocked. "These two amazing ladies have just purged our entire land of the Grey Ones! And you dare to invoke that barbarity! You should all be cheering in the streets!"

"There's weeping in the streets, Reneer."

"Weeping? What? Why?"

"Constables! Take their weapons," Greegrim said.

The constables closed in. For a moment, Erzelle saw not the forest but the black halls of the *Red Empress*, the Chef's men wrestling her to the floor, tearing her mother and father away to be eaten.

The magical black fire still burned at the edge of her soul. She clawed to reach it, but the band around her neck pulsed and the flames shrank away.

At the same moment, Olyssa shouted in her mind. *No, Erzelle!*

They'd taken Olyssa's pipe away, and her knife, were clamping her wrists behind her back. She wasn't even resisting, her dark eyes blazing at Erzelle.

Never use that power on living flesh! Never!

What do you care? Erzelle cried back as the teeth of the handcuffs bit into her own wrists. *Why aren't you fighting them?*

Olyssa looked away. The hair pick remained in the dark tangle gathered at the back of her head. The constables hadn't recognized it as a weapon.

I'm done fighting for nothing, Olyssa said.

Four constables grappled with Reneer to pin his arms behind his back. He spat out every syllable of his reproach: "You talk about the Bear Trap! My grandfather will have *you* in the Bear Trap for this, Greegrim! My grandfather—"

Greegrim slammed the butt of his pistol against Reneer's jaw.

"Stop it!" Erzelle shouted. A rough hand covered her mouth, reeking of sweat.

Reneer flexed his jaw, spat blood. Greegrim leaned in.

"Idiot. Your grandfather approved the order."

Reneer's eyes bulged. He kept opening his mouth — but had no words to bat away that taunt.

Greegrim raised his pistol, poised to strike again.

"Marshal, may I speak?" Olyssa's musical voice riveted everyone.

"Not if it's to cast a spell." He spun the weapon in his hand and aimed it at her forehead.

"You have my oath it's not."

"What's that worth to me?"

"I can't put a value on it. It's all I have to offer."

Greegrim fixed her with a glare. Beneath his cap his hair was plastered to his forehead, slick with sweat. As the silence stretched, Erzelle noticed how the other constables panted from effort or excitement. Beyond the circle of oozing trees that formed the theater for this play, the sky taunted her with a gorgeous sunset.

The marshal uttered a dismissive grunt, but didn't break eye contact or lower the gun. "Go on then."

"Reneer speaks truth," Olyssa said. "The Grey Ones are gone. You'll never see another in these woods. The man you just struck helped rid the world of them."

"Ha!" Greegrim's teeth seemed too large to fit in that squat jaw. "Then who is this woman like Death gone for a walk who appeared in the council chambers, twenty damn feet tall at least, with burned flesh and smoke for hair and a mark on her forehead just — just — like *that* one!" He tipped his head to indicate Erzelle. "She tells us in a voice like thunder that our truce is broken and her next machine, whatever that may be, will be made from us! And she shows us clockwork made from wriggling ghouls, and she shows us that worm's smugly grinning face!" The gun waved toward Reneer for emphasis. "And when I say 'us,' I mean all of Fabelford! We could all see her, in our minds. Every single one of us, from the doddering old men and women screaming in their beds to the infants screaming in their cribs. Then she vanished with a burst of fire made from darkness, like nothing anyone has ever seen before."

Reneer blanched. Erzelle felt as if her innards had flipped. Even Olyssa's voice sounded unsteady. "She's not one of the Grey Ones. She's their maker."

"Fine comfort that is! With any luck we'll give her you three and she'll let us be."

Olyssa shook her head. "It won't work. She won't care. No kind of bribery will stop her. Hurting us won't save you."

But I stopped her! Erzelle protested.

Only for now, Erzelle. She'll return. She'll make the vulpines pay dearly.

"And who are you to say what she'll do?" Greegrim barked. "Your little witchling there bears the same mark. I knew I never should have let you roam free in our lands. I knew it!"

"We didn't do anything to you!" Erzelle protested.

"Shoot the next one that speaks," Greegrim said. A constable placed the business end of his rifle against the back of Olyssa's head. Another did the same to Reneer. Erzelle felt cold metal press against the back of her skull.

Her rage grew. She never, ever wanted to be a captive again. She reached for the black fire. Again her necklace pulsed and the power stayed beyond her grasp. She could have screamed in frustration. If she did, she would die.

No, Erzelle. Not like this.

Why do you keep blocking me? she demanded.

I'm not, Olyssa said. *I can tell when you're drawing on the black fire.*

Confused, Erzelle dropped her accusation. *What are we going to do? I don't want to go with them. I don't want to be locked up.*

Olyssa didn't respond.

I bet they can't stop me if I fight. I bet you can't stop me.

My father couldn't stop my poor sister.

At that moment Erzelle didn't care. She grasped for the fire that she felt as her wrath coalesced.

She could feel the black fire surging. But the necklace the antlered man gave her pulsed again and her effort failed.

What are you doing to me? she demanded.

I don't understand what you're talking about.

Erzelle tried again. Another pulse. The fires kept their distance. What was happening? Why was it so easy before?

"Walk," Greegrim said. "Not one more word."

The prisoners were marched along the paths back to Fabelford, with rifles pressed between their shoulder blades. The night brought rain before they reached their destination.

—⟨⟨⟩⟨⟩⟩—

If Fabelford aboveground held a quirky charm in its hidden streets, the city's holding cells offered only misery.

In the cage-like chamber just beyond the grungy jail entrance, with all those guns still trained on them, Olyssa abruptly said to the Marshal:

"What you're doing won't help you. We can help you. You should let us go."

Erzelle's breath caught and her hope rose. The upending of all Olyssa's ideas about long lost Lilla had seemed to smash her brutal resolve, transformed her into something almost unrecognizable, as if Erzelle had rescued a complete stranger and not her beloved teacher from the black webbing. But now Olyssa's words were spoken in direct defiance of Greegrim's order. This, at least, was familiar. This was Olyssa as Erzelle knew her.

Instead of demanding Olyssa's execution, the Marshal curled his upper lip in a contemptuous scowl.

"You've done enough, witch-woman. Rune-cell, third level."

A contingent of six constables led Olyssa off. She didn't resist or look back at Erzelle and Reneer as she disappeared down the dark hall.

Erzelle tried mindspeech. *What are we going to do?*

No answer.

The other constables waited until Olyssa was out of sight before dragging Erzelle to "rune-cell, lowest level."

All this time, Erzelle kept trying to reach the black fires, but to no avail. They flickered, tantalizing, at the edge of her awareness. If she strained hard enough to bring the power flowing nearer the band given to her by the antlered man twitched as if threatening to tighten and the fire receded.

Both he and Olyssa had claimed the necklace was supposed to save her life, but how could that be when she so desperately needed the power back?

She glanced back over her shoulder at Reneer before they shuffled her out of sightline as Greegrim growled something about an "expedited hearing, one sure to make your mother weep."

"I know how much you've lusted for that," Reneer returned, then grunted and doubled over as Greegrim punched him in the stomach.

The Marshal bent to snarl in his captive's ear, "Joke with the Bear Trap when the time comes."

And then the constables shoved Erzelle through another vault door, down another dark stair, and she heard no more of the exchange.

The grille over the thin horizontal slot at the top of the iron door admitted barely a sliver of light. A metal panel riddled with holes served as Erzelle's cot, her toilet a drain in the floor. The accoutrements of the *Red Empress* mollycoddled her by comparison.

In the dark cell, Erzelle again reached for the fires. The band around her neck didn't pulse when she grasped for the power, but still her effort failed.

She sat on the metal cot with her back to the wall, shut out the nausea-inducing stench of ammonia, and willed her mind into a hungry void for the black fire to fill.

They were going to kill Reneer. Olyssa offered no solution. She'd gone meekly to meet her fate.

All the rage Erzelle had felt, at the Chef and his men, at the murder of her parents, at Olyssa leading her into the dangers below the temple, at Olyssa for being so stupidly wrong and blind about her sister, at Olyssa for doing nothing to stop the vulpines from imprisoning her again, putting her right back where she started — she aimed this fury at the wall that kept her from her fires, imagined her teacher on the other side of it, her rage a lance she slammed against the barrier with all her might, trying to make Olyssa pay. To hurt her.

An answering response from the fire, a momentary burst of energy, like a far-off flare.

Nothing else happened.

The cell seemed to shrink around her as her frustration and confusion deepened. The darkness, the stench, the clammy air conspired to derail her concentration.

The necklace somehow kept her from summoning the black fire. She tried to undo its clasp but couldn't find it — it was as if it never had one, had been created already fused around her neck. She plucked at it — the band lay flush against her skin, its odd rubbery texture the only way she could detect it at all. She couldn't even work a fingernail underneath it.

She covered her face with her hands, shutting the cell out of her mind, and tried again. The necklace did not pulse. A wall remained between her and the black fire.

Erzelle beat imaginary fists against the barrier. Again, the fires surged, but nothing leaked within her reach.

She clawed at the necklace, to no avail, scratching her neck in several places. The black fire taunted her.

It won't work.

Erzelle sprang from the cot at the sight of Olyssa in the middle of her cell. Nothing alleviated the gloom, but Erzelle could see her teacher as if she stood under a floodlight.

"Are you doing this?" Erzelle shouted before she remembered herself. *I need the power. We need it. Why are you stopping me?*

Olyssa's mouth didn't move. *I'm not. I never have been. These vulpines must have dealt with powerful magic before. My cell is covered floor to ceiling with runes that block the streams of magical power. I'm sure yours is too.*

Erzelle couldn't resist the temptation to wave a hand through Olyssa's body. Her teacher wasn't present in the flesh. Flustered as Erzelle was, she elicited a small thrill from getting away with a disrespectful gesture, even though Olyssa didn't acknowledge it. *How are you doing this?* she asked. *How are you here?*

The barriers they've made have holes I can work a thread through. It's very difficult without my pipe. It took a while to find the way through the wards in my cell, even longer to get through the ones in yours.

Teach me to do it! Erzelle stomped a foot. The sole of her boot made a dull thud, swallowed in the darkness.

Olyssa frowned. *If you understood tapping the darkness you'd know why I can't. You did so much in such a short time, but you had no time to really learn. What I'm doing requires a trickle of energy maintained for a long time. What you can do requires a floodgate to open.*

Then help me open it!

You don't understand. This cell shuts the power away from you. If you succeed in drawing on it, the runes will keep your power from leaving the room. It will build and build in here until it implodes on itself, and you.

This makes no sense. Something was blocking me before they brought me here. This necklace! Erzelle grabbed at the band around her neck. *When I reach for the fire it acts like it's alive and stops me.*

Really? Her teacher's frown deepened as she regarded Erzelle. *Does it still?*

Not since they put me here. But I'm still blocked!

The runes on the walls block you now. Olyssa inclined her head to indicate the necklace, her nose crinkling in distaste. *My father said that band would save your life. I can only guess it's meant to stop you from doing what Lilla did. Drawing in so much power that it murders you. It would be just like him not to tell you what it does.*

Erzelle absorbed this, confused, wanting to retort, uncertain what to say. Without the antlered man's help neither of them would be alive. Didn't Olyssa understand that?

Olyssa turned her head and narrowed her eyes as if reading the runes she claimed were there. *If the vulpines can make something like this, perhaps they won't be helpless when my sister strikes.*

What makes you sure she will?

Her teacher met her eyes. *You know.*

If Erzelle could glean one thing about both sisters from the memories she'd shared and the actions she'd witnessed, it was determination at all costs. Lilla would keep her pledge.

What about us? Erzelle's rage returned. *Will we be helpless when she strikes? We're trapped!*

Olyssa closed her eyes. *I'm sorry.* She shook her head, arguing with someone Erzelle couldn't hear. Herself. *I couldn't ... I can't ... I still can't accept ... I refuse to believe that she left with Noffreid of her own free will. That she let herself become ... That she chose ...* Her effigy paced the cell, agitated, before turning to look at Erzelle again. *After what I've learned about my sister, after years of searching for her, I thought death might be a better option. I've dealt it freely to many others. How hard could it be?*

And yet, Erzelle, I'm alive. I must not have wanted death so badly. And I know the reason. It's become clear to me that there are other things in my life now that matter to me just as much. I'm sorry I didn't come to my senses sooner. I've found you again. That's a start.

Erzelle pondered the enormity of this. Responses tumbled through her head, too quickly and slippery to pick only one, until she said, *What do we do?*

An explosion, muffled in the far distance.

Erzelle stared at her teacher. *Did you do that?*

No. Olyssa vanished. Through the grille in the door Erzelle heard shouts.

Erzelle retried to reconnect with Olyssa. Nothing. Not even a hint of her presence.

A crash like a ton of metal toppling. The staccato thunder of gunfire. A new smell cut through the ambient urine stink — smoke. She reached for the black fire again. Useless.

Olyssa reappeared, startling Erzelle so that she banged a knee against the cot. "Ow!"

I'm going to try to find Reneer. If he's still alive. Work with me.

"How?" She was too angry, too frightened and her knee smarted too much for her to bother with the mindspeech. "I can't do anything! How can I possibly work with you?"

Listen to me. I want you to imagine that we're playing the concerto together. Play the melody and I'll build the harmony, just like we've done before.

"How? My harp's gone!"

Another distant explosion. Footsteps thudded past her door as a man's screams echoed down the hall.

Erzelle, don't let your anger control you. I know it's hard but you have to tamp it down. Think about the music we practiced.

"What good will that do?"

It will let me drawn on your power and reach out further than I can on my own.

Erzelle boiled. "How can you do that when I can't?"

For the same reason I can reach you in the first place. You weren't born to tap the darkness. I was. I can weave on a microscopic level where you can only tear huge holes in the fabric. But to reach Reneer too, to do anything more, I need to draw on the strength my father gave you. I don't have it on my own. I can't explain it better than that, not in the time we have. Erzelle, I know you have good reason to be angry with me, but please, don't fight me now. Do as I ask.

Erzelle wanted to throw herself at the walls inside and out — and the sheer ridiculousness of that thought, pitching a tantrum like a two-year old as Fabelford shook apart, helped her take a step back. In such deep water she shouldn't reject a hand meant to pull her to the surface. *Okay. How?*

Like we always have.

My harp's destroyed.

I don't have my pipe, but I know every note even without it, just as you do. Imagine the notes. Imagine the harp's weight in your lap, your fingers on the strings. The music will come to you.

Erzelle sat on the hard bunk and held out her hands as if the harp rested between her knees. She plucked a note, heard it in her head, and right away Olyssa answered with sweet notes of her own. Even as she proceeded, Erzelle couldn't help but think how silly she must look, miming in the dark.

The music in her mind changed timbre as the dark energy swelled at the barrier, demanding release. Then a current rushed through her, a filament of black fire, winding around the notes in her head.

The current carried her out of the cell.

Born aloft on the phantom music, she had a sense of rushing past many nodes of sound that reverberated in her mind rather than her physical hearing. She heard whispered words, a repeated scream, wet slobbering sounds, the crackle of flame, barked orders, a symphony of chaos. Embedded in the flow of notes and magic, her awareness kept moving, hunting the right frequency.

Even without completely comprehending how they searched and what they searched for, she recognized their quarry at the same moment Olyssa did.

Reneer!

They hovered disembodied in a cylindrical chamber, its walls ringed by three stories of empty balconies. An octagonal block squatted in the center of the concave floor, a huge carved stump supporting the device that held Reneer, chained, inside.

Two giant half-open bear traps stood back to back, gaping like steel shark mouths. Reneer was pinioned there, spread-eagled over the lower jaws, so that on one side the trap's lower teeth stabbed painfully into his shoulders, while the teeth on the other side pierced the backs of his knees. The upper jaws of both traps arched over his belly. When they snapped down, they'd sever his legs at the knees, his arms at the shoulders and behead him all in one stroke.

All over, splotches of blood matted his pelt, stained his torn clothes. It clotted around his lips and dripped from his forehead. The constables had worked him over mercilessly.

Erzelle's body still sat on the floor in the cold cell, but her connection to it seemed no more than a half-remembered dream. Here in the execution chamber, no cloth or air touched her skin, no weight burdened her bones. The scene before her, too, felt dream-like — until Reneer's head lolled in their direction and his eyes widened. He *saw* them.

A raised platform encircled the depression that held the Bear Trap. To Erzelle's right four armed constables guarded an iron door, the only way in. To the left another cluster surrounded a pale-haired fox woman who knelt at their feet, murmuring as her trembling hands spread herbs over a circle carved in the floor. No question the silently weeping woman in her nightgown was Braeca.

Braeca's quartet of guards kept all their guns trained on her. Greegrim stood over her too, his pistol drawn. Olyssa and Erzelle had caught the Marshal in mid-sentence: "—sure she'll enjoy seeing you die as much as I will."

He noticed the look of surprise on Reneer's face and laughed. "What? Did you just figure out you can't get out? What are you staring at?"

Erzelle could sense Braeca's spell. Her mutterings provided its rhythm, out of sync with the concerto.

That's the woman who helped me make a new reed, Erzelle said. *What are they making her do?*

Greegrim's eyes bulged. "Who said that?"

Keep following the notes, Olyssa said. *Don't stop. Don't speak.* And then she said, "Let them go and let us help you. Summoning my sister to show her a corpse won't save you."

All the constables turned their heads at the same moment Greegrim did. Braeca overbalanced and fell on her side, staring.

Everyone in the room clearly could see Olyssa towering on the platform, and Erzelle beside her. It took Erzelle an effort as vigorous as what she'd thrown against the rune barriers to stay focused on the procession of notes and the energy they carried. She heard, in her mind, Olyssa's answering harmonies, even as her teacher took a step toward Reneer.

"Marshal, let them both go."

The flow of energy amplified, insistently tugged at Erzelle, as if a finger hooked into her mind and pulled.

The constables raised their rifles.

Don't stop playing, Olyssa said. *They can't hurt us.*

At the same moment the armed guards took aim, Braeca started, her eyes abruptly riveted on Olyssa's face. A communication in mindspeech? The apothecary squeezed her eyes shut and crawled toward the edge of the platform as Olyssa held out both hands. Bright flames flickered as if candlewicks sprouted from her fingertips. The tugging sensation in Erzelle's mind doubled and redoubled. The fiber-thin current of black fire rushed faster.

Greegrim pointed at Olyssa and Erzelle. "Kill them!"

Don't stop, Erzelle!

Braeca pulled herself over the edge of the platform and dropped to the concave floor as both groups of constables opened fire. Olyssa stood with arms outstretched, flames balled in both fists, and walked toward Greegrim and his men. At the same time, in the same pose, she strode toward the men guarding the exit. Erzelle couldn't reconcile what was happening until she perceived how tongues of black flame limned the shadows of Olyssa's dual forms. Olyssa's harmonies wound multiple threads through the melody Erzelle maintained, streamed into her and *through* her, and tapped the dark fires that she herself couldn't reach.

As Olyssa shaped Erzelle's power, she wove a rapidly evolving illusion, so that each separate group saw Olyssa walking toward them with hands aflame. As the bullets passed through her, she grimaced as if struck. Then laughed, that clear, beautiful laugh, and rose into the air. Both Olyssas levitated as she drew still more on Erzelle's power, and the constables reacted in panic, firing off more rounds — then reeling back bleeding as the two groups shot their comrades-in-arms through the mirage Olyssa created.

Erzelle fought to concentrate as Olyssa pulled even more power from her. A sound of chains rattling as Reneer's manacles came undone of their own accord. Instantly he flipped to all fours, was backing out of the Bear Trap.

Bleeding from an ear but still standing, Greegrim spotted Reneer in motion and leveled his pistol.

Olyssa groaned in genuine agony as she drew even harder on Erzelle's magic, and Erzelle slammed against the barrier holding her power back as the fire in her teacher's hands erupted at Greegrim, no longer illusory. The Marshal howled as Olyssa blasted the weapon from his hands. The blast smashed Erzelle's melody apart. The threads of black fire snapped, hurling her out of the scene.

She lay on the floor in her cell. Her head throbbed. She coughed, inhaling smoke.

She tried to stand up, but every motion made her dizzy and set the pain in her skull screaming. She tried again, this time regained her feet. She couldn't stay here. She couldn't get out.

She staggered to the cot, took her seat and again imagined herself playing the harp. She called up the notes of the concerto, first trying to pluck her part, next Olyssa's, playing both simultaneously, trying to access her own power as Olyssa had done. But she couldn't keep all of it in her head. The thickening smoke sent her coughing and thwarted her concentration. The black fire remained out of reach.

Minutes dragged by and she heard nothing from Olyssa. Every moment she was more certain that their effort to save Reneer had failed, and she would never hear from her teacher again. She might as well have remained sealed in the *Red Empress*, a brief, ignorant life and horrible death far better than this present futility. For a mad moment she wished it all undone, wished she'd been fed to the ghouls and her worries ended.

A shadow blotted the scant light passing through the grille, accompanied by a wet, gurgling moan.

Erzelle abandoned all attempts at meditation and retreated back until pressed against the wall.

A hand slapped against the door. Another moan.

A ghoul.

She held her breath, wondering if it smelled her, or if it would wander off if she stayed quiet long enough. The memory of Olyssa's words sliced through the ache clamping her skull: *My cell is covered floor to ceiling with runes that block the streams of magical power. I'm sure yours is too.*

If the door opened, maybe it would break the seal that blocked her magic.

"In here!" she cried.

The hand disappeared, replaced with a head as the thing outside tried to peer in.

"I'm in here. Get me out."

Silence, until the ghoul moaned again, its mouth pressed against the grille. It started pounding on the door. It mewled, made a gargling laugh, threw its whole body against the metal, the impact loud as a sledgehammer strike. Growling, it slammed itself again and again into the door.

Erzelle reached again for the black fire. No good.

A scream shredded the air from down the hall, punctuated with a cackle. The thing at the door gargled again as footsteps came running. A new shape eclipsed the grille completely. The cackler shrieked into the cell, inflaming Erzelle's headache like a dagger through the eye.

The pounding resumed, double-time. Through the din Erzelle thought she heard more running footsteps.

At once, the banging stopped.

The light didn't return. A whole crowd of the creatures pressed against the door. One of them gibbered, the sound muffled.

The door creaked. They were straining against it, applying constant pressure. Erzelle might have laughed if she couldn't so clearly picture what would happen if their efforts paid off. Her idea had spectacularly backfired.

A squelching noise as something soft was crushed against the grille. The creak and grind of metal bending, tearing, snapping. The grille clattered to the floor. An object plopped into the cell through the pried-open slot. The reek of rotted meat intensified. Erzelle could see nothing. She tried again for the fire as the cackler shrieked into the opening, piercing her eardrums.

The power seemed closer — but still out of her reach. Maybe if she moved near to the door. She didn't dare.

Whatever had dropped to the floor scurried toward her. It wriggled onto her boot, an enormous, fleshy spider. She kicked at it, heard a thunk as it landed elsewhere in the cell, a scuttling as it came for her again. She climbed onto the cot as a chorus of voices howled right outside her cell. She wanted to scream too but her voice had fled.

An unexpected light from without the door made her shield her eyes. The ghouls promptly abandoned their chosen post. A familiar melody, played on a pipe, poured into her cell.

Erzelle kicked the scuttling thing away again, ran to the slot and shouted, "In here! I'm in here!"

In the commotion outside she made out the hiss of someone being dragged, Reneer yelling, "Open it!"

A rasped response: "... hell with you." Greegrim.

A blunt object struck flesh. Two times. Three. The third time the Marshal yelped. Reneer growled. "I said open it, worm!"

Greegrim uttered a word Erzelle didn't recognize, though its guttural syllables reminded her of Braeca's chant to dispel the attack in her apothecary room.

A click within the wall and the door slid aside. A flashlight beam blinded her. Braeca swept in, her mane of pale hair like a halo, and scooped Erzelle from the doorway, clutching her in a fierce embrace.

"We've got you," she said.

Erzelle hugged Braeca back as the barrier that blocked the fires fell away.

Reneer, his grin smeared with blood, gripped a kneeling Greegrim by the uniform collar and pressed the barrel of the Marshal's own pistol against his temple. At one end of the corridor smoke leaked around the edges of a sealed door. At the other stood Olyssa, playing her pipe with the reed Erzelle had made. Between her teacher and her companions stood more than a dozen ghouls, lined up along the walls to either side like a gore-drenched honor guard.

The ghouls were all vulpines, recently wounded, strips of skin and pelt torn from their faces, hands, necks, forearms. All but two wore the ludicrous green stripes of prisoners. One was a constable in black with a badge of rank on his chest, a rifle over his shoulder and a sword belted to his side, his jaw torn loose on one side, exposing a shock of long teeth. One was a woman in jeans, her sweater and pearls stained bloody, one arm ending in a shredded stump. All held at bay by the pipe music.

Something tickled Erzelle's ankle. She turned to see the mangled, crushed, severed hand that had attacked her in the cell scrabbling at the pant leg of her coveralls. She struck at it with her heel, flipped it away from her, and drew the black fire into her easily as a breath, meaning to obliterate it. The band around her neck stayed dormant. Nothing would stop her this time.

No! Olyssa interjected. *Not here.*

Erzelle trembled with the delicious wrath inside of her. *Why not? Why should I even listen to you?*

If you won't listen to me, then talk. Tell me what your plan is. Olyssa's voice contained no ire, and Erzelle had no answer. Olyssa went on, *Help me get us out of here. You know this tune. Please play it with me.*

Erzelle didn't know whether to laugh or scream. How could she concentrate, the way her head throbbed, the way the black fire coursed through her, the way the smoke congealed overhead? How could Olyssa expect this from her now?

Just think of the notes. They'll come as easy as walking.

She called up the imaginary harp, flowed through the opening bars. Olyssa was right. That sensation of fingers hooking into her mind returned, but much stronger, in many more places, and the pressure building in her subsided. Olyssa's playing sped up and took on more complexity as she drew on Erzelle's power.

The vulpines started, even Greegrim, as Olyssa projected to all of them. *I need you to show me, in your mind, the way out.*

"Never!" the Marshal spat, but even as he spoke so did Olyssa, sounding amused. *The fool just showed me everything, trying not to think of it. We don't need him anymore, and if we let him go he'll cause us trouble. It's your choice what to do with him.*

Greegrim rolled his eyes toward Reneer. "Kill me then."

"You just had to spoil the moment, didn't you?" Reneer sounded genuinely disappointed. He shifted his grip on the pistol as Braeca said, "Don't!"

Erzelle had to give Greegrim credit. Every inch of him a mess of grime, blood and sweat, both his hands reduced to charred cinders by Olyssa's spell, his own gun aimed pointblank at his head, he didn't cower.

In the pause caused by Braeca's outburst, Erzelle said, "We're going to stop this."

Greegrim roared, "It's your fault it happened!"

Reneer spun the pistol and hammered the Marshal in the head with its grip. Greegrim slumped to the floor. Braeca glared, and Reneer replied with a grin. "Don't worry. He might still live, if the flames don't get him, or the ghouls. As nice as he's been to you," and his words dripped with sarcasm, "I suppose I owe him that."

The ghouls won't get him so long as Erzelle and I are together. We need to get above ground. Olyssa turned on her heel without waiting. Erzelle hurried to follow her, Braeca close behind.

Reneer stopped by the ghoul constable. He called, "You're sure they won't bite?"

Yes, Olyssa said.

Erzelle glanced back to see Reneer divesting the ghoul of his rifle and sword before hurrying to catch up.

Though Olyssa's playing never grew any louder, the notes carried everywhere. As they ascended through a stairwell as yet unclaimed by smoke or fire they found more ghouls, constables and prisoners who'd been bitten, standing glassy-eyed, drooling, making no move to harm them. On one landing lay a vulpine woman's corpse that had not turned, her red eyes wide and unseeing, her neck savaged. Three ghoul prisoners with mouths black with blood loomed beside the body.

Reneer drew the sword from its scabbard, held it level over the woman's neck, braced to strike.

Save your strength, Olyssa said.

Still he wavered, until Braeca put a placating hand on his back.

Past the top landing they walked through the cage-like reception chamber and entered the lair of the constables, a bureaucratic space of desks in rows, clocks staring indifferently from the walls and an odd vertical panel full of plug-in wires that Erzelle recognized after a beat as a phone bank.

They walked around the bank to find a rotting gnome with spidery limbs squatting on top of the desk behind it.

The creature's torso was at most half the height of a human's, but its long, folded legs resembled those of a rabbit. It crouched straight-backed, its knuckles resting on the desktop like an ape's. Its head was half again the size of its body, round as a doll's, tattered amber skin stretched taut, and in that oversized head its jaw was even more disproportionate, full of sharp, fresh-blooded teeth. Pinhole pupils dotted bulging yellow eyes.

Braeca recoiled from the creature as if struck. A smell rose from it like nothing Erzelle had encountered in all her years trapped with a ghoul-hoarding cult — a mix of rotten eggs and vomit. The effort it took to stave off gagging almost threw her completely out of the mental weaving of melody and harmony she shared with Olyssa.

"And just what is this little devil?" asked Reneer in an oddly mild tone. "I've never seen anything like it."

At the same time Braeca asked, "What is it?"

Something Lilla created and sent to spread the ghoul plague. Then Olyssa spoke to Erzelle alone. *Without your strength boosting me I don't believe they'd hear the pipe's song.*

With a growl Reneer raised the sword he'd pilfered and slashed at the gnome-thing's outsized skull. It jerked its shoulders but otherwise didn't move as the arc of Reneer's swing ended with the blade embedded in the middle of its bulbous forehead. The fox-man yanked the blade free and the creature slumped sideways, its spindly limbs curling like a beetle's. He struck again and the huge head rolled loose, thumped to the floor where it wobbled and spun, huge teeth coming to rest against the desk leg.

Reneer's own teeth were bared. "You won't hurt my people again."

Reneer, don't waste your energy, Olyssa said. *There are too many.*

Erzelle hadn't understand what Olyssa meant by *too many* until her teacher nodded her head to indicate the rest of the room. There were more of the huge-jawed gnome creatures, one huddled under a chair, another atop a file cabinet, their unblinking gazes following Olyssa.

Reneer stared at each one in turn, eyes wide with dismay. When he looked to Olyssa she asked, *Can you guide us through the city?*

"Yes," he replied, his voice strangled.

We'll need to keep moving. Spread the song as far as we can.

"I'll take us toward the north border," Reneer said.

He led the way, sword brandished, Olyssa behind him, Erzelle keeping close to her, Braeca bringing up the rear. They emerged into a smoke-clotted night, stars wavering like embers where they weren't cloaked by the netting over the streets. As their procession advanced they spotted even more of the gnome-ghouls, glaring from smashed windows alongside the vacant-eyed victims they'd bitten.

The complexity of Olyssa's melody deepened, building in layers as if she accompanied herself with multiple harmonies. Each note plucked at Erzelle's mind, an urgent caress. The range of her teacher's spell widened through the city as if it were a net borne on fog, a lullaby to pacify the attacking ghouls. Erzelle experienced this as a continual stretching of her own awareness, a sensation not far removed from how her consciousness had filled the egg-chamber after the antlered man touched her.

Yet it didn't dim her awareness of the carnage they trekked through. Every new scene they confronted made Erzelle's eyes sting, throat tighten, chest burn with anguish. A plump father and mother wailing in the cobbled street, clutching a girl Erzelle's age between them who had savage bite wounds on each of her cheekbones, huge eyes staring glassy, mouth hanging open, still able to stand but no longer breathing. Not twenty paces away around a curve, a bloody-faced mother and father standing side by side, the headless remains of their tiny daughter in her nightgown sprawled between their feet.

A luxurious home at the next corner with windows along both of the cross streets had become an oven, flames dancing on the carpet of the main room, climbing over pastel furniture, smoke churning under its ceiling. An old fox-man with long wounds gouged in spirals around his sagging neck and chin stood unmoving in the flames, his bathrobe burning.

In the middle of that intersection, a quintet of the gnome-like ghouls faced each other as if they were about to hold hands and dance a ring around the rose.

Erzelle struggled to think around the music that filled her head and turned within it like the drum of a music box. Where had these creatures come from? They had emerged from nowhere to infest the city, crouching alone, in pairs, or even in clusters of half-a-dozen, stalled in the streets and tunnels where Olyssa's spell enmeshed them. Erzelle pieced the puzzle together when a spill of leaves caused her to glance up and notice a long tear in the camouflage netting, smaller rips surrounding it. They had come from above.

Around another bend in the twisty streets of Fabelford, one of the small cars Erzelle had seen the previous morning had crumpled head on into a wall. Blood splattered the smashed windows. Nothing moved inside the cab.

Erzelle had enveloped Lilla in fire and it failed to prevent any of this. These lives were on Erzelle's hands just as much as the witch's. *We let this happen.*

We couldn't have stopped it, Olyssa replied. But did a tremolo of uncertainty undercut her impassive tone?

At a cry behind her, Erzelle turned to see, within a bright lit tunnel, a rotund fox-man wearing no more than a stained pajama top, hacking one of the gnome creatures with a butcher knife, shouting at the top of his lungs each time he struck. Behind him lay the remains of a willowy woman similarly chopped apart, the top of her head separated both from her torso and her jaw. Her tilted eyes tracked Erzelle, Olyssa, Braeca and Reneer as they hurried past.

If the survivors weren't fighting fires or righting the wreckage of their homes in the walls, they huddled together in the streets, round-eyed and trembling. One roving party of about half-a-dozen vulpine youth tended to the newly-turned ghouls in orderly fashion, dismembering them with axes and machetes and stacking the pieces in a long cart.

Others paused and stared, recognizing the source of the music that had brought the rampage to a halt. Once, a woman broke away from a crowd to intercept Olyssa, repeating, "Thank you! Thank you!" but Reneer shook his head at her and hissed, "Don't interrupt!" She smiled thinly, nodded and retreated.

The ghoul lullaby echoed from every wall, but also flowed out further, drifting far and away into corners of Fabelford the four companions never went near. Erzelle knew this because the ever-more intricate harmonies Olyssa structured around her melody made a shape in her mind that remained in focus even as its convolutions deepened. The music spread through the city like water filling an anthill, creating a contoured image in her mind of every street, house, hall and sewer it spilled into, and within this image, spots appeared like black stars. These were the ghouls frozen in the spell's web. Once Erzelle understood what they were, her heart leapt with each new creature trapped.

The more elaborate the spell became, the more room it took up in her mind, the harder it became to think or track her surroundings.

The street they traversed dimmed. At first Erzelle thought the darkening of her vision a result of the spell, not a shadow cast by something overhead, until Braeca snatched her and pulled her beneath an awning.

Whatever it was, it made no sound. Erzelle risked a peek up through torn netting. A triangular shape cut a swath from the constellations as it circled over the city. She could only guess at its size.

It distorted Olyssa's spell, stirring discordant eddies against the current of music.

Between the cobbles they stood on and the thing in the sky jutted narrow regiments of awnings, their scalloped half-shells shielding shop stoops. Reneer guided Olyssa beneath one of these across the way from where Erzelle and Braeca hid. Though Olyssa hadn't ceased playing, she'd caught sight of the shape too. She projected to her three companions:

My sister will know we're interfering. Take us to the highest place you can.

"The observation tree," Reneer suggested. Braeca took a deep breath and nodded.

The pair of them began steering the two sorceresses back toward the city's center.

Hurry, Olyssa urged.

The tune Olyssa played with both mind and fingers grew intricate as cosmic clockwork. Consumed with keeping her own small part going, Erzelle walked only when Braeca took her by the shoulders and directed her. The streets, the tunnels and the figures that populated them softened to blurs as Olyssa shared more of what she saw through the spell with Erzelle.

This sharing of vision approached the closest yet to the intensity of perception she'd experienced right after the antlered man opened her to the black fire. This time, though, Erzelle had no control. She was merely a passenger peering through the windshield.

A cord of magical darkness bound each of the spidery gnome-ghouls spread through the city to the dark shape gliding in circles above them. Those victims who'd been bitten and succumbed, too, were strung by those invisible lines to the floating object overhead. The notes of the spell didn't reach the object itself, but the cords twirled and twisted in response to its motion.

What was it? Something to not just spread the plague but tether its ghoulish crop? The threads it pulled were like marionette strings, with the puppeteer's invisible hand guiding the immense controller above.

Can she see us, through that thing? Erzelle asked.

I don't know.

Even as Olyssa answered, the pattern of the thing's flight changed, its smooth course suddenly full of swerves and sudden pivots and dips in altitude, as if it yanked at its charges and felt resistance.

The council hall, a wide cylinder, was the only building Erzelle had seen in Fabelford taller than two stories, with mock Corinthian columns engaged with its walls, illuminated by artificial lights spaced between them. From the turf mounded above it rose an astonishingly huge sycamore tree, a true giant even among the forest mutants, its canopy of jagged leaves pressed to the stars as if striving to hold them in place.

A vulpine constable challenged them at the doors. Reneer raised his sword and shouted, "Step aside if you want to save this city!"

While the young constable wavered — Erzelle thought he was perhaps only a few years older than herself — Braeca said, "You hear her playing. You've seen what her music did. Please help us."

The constable lifted his rifle and stepped out of the way.

"Show off," Reneer muttered. He shot a sidelong glance at Braeca as they huddled inside. She parried with an arch smirk.

Erzelle wanted to chuckle but it took enough of an effort just to stay upright and moving. Braeca ushered her through a dim anteroom into the immense council chamber, its configuration of balconies and central dais eerily similar to the execution room. Erzelle appreciated how terrifying Lilla must have appeared, manifesting beneath its high ceiling in a larger-than-life illusion. They went through a back exit and into a stairwell built around the trunk of the sycamore tree, whose roots proved to be buried under the building rather than spread through the roof atop it.

Made of ropes and pegs, the staircase spiraled up the trunk. Reneer held Olyssa by the waist to guide her up, step by step. When Erzelle noticed this from the corner of her eye she was briefly startled that her teacher would tolerate such intimate contact.

Braeca held Erzelle by the elbow and shoulder, and patiently murmured to her when to step up. Their ascent proceeded all too slowly, but perhaps the blessing was that Erzelle had no room in her mind to consider the increasingly precarious height. Her feet slipped on the narrow pegs of the stairs more then once. Braeca showed surprising strength in preventing her from toppling, though each time the fox-woman heaved a sigh afterward, a wordless routine to bat down panic.

As they climbed through the ceiling and emerged under the canopy, the rope stair continued twisting up toward a platform built into the topmost branches. Frustration churned in Erzelle like bile, that she couldn't move faster — that her mind couldn't hold anything other than Olyssa's spell, that she couldn't duplicate the control she'd had back in the egg chamber. What if Braeca and Reneer weren't here to help them? How could she and Olyssa fend off an attack? She hated the feeling of helplessness spreading through her body like cracks in glass.

Embroiled in those clouded thoughts, Erzelle didn't notice that they'd reached the treetop platform until the second or third time she stepped on plank instead of peg. The platform rested on an elaborate scaffolding constructed near the living crown of the massive tree. Its design allowed the leading branches to jut through strategically placed gaps. As a result the structure remained hidden under dense foliage, yet afforded a spectacular view in all directions.

Tonight, the view it presented was hellish.

The darkness below was interrupted by long furrows of light and flame. Streets once hidden beneath the hill were no longer disguised by the nets strung over them, but spouted pillars of smoke like ink poured up against the will of gravity. A charnel house stink gushed toward the stratosphere. In a couple of places steam rose and water fountained where firefighters actively fought to douse the blazes, but these efforts seemed comically inadequate. If there were more cries of anguish or shouts for help, no such sounds penetrated the fog of Olyssa's music.

The screech of an infant signaled they weren't alone on the platform. A couple of families had taken refuge up here, a stout mother with three kits and a younger couple with a baby they struggled to quiet with pacifier and blanket.

Tell them to leave! Olyssa thundered.

Reneer immediately carried out her order and was met by loud protests from both the young man and the mother of three. He snarled back, "Do it, now! Can't you feel what's happening?"

Indeed, the configuration of the spell changed as, aided by the higher elevation, the notes of Olyssa's pipe reached the thing swooping overhead. Drifting away from the tree, it spun completely around, twisting all the threads of magic hooked into it. Its course changed from swerves to a straight line. It was flying right at them.

The two families refused to leave. The young man was growling, "There's *no way* we're going back down there!"

Erzelle broke her silence, spoke both out loud and in their heads. "You'll die if you stay!"

All the children started to wail. The stout mother stared at Erzelle. At her forehead. Pointed at the symbol there. "It's her!"

Reneer had hastily steered Olyssa toward a bend in a large branch that she could use as a seat. He ran at the gaggle of refugees, waving his sword. "*Get down from here!*"

Erzelle! Olyssa demanded. *By me!*

Erzelle tried to make her legs move but had lost the focus of a moment before, even as the mother of three screamed something at her that she couldn't make out. The notes took up so much room. She elbowed weakly at Braeca's back. Braeca had placed herself protectively between Erzelle and the apoplectic vulpine. The children screamed louder.

The young man started forward, also shouting. Reneer braced with swordpoint aimed at the man's midsection. Erzelle nudged Braeca again, and this time she turned her head. Her eyes bulged.

She shoved Erzelle down and threw herself on top of her.

The flying creature passed just yards over their heads, rustling the sycamore leaves.

Underlit by the burning homes of Fabelford, the monster glistened. Translucent sheets of skin like crepe paper stretched from the central spine of its underside to the spiked tips of its wings, black veins wormed through all its layers. Larger than the plane that had flown Erzelle and her parents from Minnepaul to the *Red Empress*, its outline that of a manta ray, every part of it made from living corpses, just like the machine under the mountain. Elliptical formations like octopus suckers lined either side of its ventral spine, revealed by a flare from below to be formed of pairs of lower jaws arranged in pantomimes of exaggerated screams. What appeared to be streamers unrolled from these toothy ellipses, dragging like jellyfish tendrils through the branches and across the platform.

One of the tendrils touched the young mother clutching her infant and curled around them both with shocking speed. The baby's howls cut off.

Peering out from under Braeca's shoulder, Erzelle got a closer look at a tendril as it slithered past, though comprehension eluded her as she strained to keep from breaking her inward melody. Her brain tried to reject what she'd seen: ropes of tongues strung together with nerves and studded with teeth like the horns of poisonous slugs.

Reneer whirled and slashed the sword through another tendril as it passed, then jumped back as the severed length reared up, a grotesque parody of a serpent.

Another whipped between two of the plump mother's children, grazing them as they shrieked.

Erzelle already knew that whatever this flying creature was, Olyssa's spell had no effect on it.

That thought made her miss a note.

Olyssa clutched at her mind. *No! Play!* At that moment, Olyssa's weave became its most complex yet, as if the pipe uttered twenty voices at once. Most disorienting of all, Erzelle felt the pipe take shape in her own fingers too, as if she and not Olyssa were the one playing all the parts. The notes curled up around the flying monster like the fronds of an anemone curling around a fish, yet in another second it would escape their tenuous grip.

Projecting **Braeca, keep me safe!**, not knowing if the thought was heard, Erzelle gave her mind over completely to the spell.

Each note pulsed with darkness, then brightened to the faintest blue glow before vanishing as the power within them drained out again. Erzelle's consciousness flew and died with them, her awareness fractured into a symphony of strobes and stutters as she cast the net of herself around the machine of stretched skin and woven nerves. Motes of her being darted into the gaps between its slime-slicked vertebrae and pierced its layers of putrescent tissue. This intimacy with the animated monster's rotting innards suffocated and sickened her, causing her to quicken her playing still further, the notes dying and renewing at a presto pace. The strands of power that connected to the ghouls on the ground threaded up through the monster's inner workings. She followed those threads into its depths toward their ultimate source. Her ears detected a horrible screaming near the place where her body lay, but her brain refused to engage in further interpreting what that meant.

The flying monster's interior continued past what should have been possible, its insides larger than its outsides. She plunged past a columnar maze of contracting sinew and billowing sails of skin, darted through curtain after vascular curtain, emerging into a yawning cavern like the inside of a titan's rib cage. The sweep of her and Olyssa's combined magic through this space revealed its function: it was the waiting gullet for the ghoul harvest, that would hold the prizes Lilla chose to bring back to supply her machines. This flying monster was a construction of Lilla's ghoul magic as powerful as the one they'd destroyed underground.

Like ash spewed from flame Erzelle and Olyssa's notes shot to the cavern roof and thence through it, through a wall of viscous meat into a sinus strung through with clustered ganglions of brain matter, thick cords stemming from their centers to wind together into a single pipeline. Smaller cables of nerves branched out from it. They'd found the driving intelligence — such intelligence that something dead and programmed could possess, at any rate — that governed all the ghouls below them in Fabelford. Erzelle's hatred of what this intelligence represented, of the destruction it had wrought, seared her inside and out, and she drew deeply on the black fire, meaning to spew it all through the works and burn the monster from the sky.

NO!

With that one word, Olyssa slammed a vault door between Erzelle and the black fire.

Erzelle screamed back: ***WE NEED TO DESTROY IT NOW!*** and tried to thrash free, but she and her teacher were so intricately entangled that it wasn't possible, not without losing all grip on the monster and tearing their spell apart, as well as freeing all the ghouls pacified within it.

We have to find the place it came from!

Erzelle thought her rage might blast the spell to pieces anyway. *Do it, then! NOW!*

Mentally if not physically distant from Erzelle, that awful screaming had not abated. For an instant, Erzelle heard it as if someone were shrieking directly in her ear. Then Olyssa drew them into the monster's central nerve cord and the stream of dark smoky energy within it.

Erzelle absorbed a rapid flutter of images. Stars streaked into lines of light. A plain blotched with swaths of fire seen from high overhead. A column of spinning cloud roaring with the volume of a thousand engines. A mountain ridge jutting from the curve of the world like rows of broken bone. A single spire rising incongruously from a pit of rock, a tower out of a fairy tale, crowed with an odd dome. The cadaverous face of Lilla, eyes widening and lips curling as she recoiled in shock.

In the next heartbeat, Erzelle once more stared out of her own eyes, feeling as if she'd been ripped from her skin and stuffed back in again. She was on the floor of the observation tree's deck.

The shrieks continued, further away. The monster was gone from overhead. Braeca cradled her in a crushing embrace.

The music had stopped.

The spell unraveled as if it had never been.

Erzelle tried to sit up, to push Braeca away, and saw the dark fluid that stained her pale fur. The right sleeve of the fox-woman's blouse was ripped to tatters. Blood flowed down her arm. The tendril's teeth had torn her flesh. She looked up at Olyssa with eyes wide and glistening.

Olyssa loomed over them, pointed the pipe at Braeca's arm. "Are you wounded anywhere else?" Her tone promised death.

Braeca shook her head.

"Don't lie."

A feeble whisper. "Not lying."

Behind Braeca, Reneer stood with chest heaving, leaning on the pommel of his sword as if the weapon were a cane, small bits of tongue-tentacle twitching on the boards all around him. Behind him a boy wept over the prone body of his older sister, whose face was missing. There was no sign of his mother or his other sibling, or of the couple with the baby.

Olyssa turned to Reneer. "Cut her arm off."

Reneer's jaw dropped.

"Cut her arm off now or I kill her before she becomes a ghoul. You, get off Erzelle, now."

Braeca tried to stand, ended up collapsing to her knees as Erzelle scrambled out from beneath her. The fox-woman whispered, and shook her head. Erzelle made out words: "... take care of mother. No one else ..."

Only then did Erzelle remember the elderly and sick woman whose voice she'd heard when she'd been in Braeca's house. Braeca had been brought by force to the Bear Trap chamber, and had stayed with them, helped them, without a word about her own needs.

Below, in Fabelford proper, new chaos erupted. The noise hurled in from all directions, cries and breaking glass and the clatter of metal. The ghouls were free. The monster was having its way with the city.

How many lives had Olyssa's need to find her sister cost? And soon sweet Braeca would be among them.

In the egg-chamber, Erzelle had healed herself. Healed Reneer. How she wished she could heal Braeca now. She wanted to scream, and Reneer's voice echoed her despair as he shouted, "I can't do this!"

"There is no choice."

Braeca straightened her back, extended her wounded arm and squeezed her eyes shut.

Reneer glared at Olyssa, his chest heaving harder, forcing a sob from his throat. Then he bared his teeth and slashed the sword down.

Erzelle squeezed her eyes shut and covered her ears. Braeca's cry of pain drowned out the screams from the city.

She opened her eyes again to see Olyssa tossing her belt to Reneer. "Bind her with this!" Then she turned on her heel. *It's coming back.*

Her order had jarred Erzelle. She couldn't believe Olyssa could be so callous, after what her quest had brought down upon the vulpines. She wondered for a moment what would happen if she channeled the black fire at her teacher, flipped her off the platform in a fireball of darkness to plummet to the chaos below.

She answered her own question: *Lilla wins.*

For as brief an instant as the last, all her rage turned inward.

She would demand an answer from Olyssa, why finding Lilla had been more important than maintaining the spell and saving the lives of Fabelford — but later. When the threat was ended.

The flying monster swept back toward them, its shape expanding against the stars as it approached. Erzelle heard a woman's unceasing shrieks, growing louder as the thing bore down on them. The tongue-tentacles still extended from its underside, silhouettes struggling in their coils.

Play our concerto, Erzelle. Play your hate for these monsters and what they've done, your hatred for how the world changed and the terrible things that change meant for me and you. Give me all of it.

Olyssa brought the pipe to her lips. Even as Erzelle formed the imaginary harp, started to pluck the notes once again, her heart tore as she realized what was about to happen. What it meant for the still-living victims dangling in the monster's tendrils.

There's no choice, came Olyssa thought, and the thought was Erzelle's as well. She embraced the music with all her might as the power siphoned out of her.

The nose of the flying thing erupted in a ball of flame, black at its center, deepest ghost-blue at its edges. The black fire traced all the same paths the sorcerous notes had followed before, punching through the veins and membranes in a thousand places. The monster revealed its own voice, a shriek like sheets of metal grinding together and shredding.

Any barrier left between Erzelle and her power crumbled away as Olyssa seized on it and channeled. She lifted Erzelle's fury as if it were a solid block, shaped it to a million-armed inferno and catapulted it at Lilla's creation.

That dark and fiery spell wrapped around the monster and snatched at every cord of magical power it dragged, followed each one down to the ghoul-puppet at the other end and ate it whole. Throughout Fabelford, black fire consumed both the fanged gnomes and the newly dead and walking. Erzelle saw each immolation as though it were right up close, felt the dead flesh disintegrate against her wrath.

The monster in the sky burst in a black nova.

Even as the shriveled faces seared into her mind, Erzelle longed to burn everything her power touched. She wanted to latch into the walls of the vulpines' homes, into the tunnels beneath, into the bedrock under that, incinerate every stone.

Her necklace pulsed, or maybe it was her own pulse pressing against it.

In that instant, Olyssa redirected their focus. Still intact by sheer force of malevolent will, the conduit of power that linked the monster back to Lilla trembled, agitated, as something tracked along it toward the two sorceresses at impossible speed, a new magical assault. Shouting as one, Olyssa and Erzelle poured their own power into the conduit, sent the black fire coursing down its length in response. Lilla's howl of surprise deluged their minds.

Erzelle didn't learn what happened next, because Olyssa simply stopped playing and lowered her pipe. She was shaking.

Fabelford had fallen quiet.

"If only you'd never had to see any of this," Olyssa said, not looking at Erzelle. She sounded like she had when she'd emerged from the hold of the *Red Empress*. "Would that you never had to live in this world."

Erzelle's mind filled with the convulsions of innocents burning.

Behind them, Braeca moaned.

She shuddered in a fetal position as Reneer cupped her head in his hands. In addition to the tourniquet of Olyssa's belt, he'd bandaged the stump that was left of her arm, now truncated just below the shoulder, with strips torn from his shirt. Beyond them the young boy sat glassy-eyed. His sister's faceless corpse had vanished, replaced by a spill of ash. Braeca's lost limb, too, was nowhere to be seen; neither were the severed tentacle bits.

She's safe now, Olyssa said. *The fires would have taken her if she had been tainted.*

As casual as if observing the weather. Even now.

Reneer looked up at Olyssa and Erzelle. His shoulders shook as a sob escaped. He turned his face away.

Erzelle found her anger again. She shoved her teacher, and though Erzelle barely budged her bodily, Olyssa jerked back and stared.

Erzelle no longer cared what she said aloud. "Why didn't we strike the first time? Why did you wait? The spell would have stayed intact! We could have ended it then!"

Olyssa's eyes glistened in the starlight. "What do you think happens next?"

"How should I know?"

"What do you think my sister and Noffreid will do, now that we've destroyed their plan and their ghoul harvester?"

A flash from the vision inside the flying monster: Lilla's gaunt face contorted in surprise. Her outraged scream when they'd struck at her through her own conduit of energy. Nausea sank through Erzelle as realization set in. "Strike back harder."

"With much more force. And how do we stop it?"

More flashes from the vision: the burning plain. The roaring funnel cloud. The fairy tale tower.

"We go to them." Erzelle's insides clenched. The full import of what Olyssa wanted to do hammered down on her. "We stop them where they are."

"Do you see now why I had to find her?"

Erzelle had never heard Olyssa sound so hurt before — or perhaps had always been too awed and intimidated by her teacher to recognize this tone for what it was. The pain assaulted her own anger like acid on rock, not melting it away but eating into it and dissolving its surface, uncovering memory after memory that reminded her how much she owed this woman.

Erzelle sighed, resolved, and asked, "How are we going to get to them?"

"The same way their ghouls came here. We'll fly." Olyssa turned toward Braeca and her voice softened. "But there's something else we need to do first." She called to Reneer. "We're going to heal her as best we can."

He sniffled, nodded, and started to get up.

Olyssa stopped him. "You can stay where you are." She turned to Erzelle. "The concerto."

By rote, Erzelle summoned the first few bars. Olyssa chimed in.

They used their song to heal Braeca's wound, gently closing veins and arteries and nerves, folding skin together. It was nothing as complex as what Erzelle had done in the egg chamber, but even the two of them together didn't have access to the level of timeless cognizance Erzelle had been granted in those first crucial moments of her power.

Erzelle longed again to have that level of understanding back. To be able to do something *more* — the better to help. Braeca had been hurt, mutilated, protecting her. She couldn't make Braeca's arm return, but she wished ...

Braeca stopped shivering as the spell finished its work.

"I'm so sorry," Olyssa said. "My deepest apologies. To both of you. We're about to part ways. Maybe it will be better for you once we're gone."

"Not likely," Reneer said bitterly, still cradling Braeca. "When all is said and done, we're fugitives and she's missing an arm ... hang on now." His head snapped up, eyebrows raised in astonishment. "Parting ways how?"

"You'll see."

Reneer started to retort, then stopped as Braeca sat up. Olyssa walked over to the nearest great branch of the observation tree. Erzelle went with her, unable to meet Braeca's eyes. She distracted herself by asking her teacher, *You said we'd fly. How can we make a flying machine? The same way Lilla did? We can't!*

Her agitation at the thought of stringing together a new monster out of ghoul parts was swiftly counterbalanced by a realization that she and Olyssa, by eradicating all traces of the stuff, had just made such an endeavor impossible.

I would never, ever, ever consider such a thing. But I think I know another way. Olyssa regarded her, face in shadow. *Understand something, Erzelle. I'm learning as I go, too. Most of this is as new to me as it is to you. I can't forgive my father for what he's done to you, but the power he's bestowed on you makes an incredible number of things possible that I could never do without your help.*

I once saw my sister do something that might prove useful to us now. Please, play for me again.

Erzelle stared back, turning Olyssa's words over in her mind. *Could never do without your help.*

Okay, then.

Erzelle sat on the boards of the observation deck, her back to the guard rail, and tried to summon the tactile memory of her harp — its weight in her lap, its smooth wood, the tension of its strings. She was sure she could do so much more if she had a real instrument to play, like Olyssa did.

She found that vivid memory in a unpleasant place. She didn't just imagine her harp, but imagined herself in the last place she ever wanted to return to, the dining hall stage in the *Red Empress.* She wouldn't allow her mind to populate the hall. She pressed on, focusing on the one thing good, that gave her will to live throughout those years.

Lines appeared, not just before her mind but before her eyes. Despite the shade from the tree that blotted the starts she could perceive harp strings perfectly.

Black fire hovered between her hands, billowing out into the shape of a harp, as if a container in that form had already existed and only needed a substance to fill it. She heard Braeca gasp and Reneer swear, but didn't look. Instead she told Olyssa, *I'm ready.*

Perhaps she only imagined that Olyssa's response contained the inflections of someone startled and impressed. *So you are. Let's begin.*

Erzelle plucked fire from the strings of her harp. Her teacher sculpted each burning note on her pipe. The tune evolved into something Erzelle had never heard before, deeper into the tenor range, imp-quick and threaded with with dark motion like blood through capillaries. The fire agitated the air, sliced into the wood of the observation tree with the precision of a razor and the force of an ax, infiltrated the same wood at the cellular level, transmuting its substance into new energies.

The branches above and around them gently peeled, bent, broke apart in even sections. No cracks or snaps accompanied this disintegration. No jagged chunks of tree fell to the deck. It was as if the nearest branches were stripping themselves bare, willingly surrendering their pieces. Magic shaved away unnecessary mass as the remaining pieces shed from the tree drifted together and locked, a self-assembling jigsaw.

Erzelle found herself inside memories that weren't her own.

The first she recognized: the woman made of leaves, wings stretching as she began to lift a felled tree so much larger than herself.

The second, she did not: a forest blurred to either side of a well-worn path. She peered out through Olyssa's eyes, felt Olyssa's hair bound up from her shoulders, the wind rushing against Olyssa's skin, tugging at her shirt. She savored with her host the thrill of speed, the joyous power of the horse whose back Olyssa straddled, the flow of its mane down the chestnut sheen of its neck.

Ahead galloped another horse, pale and spotted, hooves kicking up dirt from the trail. Lilla let her own hair whip back freely, turning once to look back with bright green eyes and a devil's smile, a look unimaginable on Olyssa's face though her features copied her sister's almost down to the dimples. Lilla's laugh combined glee-filled teasing and defiant contempt as she squeezed her knees against the flanks of her beloved horse to urge him on faster.

Olyssa urged her own steed on — such mockery would not pass unanswered. Deep down, though, the rivalry didn't matter — what mattered was that they were together, sharing this exuberant rush.

More scenes in a cascade, variations on a theme. As the memories overlaid like harmonies, the concerto's rhythm adapted the thunder of hooves. Notes rose in crescendo like a flight over hills, across fields. Scales soared like leaps over streams. Tempos slowed their pace like beasts led on foot through new turf. A new path formed, lined with Olyssa's remembrances, a bar awaiting music to trot down its length before bursting into a gallop.

In the end, two sisters were lying in the grass as their horses grazed.

The arrangement of notes slowed to pastoral grace, the finale fading with that last memory.

Tears wetted Erzelle's cheeks. Hers or Olyssa's. She wasn't sure. But she understood, when she regained her own body, why Olyssa had delved into those memories.

Sculptures of two horses stood side by side on the deck, woven of strips from the great tree carved to the thinness of straw. In the moonlight they appeared identical. Strange shadows moved behind their hooves, at every fetlock, hock and knee, and the undersides of their bellies whorled with shifting black, just like the harp hovering between Erzelle's hands. The burning darkness filled both these wooden horses without igniting and consuming them.

Olyssa continued to draw on her power, to play, to shape. Each steed developed reins, a saddle, stirrups, fused to the main body. Her thoughts cut in over the multiple melodies. *We have to make them free to run on their own, without requiring our constant attention, or this will never work. I know this can be done. My sister did it with her monsters ... and she did it when she made my pipe. But Erzelle, on my own, I don't know if I can manage the same. When my sister made the pipe, she lost something of herself.*

Erzelle comprehended at once what her teacher was asking. She recalled Lilla's words as if the memory were her own: *When the black fire left me and my mind cleared, I was holding it.*

She didn't know what agreeing to this new magic might take from her. She suspected Olyssa didn't either. But she considered Braeca's sacrifice for a twelve-year-old girl she'd only known a day and breathed, and said, *Do what you have to.*

A brief sensation of shrinking. Of having a portion of herself swiftly broken off. Alarming, but not painful.

Olyssa faltered for a fraction of an instant as it happened. Erzelle knew: whatever Olyssa had taken from her, she'd given more from herself.

Dark flames leaked first from one steed's eyes, then the other's.

Each horse dipped its head and shook its mane. The gestures produced a rattling, like shaking sheaves of straw.

The images Erzelle had seen after they plunged into the brain-center of Lilla's monstrous flying harvester flickered through her mind again. The burning plain. The storm funnel. The tower within the pit of rock. A route and a destination. Olyssa was giving instructions to these new creatures of wood and black fire.

Thank you, Olyssa said once she was done. *For now, I can play alone.*

Startled, Erzelle stopped plucking notes with her mind. The harp floating between her hands evaporated, as did her trance state. A chill shivered through her, amazement at the act she'd just taken part in, what she'd helped create.

She turned to find Reneer standing right behind her, Braeca leaning against him, both staring open-mouthed as the wooden horses stamped and shuffled in near-unison. The boy who remained with them on the platform had not stirred, a lump of shadow in the background. Left alone, his family gone. That thought, and the sight of Braeca covering her mouth with her remaining hand, of Reneer steadying her, crushed the wonder of the moment.

They're ready, Olyssa said. She stopped playing. The horses didn't fly into pieces.

From the way the fox-people looked at Olyssa, Erzelle knew they'd heard her too.

Stars peered through the gaps between the leaves, which were more numerous now that one large branch of the tree had been consumed to create the horses.

Sitting cross-legged on the planks, Erzelle's feet had fallen asleep. The boards of the rail dug into her back. An icy breeze made her notice she was shivering. She struggled to stand, had to suppress the urge to flinch when Braeca reached out to stop her from toppling.

"Goodness, woman, rest for once," Reneer said. Braeca replied with a nervous titter that brought a lump to Erzelle's throat.

Surprising even herself, she addressed them.

"We won't let this happen again. I promise you."

Reneer flashed a smile at her but didn't quite manage to complete it. When he started to speak, he didn't get beyond the first syllable. It was Braeca who broke this silence. "We know you'll do what you can."

Erzelle wanted to thank her but the words seemed so inadequate she couldn't bring them to her lips. Instead she found herself blushing.

Before she realized what she was doing, she rushed over to the fox-woman and hugged her tight. Braeca hugged her back as best she could, saying nothing.

Erzelle let go and turned to Reneer. She wanted to hug him too but wasn't sure if she should.

He completed his smile at last and impishly tousled her hair. She giggled like a six-year-old, at once relieved and embarrassed.

"You make me proud, young miss," he said. "Erzelle." Then he dug into his pocket and produced a folding knife — the same one he'd given her to make the reed, that she'd used to cut Olyssa out of the web in the egg-chamber. "I got this back from Greegrim — bless his heart, he's so generous. You made good use of it before. You might need it again."

Erzelle didn't know how to address what Reneer had said, feared she might start crying if she tried. She took the knife. "Thank you."

Finally she tore herself away. She went to Olyssa — wincing at the lingering pins and needles in her step — and stared at their paired creations, whose shoulders were higher than her head. Then it occurred to her —

I've never ridden before.

In the dark, she thought she saw Olyssa smile. **With these horses, that won't matter. They don't have to be broken in.**

The horses knelt.

Reneer asked, "Could you take more riders?"

Olyssa regarded him, then slowly shook her head. **Alas, no. And besides, you've been through enough. I won't put you in any more danger. I know my sister will be ready for us.**

"We're still in plenty of danger here."

I know. I wish I could undo that.

"Sure you can't take us with you?" He managed a grin that Erzelle thought bright enough to outshine the moon. "Surely you'd welcome the company?"

Something in Olyssa's posture suggested that she'd have said *yes* if she could … and didn't know what to say instead.

Reneer cocked his head, eyes sprightly sly. "Well … it's a good thing you're taking Erzelle along then. You'd be lost without her."

Olyssa placed her pipe in Braeca's discarded herb quiver, glancing at Braeca, who nodded her permission. Slinging the quiver across her back, Olyssa offered Reneer the slightest of smiles and said, *You're right.*

She turned to Erzelle and gestured at the horse on the right. *That one's yours.*

Though the horses' joints and bellies shimmered with magical fire, the boards beneath them didn't burn. Even so, Erzelle still minded where she stepped as she approached it. The beast's immense size made her wonder how she'd pull herself onto its back. She thought its skin would prove solid and slick, like polished wood, but instead it yielded to her touch, with a texture akin to sackcloth. The surface remained tense, like cloth pulled tight, and beneath it there was warmth, but no muscle mass or pulse. It afforded her handholds and footholds as she clambered up.

Once in the saddle she figured out how to put her boots in the stirrups. They adjusted to the length of her legs and tightened comfortably around her feet.

Hold the reins, Olyssa said.

Erzelle leaned forward to pick them up. Already mounted on her horse, Olyssa tilted her face to the night sky, and the creatures stood. Sycamore leaves brushed Erzelle's hair as her new elevation put her in range of a branch. She gripped the flexible wood of the reins harder, and as if in response, the reins wrapped around her wrists of their own accord.

The horses walked toward the edge of the platform. Erzelle thought riding a flying carpet might feel similar to how her horse felt moving beneath her. No clip-clop accompanied its steps, just a soft rustling sound.

The view beyond the rail showed fires in the streets of Fabelford, higher and brighter and hotter than before. Erzelle wanted to weep.

Then the horses leapt out through the sycamore leaves and over the rail.

No plummet, no loss of altitude, not even a hint of unsteadiness. It was as if her steed continued to tread solid ground.

The pressure in her ears abruptly released, like when she'd flown on the plane from Minnepaul, the hubbub from below at once amplified to a cacophony of shouts, of flames muttering, steam hissing, engines roaring.

She risked a peek down. The moonlit trees and the streets beneath them dwindled. Her horse's hooves struck against the air as if it were rock, and when they did black disks of magical fire flared beneath them at the moment of impact, vanishing the instant a hoof lifted, a spontaneously formed invisible stair. Erzelle knew without having to puzzle that the horses themselves generated these phantom footholds, just as she knew she could call the harp of black fire back with a thought, just as she knew how to find notes on its strings with her fingers.

Tilting her head brought her nothing but stars, with a hook of moon floating close enough to grab, it seemed. She looked over her shoulder, tried to find Reneer and Braeca but they were hidden by the night and the sycamore leaves. Smoke taunted her from below, a bizarre contrast to the bitter cold wind that buffeted her cheeks.

Beside her Olyssa had her eyes fixed on the horizon, where a constellation formed around two bright stars twinkling like the glint of light in spectacles, a curious onlooker shrouded by darkness. For a fleeting instant the jeweled end of her teacher's hair pick glittered in the moonlight.

Brace yourself, Olyssa said.

Exhausted enough to collapse into dust, distressed and disgusted with the horrors of the past two days and nights, Erzelle still laughed with exhilaration as the horses bounded forward.

The lights below blurred, shrinking swiftly behind them.

Their steeds galloped at a speed impossible on the ground. The wind against Erzelle's skin became a gale. She should have been torn from her perch, but the stirrups and reins gripped her tight of their own accord and the saddle curled up to brace her back.

The horizon curved before them in a futile attempt to eclipse the night's tapestry. She greeted it with whoops charged with the terror and excitement that coursed through her in one inseparable stream. If Olyssa made any sound, Erzelle couldn't hear over the rush of air. Her body refused to believe she was safe and secure, so she held on white-knuckled as they raced west.

A thin band of light appeared ahead and to the south that resolved into a lake, its edges too regular to be natural, its waters glowing. Long sinuous shadows moved within it, sometimes breaking the surface, too far away for Erzelle to make out what they were.

What are they? she asked, and Olyssa replied after a time, *I don't know.*

The structure faded behind them into the night.

—⌒·⊙ₒ⊙·⌒—

Fast as they moved, they didn't outpace the sunrise at their backs.

Its first rays revealed in full the unnerving beauty of the beasts they rode. Pale as dried wood, skin like wicker mesh, black flame streaming back from their eyes, their nostrils, their hoofs, the bends in their joints, and churning through the thinner mesh lathing of their undersides as if the wooden hide there simply served as grates beneath a furnace. Oversized puppets without evident strings, straw sculptures rippling with movement, they were identical, both modeled after the horse Olyssa had so loved as a teen. Erzelle wondered why her own mount wasn't modeled after Lilla's, then quivered inside as the thought brought revulsion.

Black fire flashed as their steeds' hooves pounded against a non-existent surface. *I'm dreaming this*, Erzelle thought.

She wished it could be so, that she could wake up suddenly, her mother practicing her harp in her study, her father puttering and fussing in the front room before leaving for his office, double-checking that he'd retrieved all the papers he brought home the previous evening.

But she knew better. Never in Erzelle's life had she dreamed anything so bizarre. That attested to the reality of what she saw, heard, felt, as much as anything else.

Besides — blinking, shaking her head, did nothing to alter the strangeness of the landscape scrolling hundreds of feet below them, a plain of lush fields marred by pools of burning tar. Occasionally she spotted ruts of road winding through this oddly fertile hell, even clusters of houses around one of the largest pits. The forms moving around them seemed too large to be human — even from this high up — though if the vulpines were human after all, as Reneer insisted, perhaps these were too. Erzelle tried to imagine how she and Olyssa appeared to them.

Olyssa didn't speak, instead acting as sentry, constantly scanning the skies, the ground, every once in a while glancing over at Erzelle to proffer her a grim smile.

The weight of exhaustion tugged on Erzelle with increasing persistence. The notion that she might grow accustomed to this terrifyingly, joyously impossible ride seemed ridiculous — but she did. Without realizing she was doing so, she leaned against her horse's neck. The reins wound up her arms to her shoulders. Like this, at last she dozed. In her mind a soothing piper's tune played, rocking her with the rhythm of the horses' stride.

Occasionally throughout the next few hours, her eyelids would flutter open. Or perhaps she dreamed all along, because each time she beheld something new and odd:

A school of winged humanoids that paralleled their progress from a distance of about a quarter mile, just close enough for Erzelle to make out the round eyes staring from the sides of their heads like those of fish.

A lake that reflected the sky to perfection, a dark rock jutting from its depths. A tower glinted at its peak, not like the fairy tale one rising from the pit of rock that Erzelle had glimpsed in her vision. Light refracted through its walls into rainbows, and inside it dark things crawled, a crystal vase filled with ants.

The earth, bubbling brown and black. Across it rolled a fortress mounted on tank treads tall and wide enough to flatten whole villages. A cylindrical iron crow's nest atop the works turned ponderously, tracking them with a single telescope eye.

Erzelle, wake up!

Still daylight.

Erzelle gasped and sat up straight, winced at the pain in her neck and the searing cold. How had she slept with that wind trying to strip her nerves bare? The tune she'd heard as she dreamed no longer played.

Ahead a dense wall of ominous clouds dominated the heavens, extending upward for miles, a parapet hiding the sun. Lightning bolts of neon indigo split the darkness beneath it. Seconds later the accompanying thunder blasted Erzelle's ears, growing louder as they raced closer. It became a constant barrage as they rode beneath the ledge of thunderheads toward the heart of the storm. The ground below was a blasted wasteland of rock and mud, revealed in strobe light staccato. Much to Erzelle's surprise no rain drenched them, although the immense electric arcs that roared through the haze forced her to squint and cover her ears.

Olyssa had her pipe out. Terror and vertigo shrieked through Erzelle at the sight. She was certain her teacher would fall. The disjointed illumination from the continual lighting flashes showed Olyssa sitting with her back straight, jacket whipping behind her, as if she wasn't moving at dizzying speed with wind tearing at her. The horse's body altered to secure her, stirrups winding higher up her legs, the saddle stretching to embrace her waist, reins wrapped around the elbow she bent to bring the reed to her lips, leaving her other hand free to mute the bell.

Now-familiar hooks imposed on Erzelle's consciousness, seeking to draw on her power again.

She understood what her teacher expected. The head-splitting noise dulled her concentration, but she heard the inward tune and improvised upon it, a ghost harp manifesting in her mind's eye.

At once the roar quieted. Olyssa had built a shield around them, though it failed to blot out a mix of stenches like nothing Erzelle had encountered before: rotted fruit and overheated metal, a dense reek of copper, spoiled milk.

Olyssa stopped drawing power from Erzelle but continued to play.

Visible only intermittently but growing closer, a single spinning column held up the vault of storm cloud. Erzelle recognized it from the visions she'd seen when they accessed the flying harvester's nerve center. Though they were nowhere near it, she felt its pull, as if she were a grain of sand in the top of an hourglass tumbling toward its inescapable center. Given the distance, the titanic cyclone had to be wider than the mountain where the Grey Ones had dwelled, bigger around in circumference than the city of Minnepaul. It spun in place, lashing out with lightning, radiating rage.

Olyssa said, *That's where it all started.*

It took Erzelle a moment to grasp what she meant. The destruction of the world. *The Storms?*

Yes.

They angled south to circumvent the roaring cyclone and continue west. To their right it swelled, a pillar of darkness wide as a sea that tore at both earth and sky, thrusting into the shelf of the storm like a column into a cavern roof. When Erzelle dared to look directly at it, an animal fear stiffened her spine, as if a hungry presence stared back.

Only Olyssa's music anchored her sense of the passage of time. Though they were nowhere close to the cyclone, it expanded and expanded in the lightning-stuttered view, a sentry that would never grant them passage.

Yet even as it loomed its largest, a horizontal line of light appeared in the distance, a thin bar of sunlight drawn across the dark that defined the storm's far edge. Erzelle's heart lightened at the sight.

As the galloping horses began to put the cyclone behind them, the ceiling of the storm between it and them roiled and bulged downward.

Do as I do!

Olyssa stopped playing and gripped her horse's neck, her pipe clutched in one clenched fist, the reins winding around her arms to secure her. The ear-splitting roar of the constant thunder immediately returned. Erzelle imitated her just as the horses' ears flattened and they shot forward at a speed no living thing could ever match.

Two thin funnel clouds descended from the mass of the storm and curved toward them, reaching like tentacles. Lightning snaked in front of the riders, searing Erzelle blind.

Her eyes squeezed shut, Erzelle pictured her harp, pictured her hands picking up the tune Olyssa had dropped.

The world went silent.

She opened her eyes to stare in sheer bewilderment. Sheer horror.

The tapered tips of the funnel clouds circled them like eels shimmying around their prey, stabbed again and again at the shield Erzelle had restored. She gripped her horse as tight as she could, white-knuckled, terror icing her spine, but didn't stop playing, unable to look away as the twisters tried over and over to reach her and Olyssa.

The attackers withdrew as sunlight washed over them.

The horses reduced their pace, the blur below subsiding to reveal they were now dozens of feet above the boulder-strewn wasteland rather than hundreds. Olyssa and Erzelle stared at each other as lighting flashed and Erzelle's heartbeat slowed ever so slightly in its tempo.

Her teacher smiled thinly. **Well done.**

They were out from underneath the storm shelf. Ahead, broken mountains loomed like a shattered spine crossing the world. The westering sun hovered behind the peaks, in danger of impalement. The rapidly shrinking miles of terrain between them and the mountain ridge mounded into lifeless, unwelcoming hills.

Erzelle recalled her visions. The broken mountains, the tower among them, then Lilla.

What do we do? she asked Olyssa.

One of the mountains changed shape.

Hello, Olyssa. I knew you'd come.

A figure separated itself from the rock, its silhouette tall enough to lift a hand and cause an eclipse.

Erzelle's mind couldn't process what was happening. No living thing could be that large and move with such lithe grace, or such casual arrogance.

The green lakes of Lilla's eyes tracked their approach over a cavernous smile. Her hair could clog rivers. The horses and their riders would be bugs on her outstretched palm. Her earth red gown dragging through the valleys, she stepped over the foothills of the mountain she'd emerged from, and when she laughed snow and rock came loose on its shattered face.

Were Erzelle not secured, she would have fallen off her steed. Her grip on the reins had gone as slack as her jaw.

Tricks! Olyssa shouted in her mind. *Don't believe them!*

Erzelle picked up on a note of panic in her teacher's voice.

Black smoke writhed in the spaces between Lilla's teeth. Tendrils of it slithered from her hair, not unlike the predatory funnel clouds they'd just eluded. More spilled out from under the fingernails of her skeletal hand as she strode toward them, a rumble of earth and a whoosh of air accompanying her footfalls.

Though Olyssa rode barely ten feet away, the rush of air nearly drowned her words. "Find my enemies," she chanted. Her hooks found the edges of Erzelle's consciousness. "Find my enemies."

You want to hurt me again, Lilla said, *with the gift I gave you?*

She opened her mouth and expelled enough smoke to smother a city, aiming right at them.

Without thinking, Erzelle lifted her hands, the ghostly image of her harp fixed in her mind's eye, and reconjured the protective bubble. The smoke parted around it — but stayed in place, completely enveloping them. It pressed in from all directions at once, seeking a weakness in Erzelle's fortifications. Worse, wrapped in that swirling tar, they could no longer see Lilla.

Erzelle! With her shout, Olyssa projected a new melody directly into Erzelle's head. Not for an accompaniment, a harmony, a help. This was for her to play solo.

Erzelle seized on it, threw the notes through her harp, and the surface of the sphere of protection she had created burst into black flame.

The smoke didn't recoil. Lilla's magic fought back. The pressure at the edges of Erzelle's awareness redoubled, hardened into spines, the smoke attempting to snuff out the fire and pierce through to its source at every point.

The sensation translated into needle-sharp fangs pushing through every inch of Erzelle's skin.

An image of the Chef's smug smile wormed through her mind, beaming over at her behind her harp as the ghouls that had been her parents snapped their jaws from the gurney. *Your turn soon, pretty plumpkin.*

She shoved back with all her hate. Sped and layered the melody in her head just as she'd heard Olyssa do, accelerated by pain and rage, surges of darkness embedded in every note. She screamed as she pushed back with all the fury she could muster.

The black fire blasted outward in a shockwave. It swept the smoke away, igniting and converting it, absorbing its power as it erupted in all directions. The hillsides below churned and spewed back earth as the blast struck.

Lilla laughed, a wild thrill-ride cackle. As the bubble of flame spread, it also faded, and within minutes they could see clearly again. Could see *her* again. Death personified with a stride that that could devour miles, she'd closed a considerable distance between herself and their horses, left the mountains several steps behind. Her body blocked the sun from view, her head high as a storm cloud, ringed with writhing smoke.

The dissipating wave reached her and her towering form scattered like a column of fog in a windstorm.

Hidden inside the illusion until that moment, a phalanx of triangular harvesters like the one that had ravaged Fabelford tilted and shuddered in the sky as the last remnants of Erzelle's strike hit them. Within their midst spun two larger, uglier corpse-monsters, with long necks stretching from conical bodies to attach to heads like immense grey lotus blooms.

One of the harvesters flipped and fell with an ear-splitting screech, the black fire consuming it before it ever reached the ground. The rest remained in the air. Some dove straight at Erzelle and Olyssa. Some soared aft. Some scattered to either side.

Olyssa snarled, "Find my enemies."

The harp manifested above Erzelle in full black fire glory as her mind envisioned ghostly hands playing a ceaseless howl of fury down its octaves. She fed it all into the spell called by her teacher's chant. Her necklace twitched in warning.

Olyssa didn't play her pipe, but held it out before her like a magician's wand. The runes along its length flared red as Erzelle's fire spewed from its bell. A harvester exploded in an indigo ball, then another, then another. Erzelle tried to summon another protective sphere of dark flame even as she fueled Olyssa's weapon. But the attack was upon them before the thought fully coalesced. Her horse veered to the right and up of its own accord just before one of the bizarre flower-headed monsters plunged through the air where she had been. Overwhelmed, her head spinning past the point of dizziness, the illusion of traveling on solid ground shattered, and Erzelle lost her place in the notes.

The horse angled straight up as a disintegrating harvester fell past her. The flower-headed monster pivoted below and surged up after her. Its twin darted its bulk behind Olyssa, whose horse dashed east, away from Erzelle and the mountains, the fire from the pipe extinguished.

The concave head of the thing chasing Erzelle was made of eight flat membranous lobes that spread out like petals from a central spiky bole, bony stamens surrounding a hole that coughed Lilla's living-tar smoke. The rims of the petals were studded by the crowns of skulls, holes drilled through each one like pupils in eyeballs and Erzelle had no doubt this was precisely the purpose they served. The long flexible neck beneath flared out into a conical body longer than a soccer field, formed of trapezoidal overlapping wings that whirled nonstop, every bit of the monster made of skin stretched over bone frames.

From the orifice in the center of its flower-like face a tendril of smoke lashed out at her like a chameleon's tongue. Her horse reversed course and plummeted at a steep angle, making Erzelle want to scream and retch at once.

She didn't recognize at first the tug of Olyssa's power on hers, striving to regain purchase. Her own concentration shattered, she only knew the monster in pursuit was gaining on her as it dove to follow.

Notes sounded about her, not her own. Olyssa urgently projecting, giving her a score to follow. She tried to play it but nausea and adrenaline cooked her brain.

Erzelle hugged the horse's neck just before it spun in the air, still plunging toward the ground but at a shallower angle. The monster narrowed the distance and lashed out again with its smoky tongue. But Olyssa dashed across her path, her own foul pursuer mere yards behind her.

Erzelle realized what was about to happen the instant before it did. The burn of Lilla's smoke across her back cut short right as it touched her, as the flower-headed monstrosities, tricked by Olyssa's horses, smashed into one another at right angles with a sound like a thousand sheets ripping.

Erzelle threw back her head, cackled in triumph, and immediately reformed the harp. She latched onto Olyssa's tune, heard the whoosh of sudden fire as Olyssa directed their combined energies and obliterated the tangled monsters from existence.

Four of the harvesters remained, circling above. Black spots like spores started spilling out of them that resolved as they fell into a mass of the huge-jawed gnome-ghouls, disgorged to rain on them. Their spidery limbs splayed wide, they poured by the hundreds even as Olyssa destroyed the black triangles that spat them out.

Erzelle tried again to overlay the protective shield of dark fire, simultaneously feeding power to Olyssa's weapon. The harp reappeared in the air above her, strings thrumming. This time she succeeded. Much larger, much thicker, the sphere encircled them both.

The ghouls made popping noises as they struck it. For a second the sounds made Erzelle's stomach lurch. Then she rejoiced in it. As it went on and on, she started to giggle. Soon she was howling in laughter, even when the noises stopped.

Fire no longer gushed from the pipe. No more enemies to find. *Erzelle*, Olyssa scolded. *Erzelle!*

The necklace tightened against Erzelle's throat. She gasped as the shield of black flame vanished, her harp with it.

The sky was clear. The sun brushed the broken mountains an ominous red.

The furnace of the black fire still churned outside her mind, but muted, the same way it had been after she had purged the lair of the Grey Ones. When she tried to tap the darkness again the fires stayed out of reach, and the necklace pulsed again.

Her neck ached. Her back and shoulders felt severely sunburned.

They came to a halt, sitting on their false horses, about sixty yards above foothills tumbled into stony chaos by the magic that had just been in play.

Erzelle asked, eyes wide, *Is Lilla gone?*

No. That was all a trick, Erzelle. She's still waiting.

They hadn't even confronted Lilla in the flesh yet and Erzelle could no longer tap the fires. Her heart pounded anew. *I can't reach—*

It's the necklace my father gave you. It's blocked you again.

I know! Erzelle blurted in frustration. *How do I undo it? It tightens like it's trying to strangle me when I call to the black fire.*

Olyssa swore. *Only hell knows what my father had in mind.* She looked Erzelle up and down, worried. *I … I fear to try tampering with it. But perhaps …* She placed the reed to her lips. *Don't tap the darkness. Just think of the concerto, like you did in the cell.*

Before Erzelle could stop herself she retorted, *You think it's that easy? Don't you even care if I'm okay?*

She thought her teacher's gaze held no emotion until she heard the strain in her response. *Of course I do. But even if you aren't you and I are both long past the point of choice.*

That wasn't true. They still had a choice. They could turn back. They could flee their separate ways and hope Lilla never found them. They could leave Fabelford to its fate. Knots tied in Erzelle's belly as the heat of shame flushed her face red, humiliation that she'd even let these options cross her mind.

She summoned the notes of the concerto. Olyssa began to play.

A current of fire wound through the music, as had happened in Fabelford.

There's resistance, but I can still tap the darkness through you, Erzelle. That will have to do. Olyssa continued the soft melody, and the horses resumed a mid-air trot, their altitude gradually climbing.

Take deep breaths, Olyssa advised. *Keep the concerto fixed in your mind.*

As she played, she wove. The same way Erzelle heard mindspeech, she heard Olyssa's spell, gleaned a sense of its purpose. Olyssa was shaping something in principle akin to the horses, able to function independently of its creator's control. It wasn't, however, a solid object. Erzelle had the impression of a sphere formed of motes of sound, completely invisible to the unenhanced eye. Completed, it rolled ahead of them. Olyssa immediately started to weave another.

The path through the air their horses took wove as well, curving southwest between jagged peaks that reared toward the heavens like the teeth in a behemoth's shattered jaw, the upper tips of these fangs striped with ice.

Between the peaks lay mounds of boulders, the remains of the original, larger peaks, some of the individual rocks large enough to be mountains in their own right.

Erzelle scanned both sky and slopes for any new sign of Lilla, her ghouls or her corpse-machines, saw none and found this absence not the least bit comforting.

Their course gradually steered them west, then northwest, with the sun's red glare to their left. They galloped with the wind toward a peak taller than the others, crowned with needles of stone in a ring. Olyssa continued to weave her spheres of magic. The chill air filled Erzelle's lungs, raised goose pimples on her skin, though she hardly noticed, watching those needles of stone for monsters or worse to emerge from between them.

None did. Up close the needles proved to be stalagmites, black fluid dripping up into the sky from their uppermost tips in defiance of gravity. Though Erzelle couldn't guess what they were for, she sensed the power coursing up through them — and also that they were intended to handle a much greater capacity than the current flow.

Had she and Olyssa actually weakened Lilla in the fight? Could that be possible? Erzelle didn't dare let herself believe that idea all the way. Too dangerous.

Olyssa ceased her spellcasting. *Rest now and be ready.*

Only then did Erzelle become aware she still played the concerto in her head. It had at this late hour, after all their trials together, become second nature, like the simple lullabies her mother had taught her that she still sometimes found herself absently humming.

They rode between the needle formations unchallenged. The stalagmites stood sentry around a huge well hollowed out of the mountain. At the bottom of the hollow stood a tower, the one from the visions Erzelle and Olyssa had gleaned when they destroyed the monster over Fabelford. With its smooth, white walls, the spire appeared pristine as a fairy tale illustration, until Erzelle spotted ribs and eye sockets and realized the structure was tiled from base to crown with mosaics of bleached bone.

The odd structure that crowned the tower resolved as they descended into a half-cylinder set on its flat side, open at one end like a fish's mouth with long lower jaw extended. It reminded Erzelle of the hangar bay where she and her parents had boarded the plane that took them to the *Red Empress.*

A few seconds more and they'd descended low enough to peer into the hangar bay. Not far back from its entrance sat another of the harvesters, an outsized moth, only it was incomplete, a scaffold without skin.

Beside it stood Lilla, clad in the same red gown cinched around the waist that she'd worn when she'd seemed the size of a mountain. She should have been a tiny, single figure next to the half-built machine, under the vaulted ceiling. Instead she dominated the cavernous hall as though she were still as tall as the sky. Her flowing black hair moved as if constantly brushed by a breeze. The polished stone floor reflected her gaunt form. She greeted them with a cadaverous smile.

Olyssa put the reed back to her lips, her knuckles white around the pipe.

The harvester skeleton swarmed with the tiny huge-headed, spider-legged ghouls, and with the same kind of grotesque mosaic creatures made of mismatched parts that had infested the tunnels under the Grey Ones' temple.

Lilla followed her sister's gaze, shrugged her bony shoulders as if to say, "Oh, that?" and waved a hand wreathed in smoke.

The structure and all the creatures within it collapsed to a pile of bone dust and spoiled meat.

There. I've saved you the trouble. Her grin widened, her eyes bright with mirth. *Welcome.*

You still smile when you're angry, Olyssa observed, dispassionate as a sniper taking aim.

Erzelle tried to catch her teacher's eye. She repressed the urge to wave or shout with the witch standing not thirty yards away from them. She could not believe, after all they had just been through, that they were simply going to alight on the platform as if they were stopping in for a bite to eat.

That's exactly what they did. The horses touched down and trotted to a stop, their hooves rustling against the stone. Lilla stayed put, still smiling.

Olyssa remained on her horse, watching her sister in silence. Erzelle's gaze darted from one to the other. The resemblance made her queasy. But for her green eyes, Lilla could have been Olyssa mummified.

Olyssa always seemed to have a plan, and when she didn't, she improvised like the master musician she was. Erzelle wondered if her teacher had a plan now. Her pulse pounding faster as the silence lengthened.

Erzelle attempted communication with Olyssa alone. *What are we going to do?*

Lilla replied, "I'd also like to know the answer to that," her voice as musical as her sister's, though other qualities infested it — the rustle of dried leaves, the tinny resonance of metal. She stared at Erzelle, at the mark on her forehead, her expression unchanging, even though she addressed Olyssa. "I'm touched you kept your promise. You still have my little gift."

When Lilla had appeared as a giant, she'd accused her sister of trying to kill her with that same "gift." Still, Olyssa's grim countenance slipped.

Lilla's lips curled ruefully. "Don't shed any tears for me, dear sister. Things have gone wonderfully since I last saw you."

Erzelle remembered the event Lilla referenced — the demonstration of the leaf-woman who could lift the Walking Tree, Olyssa tossed like a doll, the exchange of hurtful words that followed.

Olyssa's fists clenched before she regained control. "Where's Noffreid?"

Lilla's expression soured and her eyes narrowed. But she only shrugged. "He's no longer with me."

"Dead?"

"Missing." After a pause, "Did you hope I'd say yes?" She bit off every syllable. "How sweet that you're so concerned."

Olyssa nodded, as if to herself, reaching a decision. The horses knelt at some unspoken command. Erzelle hardly dared to breath as her stirrups and reins loosened. Her teacher dismounted. Without blinking Lilla tracked every movement Olyssa made.

Erzelle nearly screamed as Lilla spoke inside her mind. *How nice that my father crawled up from his hiding place to mark a new subject. How long have you known the darkness, girl?*

Olyssa didn't react. She didn't hear. The words were broadcast to Erzelle alone.

Where did my sister find you? Where did my father find you?

To her horror she felt the same sort of tugging on her mind that she had whenever Olyssa drew on her. The sensation was profoundly different, though: instead of a gentle caress, a prickling behind her eyes, at the base of her neck, around her temples, beneath her scalp. The closest thing she'd experienced before had been when Lilla tried to pierce her shield spell, an assault of needles from all directions.

"Stop it!" she yelled. She spread her hands to summon the harp, and a twitch from the band around her neck reminded her it wouldn't work. Not that she would have known what to do if it had. It had never occurred to her she could be attacked through the same channels Olyssa used to bond with her.

Lilla's eyes widened at Erzelle's gesture and her mouth twisted into a scowl. The prickling, needling sensation faded, though not altogether.

Olyssa advanced, every angle of her body charged with menace. "You leave her be!"

That sickening grin returned, wry and knowing. "You'd be nothing without that one — and there's so much she doesn't know."

Olyssa's beseeching tone surprised Erzelle. "Lilla … Does it have to be this way? Surely this can't be what you want."

Lilla cocked her head to one side, furrowed her brow ridges. "Sweet talk, now, Olyssa? Be honest. I disgust you. To you I look like a *monster*."

Olyssa shuddered and her shoulders hitched. Lilla blasted her own old words back to her. "Do you still take pleasure at the thought of me rotting inside?"

Erzelle heard the barely audible, sobbed whisper. "No. I never did."

"So what now?" Lilla titled her chin up in defiance and condemnation, stretching the tendons in her withered neck. "You use the gift I gave you to kill me?"

"Do I need to?"

"Of course not. Take father's new darling, climb back on your marvelous horses, fly from here and never return."

To Erzelle's eyes, Olyssa's usual impassivity had shattered. Her tortured expression betrayed a mind at war with itself. She couldn't be seriously considering Lilla's offer?

Erzelle wanted to shake her, to yell, *What's wrong with you? Don't fall for this!* but if she did, what would Lilla do to her — or to Olyssa? She was afraid to move. But this drawn-out standoff was its own agony.

The silence lengthened. Olyssa still didn't answer, though she stood straighter, ran the fingers of one hand along the runes of the pipe, the gesture full of both sadness and threat. It was lost on neither Erzelle nor Lilla.

The sisters faced each other, separated now by about thirty feet, Olyssa grim, Lilla eerily wistful. The silence stretched until the air quivered between them. The needles prodding at Erzelle's mind never relented.

"I made a place for you at Violet Bluffs," Lilla finally confided, "and I wish I could again. You were safe, where I put you. You should have stayed there."

Erzelle's stomach twisted, remembering Olyssa twitching in the web, eyes rolling beneath closed eyelids, the black strands continuing underneath her skin, Lilla's idea of *safe*. Worse, the needling sensation in her head intensified, Lilla's probing tendrils crawling like maggots in the interstices between her and the black fire, her contact with that power still blocked.

If only she could work like Olyssa, weave tiny threads of current through the barrier the necklace posed.

Could she?

She started when a voice projected through her tumbled thoughts, but it was Olyssa's.

Erzelle, move behind me, now. Don't speak to me unless you absolutely must. I can't prevent her from hearing you. She's hunting the places we're vulnerable.

Simultaneously with her mindspeech Olyssa asked Lilla aloud, "What would I need to be safe from? From *you?* What is it that you're making?"

Though it was ridiculous to think Lilla wouldn't notice her, Erzelle tried to make her herself small, to not draw attention, as she quietly slid from her horse. When she'd lived inside the *Red Empress*, lowering her eyes and shuffling along at a quick pace as if following an order had warded off a lot of unwanted attention. She assumed that demeanor as the crawling sensation intensified. She wanted to shout, *She's trying to tap my power the way you do!* Surely Olyssa knew? She hoped her teacher could detect what her sister was doing.

She stole a glance at Lilla and on a different level of consciousness registered the witch as a dark sun, burning hotter by the second, certain to flare at any sudden move, and she could only hope Olyssa had already deduced what was happening and knew what to do about it.

"Noffreid's dream," said Lilla, still wistful. "I don't suppose you'd care for what he and I have built, if you were capable of understanding it."

"Try me. Explain it."

"No. I don't think so."

Lilla watched like a cat tracking a beetle as Erzelle walked the final steps to where Olyssa stood. Then the witch shrugged and addressed her sister. "It's *you* who should stand behind *her.*" She barked a laugh, the black smoke filling her mouth, slithering out from her hair. "You'd have a few seconds' room to run."

Erzelle's heart beat like a drum roll. Did Lilla know she couldn't access the black fire? Had these constant, maddening prickles in Erzelle's skull exposed that she was powerless?

Olyssa replied, "I spent years searching for you. I won't run."

Lilla's eyes narrowed. "Why?"

"I wanted to undo what's been done. Not just what Noffreid did, but what I did."

Lilla exploded with laughter. "You thought you could *save* me, didn't you? You didn't know I never wanted to be saved."

"You can still come back."

"But you got your wish, *dear sister*." Every word became a knife slash. "You said you hoped this power would kill me. And it did."

"That's not so." Olyssa took a step, holding up her pipe. "It wouldn't play if you couldn't come back! We wouldn't be here now if you couldn't come back. I want you to come back."

Lilla's mouth worked, but no words passed her lips. Erzelle couldn't believe it. Olyssa's earnest appeal had gotten under her sister's skin.

Finally Lilla blurted, "I don't want to!"

Erzelle's surprise nearly shook a nervous laugh free, that such an unnervingly hideous and graceful figure could sound so petulant.

In that moment of distraction, the force plucking at the edge of her consciousness jabbed into her mind from all angles. The attack froze her in place. Splitting pain erupted behind her right eye, behind her left, at the back of her head. Barriers of power descended around her like guillotine blades, and she recognized what they were doing. Cutting her link to Olyssa.

Projecting was impossible. "She's attacking me!"

"Am I now?" Lilla cackled, more smoke spilling from her throat.

Olyssa put the reed to her lips.

Her sister shouted with the volume of a locomotive crash, and yet Erzelle still heard Olyssa's notes, and felt the welcome caress of her teacher trying to draw on her. The magical trap snapped into place, and Olyssa's touch vanished.

Yet hearing the music at all, connecting that bond once again, however briefly, sparked a wild improvisation.

As she had when they were under the stormcloud, Erzelle played Olyssa's part of the concerto in her head, the same notes her teacher followed as she tapped the black fire through Erzelle. She imitated her teacher as precisely as she could, at the fastest tempo she'd heard Olyssa play. Distantly, the black fires churned, unable to respond to her summons.

Olyssa had admonished her when they were trapped in the Fabelford prison. *What I'm doing requires a trickle of energy maintained for a long time. What you can do requires a floodgate to open.*

The necklace wouldn't let her open a floodgate. But if Olyssa could work tiny trickles through her, maybe she could work the same way.

The prickling needles continued to dig into her like a thousand arachnid legs.

Erzelle didn't know if her blind faith attempt to replicate Olyssa's technique was working until the surge of contact electrified her nerves, made the hair at the back of her neck stand. She fought back all urges to throw her force into a blast, and simply continued to play. The necklace stayed dormant.

As the black fire filled the thread she'd created, she at once could see the hostile spell-strands scrabbling at her. They weren't coming from Lilla.

She seized on one of those strands, sent her stream of black fire vibrating up its length, back to its source.

With a surprised shout, a man appeared beside Lilla. Gaunt as the witch, he wore a blue-black robe with a short crop of white hair crowning his grey scalp. His huge blue eyes bulged wider as Erzelle tested the limits of her new-found skill, drove more power through her thread and stabbed her magic at the figure who had to be Noffreid. He flipped backward, landing on his spine.

All the unwelcome, invasive prickling stopped. The walls cutting her off from Olyssa fell away.

"Don't you dare hurt him!" Lilla bellowed. Her every syllable formed a jet of tarry mist that stretched toward Olyssa. Erzelle rejoiced as Olyssa reconnected to her mind, the familiar hooks returning to draw on the black fire. The complicated round Olyssa played, a musical phrase whose end note was also its beginning, accelerated as the tendrils of smoke sped toward her. A spherical pattern ballooned into being that trapped Lilla's smoke and whirled it into a ball that hovered equidistant between the two sisters.

Lilla curled her lips in a defiant snarl. Near her, Noffreid regained his feet. Erzelle's second look at him yielded surprises. He was shorter than Lilla by a couple of inches, and though she'd maintained an unnerving beauty in her cadaverous state, he most definitely had not.

But for the intelligence in his too-wide set eyes, Erzelle would have assumed him a ghoul. His skin hung in flaps from nose, cheekbones and chin, exposing dark slime beneath. His ragged gait suggested muscles strung together wrong. With his bulging forehead, sunken temples, disproportionally short arms and lopsided sneer, Erzelle could hardly believe that this was the man who'd stolen Olyssa's beloved sister. His appearance made for a grotesque caricature of the youth from Olyssa's shared memories.

His bright blue eyes fixed on Erzelle's, on the mark on her forehead. He too bore that mark, the only part of his face that hadn't rotted. Then his gaze darted left, right, up, tracking something in the space around her, though she saw nothing. It had to be magic, like the sphere Olyssa wove, though her awareness sensed no spell at hand. Whatever he was doing, it was too subtle for her to detect with only a trickle of the black fire coursing through her.

She needed more or she couldn't fend him off. Would the necklace allow it?

Lilla opened her mouth, held out her hands, blowing more and more of the roiling smoke at her sister, who snatched it all and coiled it in the web of sound she'd made, drawing more from Erzelle as she added layer upon layer. Erzelle accompanied Olyssa in her mind but didn't summon her fiery harp, afraid it would trigger the band around her neck to seal off her power.

Noffreid stalked away from his lover, eyes still focused on Erzelle. He skirted the edge of the destroyed harvester as he raised his right hand with fingers splayed. A blade of red light protruded from every finger.

Olyssa started to change her melody, and the ball of dark energy lurched in Noffreid's direction, but Lilla laughed and the amount of raw power gushing through her doubled, quadrupled, forcing her sister to play with even more complexity and draw even more from Erzelle to fend it off.

Noffreid rushed past Olyssa, giving her a wide berth, circling around to come at Erzelle with those blades of light.

In her mind Erzelle played the notes on her harp that summoned the shield of fire. It manifested around her.

Then immediately dissipated, drawn away into nothingness like a sheet yanked off a cage by a stage magician.

Noffreid worked with the subtle and small the same way Olyssa did. He'd woven something around her she couldn't detect that siphoned her fire away. He bared his teeth in a triumphant sneer.

Erzelle gave up on the shield and channeled fire at her attacker. The new trap woven around her absorbed the stream. She opened her mind to assault the new barrier with every bit of strength she had.

The necklace pulsed, walling the black fire away from her as Noffreid closed in.

Olyssa! she yelled, to be rewarded by Lilla's thunderous cackle.

The patriarch of the Family had rolled with that same kind of laughter as the remains of her parents were sliced to pieces. In her mind she heard it all again, how the customers of the *Red Empress* had laughed through the hundreds of murders she'd been forced to witness. The moans of the ghouls trapped in that hold. The cries of the vulpines of Fabelford as Lilla's ghouls slaughtered their young ones. Braeca shuddering on the planks, her arm severed.

Erzelle's fury attempted to erupt from every pore like geysers from the Earth's crust. The necklace tightened garrotte-like, shutting out the flood, maddening her.

Noffreid stopped. His baleful eyes studied Erzelle. His sneer returned. Erzelle's throat tightened with fear. He knew she was helpless.

He stepped back and switched his attention to Olyssa, who had her back to both of them, still locked in a magical stranglehold with her sister.

He folded his skeletal hands together and drew them apart again to unveil a cat's cradle of glowing lines strung between his fingers. He turned up his right palm. The glowing lines flicked upright, joined to form a shape like a dagger's blade.

Doubly hobbled, Erzelle focused all her energies, not on the barrier the antlered man's necklace pressed around her but the necklace itself, the curse that kept her power in check.

It pulsed, pulsed, tightened until she couldn't breath.

She pushed back harder, not caring if it killed her.

It broke.

A nimbus of black fire enveloped her head to foot — but Noffreid's spell still held, still kept her fires from reaching him, tying them up and drawing them away into some other space.

But Erzelle could now *see* the web he'd woven around her, beacon-bright, hundreds of symmetrical layers to divert and diffuse any energy she hurled at it. Not solid but like mesh, there were millions of gaps, too small to allow a burst of power through. Olyssa could have mastered it but Lilla had her in a death grip. Erzelle could see *that* too, the simple game Lilla played, pouring more and more of her power into the trap Olyssa made for it, forcing her to focus all her attention on it lest it overwhelm her spell and burst.

Noffreid raised his arm to strike. Erzelle couldn't stop him.

"Look out!" she yelled.

He hurled the spearhead at Olyssa's back.

The spell struck her between the shoulder blades. Olyssa cried out and fell to her knees. Incredibly, she kept hold of her pipe, picked up the tune again with only a note missed. That break was opportunity enough for Lilla. Tendrils whipped out from her sphere of smoke, lunged to rip the pipe from Olyssa's hands — but didn't quite reach Olyssa as she resumed her tune with a blur of speed that she couldn't possibly keep up long. Blood streamed down the back of her jacket.

Olyssa wove faster and faster to keep her spell from bursting apart. Another spearhead of light appeared in Noffreid's hand.

Erzelle threw her soul wide and screamed. Black fire burst from her in every direction at once, as much as she used to destroy the Grey Ones and all their traces, and more. Noffreid's trap still held, but stretched and strained against her push. She crashed her will against it, imagining as she played the harp in her mind that every note boomed with the strength of an earthquake.

The spider-threads of the spell around Erzelle shattered.

In order to avoid Noffreid's blow Olyssa scrambled half to her feet, but she wasn't fast enough. It caught her right above her hip.

Erzelle spewed black fire in a roar.

The pipe clattered to the floor. The thud of a body landing. The threads of connection between Erzelle and her teacher sliding away.

Erzelle's strike hit Noffreid with the force of a mortar shell. He flew through the air, smashed against the arch of the ceiling and fell, tumbling like a rag doll. She spun at Lilla's ear-splitting screech. A hundred smoking tendrils spiraled out at Erzelle and she met them with as many streams of black flame. She dashed forward, driving Lilla back, no attention to spare for Olyssa, who sprawled unmoving.

Lilla screeched again in bug-eyed frenzy, more tendrils sprouting from her back and belly to join the ones spewing from her mouth and hands. Erzelle had no trouble matching her. The more she poured her own power through her body, the more her heart pounded, her blood thundered, her brain sang. Her chest heaved with the ambrosia of each new breath.

You will die if you don't wear it.

Lilla moaned and curled her hands into claws. Fissures opened, closed, opened again in her neck, along her jaw, across her forehead. Every tendril of smoke divided in two and lashed forward, snaking toward Erzelle.

Erzelle tangled every one of them in her own dark fire.

Layers and layers of notes played in her head, each with lives of their own, as if her mind had subdivided and subdivided and the different slices had no need to be told their mission anymore. In places it felt as if her skin thinned and flesh parted to make more room for the fire to come through. She chose not to think on what that might mean and frankly didn't care.

She and Lilla circled each other, their entwined powers writhing together in an ellipse that swelled in the air between them, each one trying to break a strand loose to strike at the other directly. As they swung one another about in this mad dance, Erzelle noticed motion in her peripheral vision. Noffreid, on his feet, the flesh of the left half of his face hanging loose. He pulled his hands apart to reveal another glowing cat's cradle.

Erzelle aimed a stream of fire at him and Lilla caught it.

His eyes of ice fixed on her. A cone of light stood in his hand. He raised his arm.

Olyssa sprang. Erzelle hadn't seen her teacher grab the pipe or get her feet under her. Neither had Noffreid, who dodged with surprising speed as Olyssa swung the pipe like a club, whiffing it through the space where his head had been a moment prior.

He spun around and slashed with fingers wielding blades of light. Blood spattered as he sliced across her torso. Olyssa gasped and dropped the pipe again.

Erzelle sensed Lilla aiming a strike at Olyssa and shouted *No!* as she loosed even more torrents of fire at the witch.

Noffreid slashed again. Olyssa caught his wrist. He pressed the claws toward her face, then twisted, trying to snake out of her grip. With her free hand she pulled the stiletto from her hair pick, spun it through her fingers and impaled it to the hilt in his ear.

The red blades vanished from his fingertips.

They spun in a macabre tango, her clutching his wrist and the knife hilt, him scrabbling feebly at her arm with his free hand, oversized eyes rolling back into their sockets, jaws gaping. Then came the sound of bone splintering and snapping as Olyssa raised her elbow and levered the edge of the stiletto up through his half-rotted skull, her teeth bared with the effort. A mass of spongy muck splattered out through the hole she'd torn open. The hilt of the stiletto broke free. Noffreid dropped, a marionette with strings snipped, the blade still impaled in his skull.

Lilla screamed to shake the tower down. *Youalwayshatedhim youalwayshatedhim   omyloveomylove   illmakeyouliveagain* YOUALWAYSHATEDHIM

She tried now to disentangle her powers from Erzelle's, but as soon as her retreat started Erzelle's own fires surged, striking with the force of years of accumulated rage. Lilla made no effort to fight it. Instead, she absorbed it. Tongues of flame and smoke swirled from her, her mouth wide, her eyes round, her entire body contorted in shock and grief. Fissures reappeared at her neck, others along her forearms, around her eyes.

Erzelle's body was like a membrane stretched to its limits as she poured her fire into Lilla, emptied all of her wrath into her opponent. Lilla seized on her power, not resisting it but redirecting it, converting fire to fog and shooting it outward.

Sister, stop! Erzelle, stop!

Olyssa's pleas went unheeded as the smoky tendrils latched across the arch of the ceiling in a thousand places. Too late Erzelle realized that Lilla meant to pull the rock down on all of them. She tried to reverse the torrent, only to feel Lilla's will hook into her soul from all directions. Another smoke tendril coiled around Olyssa's legs and dragged her forward as dust fell from the cracks spreading through the dome above.

Unable to free herself, Erzelle sent more fire coursing out along the bonds forced on her. Fissures appeared all over her body in the exact places they yawed through Lilla. She and Lilla would die together, and about this she felt no qualms at all. If she could save Olyssa somehow that would be—

ENOUGH!!

The voice descended from nowhere, heavy as a cave collapse. An invisible steel wall fell between Erzelle and Lilla, not so much severing the battle of energies between them as crushing them apart.

Erzelle tumbled backward as if a mountain had slapped her.

Somehow Olyssa caught her and ended her bruising roll. Erzelle clapped her hands to her ears as Lilla's howl filled her head.

The last red remnants of dusk cast long shadows through the hangar. These dimmed, replaced with a haze that distorted everything. The vaulted ceiling faded, and in its stead a giant's ponderous head appeared above them, its flesh bruised and swollen, its neck a ragged stump. It hung face down, rivers of sorrow coursing through every line and crease. Without all the abuse it had suffered the face would have been handsome: aquiline nose, wide cheekbones, square jaw, smooth scalp, dark eyes that glistened.

The head dangled at the nadir of a tangle of fleshy tubes that pulsed like arteries. Those vessels branched and branched as they rose, spreading horizontally as well as vertically as they stretched into the heavens. Gruesome bulges marred each tube at random intervals. Every sack-like bubble displayed a face, some staring vacant, some contorted in agony.

All the massive head's features were familiar. It bore a family resemblance.

Toward the other end of the chamber, Lilla rasped a breath, arched her back, pointed an emaciated, accusing finger at the suspended head, then lay still.

The black fires roiled restlessly within Erzelle, craving release.

Olyssa touched her cheek tenderly. Erzelle trained her mind on that gesture as her teacher helped her stand.

"Now you see what lies behind his mask," Olyssa said, peering up at her father.

Erzelle blinked, bewildered, until the scene transformed and Olyssa's full meaning became clear. A body appeared beneath the face, huge, muscular, covered with a brown pelt. The head itself lengthened and tapered, no longer human but the streamlined wedge of a deer. The great veins thinned and hardened into antlers that stretched to the sky. Grimacing faces dangled from their branches.

The transformation left Olyssa unimpressed.

"It's been years since you dared show yourself to me." Erzelle had never heard Olyssa's voice so raw. She pointed at the antlered man, her hand shaking. "You knew all along where she was. What she was doing. You could have stopped her yourself. Instead you played another sick game!"

I couldn't stop her without destroying her. That I won't do.

Olyssa barked an outraged laugh. "You could have told me where she was. What she was!"

You would have stopped searching had you known.

"Lies!"

I see into more futures than this one. Some consequences I know.

"It's no use talking," Olyssa raised her both hands, flexed her fingers, like she'd choke the creature if she could. "Take back what you've done. To both of them!"

The antlered man lowered his head. *I asked for your help and you nearly killed both of my daughters.*

Erzelle's jaw dropped as she realized he was talking to her.

"You asked nothing!" Olyssa said. "You've learned nothing. You punch a hole through my apprentice's mind straight into your so-called *prana* with no thought at all as to what will happen. Just like you did to Lilla." Spittle flew as she shouted. "And that *thing* you put around her neck! That you said would save her life. She didn't know what it would do! It nearly killed her!"

Hearing that rant, a twinge of hurt, of resentment, shivered through Erzelle. *But I saved you,* she began.

Olyssa knelt beside her. To Erzelle's shock, she hugged her fiercely. "Yes, you did. You are the bravest person I've ever met. And everything you did could have killed you. Or worse." She pointed past the antlered man to Lilla's prone form, hardly more than red cloth over bone. "That's what's in store for you if you let him leave you this way." She stood. "Take it back from her!"

The creature regarded Erzelle, every line of its posture suggesting sadness. *Do you want this door closed?*

Erzelle didn't know the answer. Without this power, she couldn't have freed Olyssa from the web in the egg chamber or fueled the horses that brought them here. They could never have saved the people in Fabelford from further harm.

Olyssa took Erzelle by the chin, guided her gaze again to Lilla. Her voice choked. "Look closely."

Porcelain cracks had spread over every inch of Lilla's exposed skin. In some places the cracks had widened, and tarry smoke still puffed out and sucked in, a gruesome parody of breathing.

"I don't want this to happen to you."

The antlered man studied his fallen daughter, shoulders sagging. He lifted a trembling hand toward her, then withdrew it.

Don't feel sorry for him, Erzelle. He inflicted this ridiculous little hell upon himself, as if it somehow makes up for all the pain and death he caused. As if anything could exonerate him. It fixes nothing. It changes nothing.

It wasn't the creature's sorrow that brought tears to Erzelle's eyes, but the whole situation, how it had started with a petty rivalry between otherwise loving sisters, how it had played out here in the tower, and all the people it had hurt, the countless victims of the Storms — and Lilla's countless victims, even Lilla herself.

Erzelle could take center stage in this tragedy, or consign herself once again to a bit part.

"Yes," she said. "Close it."

The antlered man inclined his head but didn't reach for her. The black fire inside her disappeared, the flue shut. Emptiness replaced it. Immediately she longed for it back.

A rustle behind her. The horses, still kneeling at the ledge, unraveled into heaps of straw.

Olyssa demanded, "Now do the same for Lilla, like you should have years ago."

The great beast raised its hands in denial. *She would die in an instant. Her hatred and the power that feeds it are one. It's all that keeps her alive.*

"And why is that, father?" Her words dripped with poison. "Who made her that way? Maybe death would be better."

He didn't answer.

Unsure if she dared interrupt, Erzelle did anyway. "You wanted me to help her. Is there something we can do?"

Her glance at Lilla turned into a double take, as Lilla's skin mended itself before her eyes. She wondered how often Lilla had reached this point before, how far now she must be from human, from the girl Olyssa had once raced horses with and played music for.

She has to bring herself back, the beast said. He turned to Olyssa. *You're the only one who can make her want that. You've taken the best first step. You've rid her of the monster.*

"Noffreid?" she exclaimed, incredulous. "Don't *you* talk about monsters. You brought him to her." Olyssa added, as if surprised she were saying it, "I killed the love of her life."

The beast rumbled. *He deserved it.*

"How blissfully ignorant you are. Father, do you ever think at all, really think, about how all of this happened?"

Lilla sat up, a painfully beautiful smile of victory brightening her cadaverous face. She peered up at the antlered man, who had his back to her.

Olyssa stumbled back, her head jerking as if she'd been struck, and then put a hand to her mouth.

And Lilla's smile gaped, new cracks spreading from its corners, from around her eyes, across her throat. Her face split apart and black smoke fountained through the opening, speared through the back of the antlered man's head. The beast convulsed, and when it screamed, Lilla's smoke geysered out.

A flash of an image superimposed over the scene. That huge swollen face, the beast's true form, howling in agony as Lilla's power melted its eyes.

All of it vanished, quick as a thrown switch. The haze, the antlered man, the pendulum face, gone. Lilla, too, disappeared.

Erzelle and Olyssa were alone in the chamber at the top of the tower. All that remained were the heaps of straw that had been the horses, dust from the destroyed harvester and the corpse of Lilla's lover.

Olyssa kept staring at the place where her sister had been.

Erzelle hoped to never see her again. Olyssa, she knew, didn't share that wish, despite everything.

My sister spoke to me before she attacked him.

Erzelle recalled Olyssa's sudden start.

She said the worst thing she could do to him was kill his favorite daughter right in front of his eyes. That it was what I deserved for killing Noffreid. But she said it was father's fault that I became what I am.

She said I was his favorite.

For the first time since Erzelle had known her, Olyssa sounded utterly bewildered.

Erzelle knew what it meant to lose a family. She went to her teacher and embraced her.

Her teacher's clothes were soaked with sweat, and blood. The curls of her hair tickled Erzelle's neck as she knelt and clutched Erzelle back. Her huge body shook with silent weeping.

When Olyssa finally broke free, she retrieved her pipe and put it to her lips. Its runes shone blue. It still played.

When she saw this, she broke out in sobs.

Knowing they were sobs of joy that Lilla still lived made Erzelle queasy. She shared not a bit of her teacher's relief but she kept that thought to herself.

She put her her arms around Olyssa's shoulders and held her, until Olyssa coughed and pressed a hand to her side.

Olyssa had carried herself with such aggressive strength since the fight ended that Erzelle had hoped the wounds Noffreid dealt to her weren't as horrendous as they'd first looked. But blood was seeping through Olyssa's fingers, and the back of her jacket had darkened into one huge stain.

Erzelle's body wound tight with frustration she couldn't release, an urge to lash out at the unfairness of it all. Had she hung on to her power, she could have healed Olyssa in a blink.

When Olyssa straightened, she spoke as if nothing were amiss. "There's work to do."

Erzelle helped Olyssa to bind the wounds in her back and side, unfolding Reneer's knife to cut strips from her shirt and Olyssa's trousers. Then they went searching for the way into the tower, and found it.

Beneath the tower's cellars, in the bowels of the mountain, they found another egg shaped chamber, ten times the size of the one at Violet Bluffs. Flood it half-full of water and the *Red Empress* could have floated on the surface with room to spare.

The corpse machine that filled the chamber had to be the master that governed the others, a leviathan of flesh pistons and bone gears. Like its smaller cousin the bulk of it formed a basin that had once held a sea of the corrupt smoke. Now it sat empty.

When Erzelle and Olyssa came upon it, the contraption was under siege. A legion of ghouls clogged its works, tearing it apart piece by piece. In some places the pieces built into the machine fought back, adding to the chaos.

Erzelle covered her mouth and nose against the stench of a thousand opened graves. She and Olyssa looked down on the reeking mess from a stone balcony that circled the entire egg near its top, much like its earthen counterpart near Fabelford. While red magic sputtered within the works, an inverse forest of glowing moss hung from the egg's crown, casting the top of the chamber in a greenish pall, rendering the entire tableau morbidly festive.

Erzelle asked, "Why are the ghouls doing that?"

"I had hoped ... when we flew toward the tower I tapped the darkness through you and used it to weave several spells." Erzelle remembered: the spheres of music sent on ahead. "I hoped that my sister and Noffreid wouldn't recognize them as anything worth their concern — just as the Chef once looked at this pipe and failed to understand what it could do. What I wove were ghoul charms. I designed them to find the creatures hidden beneath this rock and turn them on one another. I had to make sure the machine was destroyed, regardless of whether we survived."

The carnage below made Olyssa's matter-of-fact tone about their own deaths all the more surreal. Erzelle had no words. She glanced up at Olyssa, whose lips were pressed tight in an incongruous frown, her brow knotted.

"I'm glad to see it worked," Olyssa finally said. She turned to Erzelle, winced, clutched her side and smiled weakly. "Thank you. For coming all this way with me."

She had to lean on Erzelle as she walked.

Lilla and Noffreid had built a lift into the tower, but as it responded only to their magic, Erzelle and Olyssa had been forced, in their search for the egg chamber, to descend a long spiral stair bored into the structure from top to bottom.

They started the ascent, Olyssa's breath becoming more labored as they climbed. They reached only the third landing up — the deepest cellar still several stories above them — when Olyssa collapsed.

She was reassuring Erzelle even as she attempted to stand and couldn't. Erzelle strained all her tired body to help, but her teacher was too heavy to lift.

"I'm all right," Olyssa repeated. "I'll be all right."

Erzelle hated feeling so helpless. "Tell me what to do!" She hated how her heartbeat surged, how her voice shook and squeaked. Her eyes burned. Her throat tightened. She inwardly screamed at herself for letting her teacher talk her into giving her magic up.

She followed Olyssa's directions, using Reneer's knife to cut new strips from their clothes to redress the wounds. When she pulled off the blood-drenched bandages she gasped. The razor-straight cuts had turned black at the edges, and wouldn't stop bleeding — in fact, the bleeding worsened as she tried to stanch it. Angry red tracks wormed up the surrounding veins.

Pale and sweating, Olyssa played a spell meant to assist the new bandages in holding the wounds closed. The binding soaked through black as she fluttered her hand at the bell.

Erzelle held out a hand. She wasn't sure if Olyssa would surrender the pipe, but she did.

Erzelle played, willing herself to perceive the energy flow that would summon the healing. She so vividly remembered how it felt, what to do, whether mending Reneer's burns or Braeca's arm. Worse than her time in the containment cell: nothing responded to her at all. The fires were gone.

Olyssa's breathing slowed as her consciousness faded.

Erzelle contemplated a future alone with her teacher's body under this charnel tower.

Keep her talking, she thought. *Just keep her talking.*

"I want to go back to Reneer and Braeca," she said. "I want to make sure they're okay. Can we?"

Though it was the first thing that sprang to her mind, she meant every word, and also the thought that followed: *I don't know how I'll do it without you.*

Olyssa's eyelids fluttered, and for a moment she looked just as she had in Lilla's web-trap, helpless, snared in a nightmare she couldn't wake from.

Then her eyes opened. *It won't be easy.* She smiled. *But I know you'll see them safe.*

"We'll see them safe."

Olyssa gazed at the glowing moss striping the underside of the staircase above. Her brow furrowed in puzzlement. *When Lilla said I was father's favorite, she told me something else. She said our father feared these machines. She didn't tell me what they're meant to do, but she said they finally would destroy even him. She said that's why he manipulated me into finding her.*

But that's not why you did it, Erzelle thought. *You did it because you love her. Even now you still do. Maybe someday your sister will understand.*

I don't think there's going to be a someday, Olyssa replied.

Yes, there will be, don't talk like this.

Even in her mind, her teacher's voice grew weaker. *Perhaps. Perhaps.*

And then the realization struck Erzelle in a searing blaze. She wasn't speaking aloud, and still Olyssa heard her. Erzelle had not been able to send her thoughts like that before the antlered man marked her.

The mark was gone. But she was projecting. Her magic still worked.

Olyssa's eyes closed. Her head lolled sideways.

Erzelle stared at her for a full half minute, unaware how fast her heart beat or how ragged her breath came. Olyssa's state and her epiphany combined to keep her thoughts from cohering. She lifted her hands. Did she only imagine the ghostly outline of a harp?

Illusory or not, what choice did she have? She imagined plucking its strings. No fires churned at the edge of her awareness.

She began the concerto.

No black fire burned within each note. But as she proceeded through the first movement, she perceived a different source, an ambient energy that burned all around her, a pale reflection of the otherworldly energy she'd channeled before.

This had to be the medium Olyssa worked in, that allowed her to make small spells with her music. Not an inferno but a faint ghostly flicker, a foxfire freed of any physical source, visible only to the mind's eye. She imagined each note sparked with that fire.

She sent her mind searching for Olyssa, the aurora within her. She found it, ebbing.

Erzelle continued into the concerto's second movement, shaping her intent, seeking broken patterns and threading new lines of power across the tears through Olyssa's life-force made by Noffreid's spell. New holes suppurated even as she sewed the old ones closed, the remnants of Noffreid's festering magic resisting her.

She played on in a fugue, every note a faint spark.

She didn't know when her own consciousness ended and the hallucinations of dream began.

Hours later, curled uncomfortably on the stone, Erzelle dreamed of a great head dangling at the end of a widening of veins. As before, the veins bulged with disembodied faces, all screaming non-stop in silent horror. The head curled back its lips, startlingly full beneath jutting cheekbones and bright green eyes. Lilla cackled, and though Erzelle couldn't hear her laughter, she saw tendrils of smoke twist out from the eyes of all the other heads as they howled and howled.

She sat up in the dark, convinced in the instant before she awakened that she heard Lilla's cackle, right there on the landing with them. But the only sound was Olyssa's peaceful breathing.

EPILOGUE

"*T*he nerve of you brutes," Reneer said. "Bringing all these guns to a knife fight."

He saw no point in keeping his mouth shut. Often his penchant for loud-mouth sarcasm got him out of scrapes simply by catching the other party completely off guard.

Even he had to admit, this time it wasn't going to work.

He wouldn't care so much if all the bullets in the constables' bandoliers were meant for him alone. For five days he and Braeca had hurried west through the woods over ever more difficult terrain. The very first day the motorbike he'd stolen had blown a tire. By the third day he's used up all the bullets in the stolen rifle trying to fell food on the hoof.

He'd hoped they'd put Fabelford far enough behind them that, given the chaos of that horrible night assault by the harvester, no one would miss them.

He was wrong. Nor did any of the black-clad constables soften their narrow-eyed gazes when he said, "You have us to thank that the Grey Ones are gone for good. You know that, right?"

Because of an overnight downpour, Reneer and Braeca had taken shelter beneath the overhang of an immense rock resembling the head of a hawk. They'd been awakened by a shout to come out with hands raised. Knowing better, Reneer had emerged with his dagger handy, only to discover a half circle of twenty riflemen already in position. Twenty! Who did they think he was?

Of course, he had last been seen in the company of two jaw-droppingly powerful sorceresses.

He tried a new tack. "I'll come with you quietly if you let my friend go."

He winced when one of the constables shouted back, "No. The witch too."

"She's an apothecary, not a witch," he said, then sighed and rolled his eyes heavenward. "Oh, what's the use? I bet you can't even spell apothecary."

Braeca sat silently, wrapped in a tattered blanket. Eyes downcast, as if she knew all along it would come to this. Reneer's stolen sword lay beside her, useless to them both.

After what she'd been through, after what he'd involved her in, what he'd had to do to save her life, the defeat in her posture wrung his heart most of all. At least he'd had time before they'd fled to browbeat his guilt-wracked grandfather into seeing to the safety of Braeca's mother. Reneer had vowed to himself that if his grandfather broke that word he would die, beloved relative or no.

Of course, first there was surviving the firing squad to consider.

The bulkiest of the constables, a mastiff-like fellow named Porgril who was doing all the barking, said, "You have to the count of one to drop your knife."

"Technically, it's not a knife," Reneer said.

A small cloud passed over the clearing, brushing it with shadow. A second later sunlight returned to welcome Reneer's death.

The constables raised their weapons.

Gunfire.

Reneer threw himself over Braeca. It wouldn't protect her, but it was the last decent thing he could do. He opened his eyes a few moments later at the realization that the shooting had stopped and he'd not been hit by a single bullet.

"Are you all right?"

Braeca nodded, eyes saucer-wide.

He pushed up off her, onto all fours, and turned around. Eight of the constables lay dead on the ground, gunshot wounds between their tilted eyes. The remainder had fled through the trees. Leaves quivered from the speed of their frantic retreat.

From atop the hawk-headed rock that sheltered them, a titanic creature hopped with alarming fleetness into the clearing. Reneer thought he might have screamed had he not been too flabbergasted by the sight of the thing.

It had four legs. Wings. A long, graceful, reptilian head, and a tail that stretched behind it over ten feet. And it was made out of straw.

Erzelle and Olyssa rode its back, their feet secured in stirrups that grew right out of the thing's flaxen hide. Olyssa, hair bound up, brandished her rifle, runes glowing red along its barrel. Erzelle stared at him, then, espying Braeca, broke into a shy smile. The star tattoo she'd mysteriously gained underground no longer marred her brow.

When Erzelle's gaze fell upon one of the downed fox-men, her smile vanished.

As usual, Olyssa was all business. "We need to get you somewhere safer. Both of you." Then she smiled, too. "There's room this time."

Reneer stared at the straw beast's broad back. Made, no doubt, like the horses they'd flown off on to someplace from whence he'd assumed they'd never return.

For once he had no quip to offer. The break in his voice surprised him when he asked, "Where on Earth would we go?"

Erzelle spoke. "We'll find a place."

ACKNOWLEDGMENTS

Here's how *The Black Fire Concerto* came to be.

It began life as a novelette called "The Reed Player" — which in the finished book is the first part, now called "The Red Empress." That novelette started from two completely different points of origin. The first is an idea for a character that's been with me a long time: a tall, broad-shouldered, dark-haired woman, deadly accurate with a firearm, who travels from town to town and has encounters along the dark fantasy and horror spectrum, only a few shades removed from Stephen King's Roland.

The second came from a fellow I know here in Roanoke, Jonathan Overturf, who I met through the local theater scene. He shared a nightmare he'd had about a restaurant where the patrons eat zombies. They would send unsuspecting tourists into the cellar, where the zombies were kept, to be bitten and then become dinner. He invited me to make use of it.

I am not sure what inspired me to apply the first to the second, but the result radically transformed both. The setting became a post-apocalyptic world where magic works. The restaurant became a moored riverboat modified into a fortress. The patrons became wealthy cultists and a black-clad crew. The gunslinger became a musician named Olyssa, who plays a unique sorcery-empowered pipe. This alchemy also required two new characters: a villain named the Chef — inspired by a figure in a nightmare I had as a teenager — who is my riff on Cormac McCarthy's The Judge; as well as a young girl, a harpist, held prisoner in the riverboat after her parents are murdered. The girl, Erzelle, ended up being the story's protagonist, the events that unfold seen through her eyes. The first draft was written in 2009. It underwent many beta readings and was bounced from many markets.

Fast forward to Autumn 2011. My buddy Claire (penname C.S.E. Cooney) approached me to consider contributing to a line of e-books that John O'Neill of *Black Gate* wanted to launch. After hemming and hawing I asked Claire to read "The Reed Player" and decide if it would work for her as a seed for a longer book. See, I always had this idea that Olyssa and Erzelle could have many more adventures — I've always wanted my own sword-and-sorcery style wanderers — though there seemed little point in generating more when their first adventure hadn't seen daylight.

Claire called me after reading it, and I believe her exact words were, "Please, please, please, make this a novel for me, please!" Or something awfully close to that. It's also worthy of note that Anita, my wife of more than twenty years, and frequent partner in creative projects, had this to say on the matter: "Oh, yes, you're doing that."

In "The Reed Player," Olyssa was searching for her lost sister. Not long after that early draft, my longtime writing buddy from Hollins University days, Cathy Reniere, suggested I should consider tying the story of the missing sibling to the story of how the entire world was transformed. There were also, in the original draft, references to a wolf-like people. Returning to this story, I made those wolf-people vulpine instead and decided to find out who these vulpines were.

My apologies if I leave anyone out, as this project has been years in the making and is still ongoing as I write this. I'm grateful to Anita, Cathy, Jaime Lee Moyer, Nicole Kornher-Stace, Sonya Taaffe, Laurie Schroeder, and Virginia Mohlere, who read the original novelette, and offered feedback and encouragement; to Anita, Virginia, Nicole, Sonya and Elizabeth Campbell, who cheered and critiqued and copy-edited as the story become a novel; to John O'Neill who took a chance on sharing this with the world; and especially to Claire, who asked me to write this story, and then worked tirelessly to help me shape it into something exponentially better than I ever could have managed alone.

—Mike Allen, Roanoke, Va., March 2, 2013

ABOUT THE AUTHOR

Mike Allen lives in Roanoke, Va., with his wife and frequent editing assistant Anita, their dog Loki and felines Pandora and Persephone. By day he works as the arts columnist for The Roanoke Times, the city's daily paper.

In his spare time he's a writer, editor, publisher and poet. His poetry collection *Strange Wisdoms of the Dead* was a Philadelphia Inquirer Editor's Choice selection in 2006. His horror tale "The Button Bin" was a finalist for the Nebula Award for Best Short Story in 2009. His poems and stories have appeared in *Asimov's Science Fiction, Weird Tales, Strange Horizons, Goblin Fruit, Interzone, The Best Horror of the Year One, Beneath Ceaseless Skies, Cthulhu's Reign, Solaris Rising 2: The New Solaris Book of Science Fiction,* and other places. Dagan Books is bringing out his first collection of short fiction, *The Button Bin and Other Stories.*

He's the editor of the critically-acclaimed *Clockwork Phoenix* anthologies of weird fiction, and in 2012 successfully raised more than $10,000 through Kickstarter.com to produce a fourth volume. He also edits the long-running print poetry journal, *Mythic Delirium,* which is about to transform into a webzine that will showcase both fiction and poetry. You can follow his efforts as a writer at descentintolight. com, as an editor at mythicdelirium.com, and as both on Twitter at @mythicdelirium.

The Black Fire Concerto is his first novel.

BOOKS BY MIKE ALLEN

Novels
The Black Fire Concerto

Collections
The Button Bin and Other Stories

Short Fictions
She Who Runs
Sleepless, Burning Life
Stolen Souls
Follow the Wounded One

Poetry Collections
The Journey to Kailash
Strange Wisdoms of the Dead
Disturbing Muses
Petting the Time Shark
Defacing the Moon

As Editor
Clockwork Phoenix 4
Clockwork Phoenix 3: New Tales of Beauty and Strangeness
Clockwork Phoenix 2: More Tales of Beauty and Strangeness
Clockwork Phoenix: Tales of Beauty and Strangeness
Mythic 2
Mythic
The Alchemy of Stars: Rhysling Award Winners Showcase
(with Roger Dutcher)
New Dominions: Fantasy Stories by Virginia Writers